“What int
Kenzie wa

Hunter’s shi… green eyes skimmed over her from top to bottom before he answered. “I don’t.”

He could make her lose her patience faster than any human being she had ever encountered, and that included Billy. Kenzie struggled now to hold on to her temper as she asked, “Then why would you be going to the scene where he was found?”

He slowly smiled at Kenzie, knowing that it annoyed her. He couldn’t explain why, but he really liked getting under her skin. “Let’s just say I have a real interest in the person who did this to him.”

“Why?” Kenzie demanded.

Hunter saw no reason to keep this a secret. Teasing Kenzie took a back seat to possibly solving a case—or at least getting one step closer to solving it.

“Because I think that my cold case might have been this guy’s first murder.”

* * *

Be sure to check out the next books in this exciting miniseries:

Cavanaugh Justice—Where Aurora’s finest are always in action

* * *

If you’re on Twitter, tell us what you think of Harlequin Romantic Suspense! #harlequinromsuspense

Dear Reader,

I'm not sure if anyone is keeping count out there, but this marks my fortieth Cavanaugh Justice series book. What had started out as a limited, five-book series refused to fade away. To be honest, the idea of a law enforcement family, whose first allegiance was to each other and then to the law they had all taken an oath to uphold, fascinated me. Possibly because I had grown up with a family that could have easily fit inside a cereal box, I always wondered what it would be like to have cousins and uncles and aunts to add dimensions to my life. Creating them on paper was the next best thing. And, like Mickey Mouse creating helpers for himself in *The Sorcerer's Apprentice*, once I got started, I couldn't stop myself. And I was further encouraged by wonderful letters from you, telling me how much you enjoyed the last Cavanaugh book and asking me if there would be more coming. Ask and ye shall receive (or careful what you wish for, take your choice).

I hope you enjoy this latest entry in the Cavanaugh Justice series. As ever, I thank you for taking the time to pick up one of my stories to read, and from the bottom of my heart, I wish you someone to love who loves you back.

All the best,

Marie Ferrarella

CAVANAUGH'S MISSING PERSON

Marie Ferrarella

HARLEQUIN® ROMANTIC SUSPENSE

ISBN-13: 978-1-335-66211-8

Cavanaugh's Missing Person

This edition published by arrangement with Harlequin Books S.A.

For questions and comments about the quality of this book, please contact us at CustomerService@Harlequin.com.

Printed in U.S.A.

USA TODAY bestselling and RITA® Award–winning author **Marie Ferrarella** has written more than two hundred and fifty books for Harlequin, some under the name Marie Nicole. Her romances are beloved by fans worldwide. Visit her website, marieferrarella.com.

Books by Marie Ferrarella

Harlequin Romantic Suspense

Cavanaugh Justice

Mission: Cavanaugh Baby
Cavanaugh on Duty
A Widow's Guilty Secret
Cavanaugh's Surrender
Cavanaugh Rules
Cavanaugh's Bodyguard
Cavanaugh Fortune
How to Seduce a Cavanaugh
Cavanaugh or Death
Cavanaugh Cold Case
Cavanaugh in the Rough
Cavanaugh on Call
Cavanaugh Encounter
Cavanaugh Vanguard
Cavanaugh Cowboy
Cavanaugh's Missing Person

Visit the Author Profile page at Harlequin.com for more titles.

To

Nancy Parodi Neubert,

Who patiently let me

Try out my stories on her

More years ago

Than either of us

Care to remember.

Thank you, Nance.

Love,

Twinkles

Prologue

She knew this location like the back of her hand. She brought them all here—while they were still alive—certain that they would view this as an intimate, secluded hideaway.

She was just as confident as they were about it, but to her it also meant that she and the person she brought here would be isolated and that there would be no unwanted interruptions.

Or any unforeseen last-minute rescues.

There never were this far out from civilization. After all, no one had ever heard her cries when she had screamed for help all those years ago.

She had chosen this place carefully, deliberately.

It *had* to be this place for the purge to be effective.

Despite that and all the precautions she took, she never failed to remain vigilant and alert. While she had always been confident, it had never been to the point that she became careless. Because carelessness would usher in error and error—any error—could wind up, in the long run, being fatal.

For her.

She had worked too hard to lose everything she had amassed because of an error.

The door to this little "hideaway" was closed and there

were no windows, at least none that allowed anyone to look inside. But even so, an unseasonable evening breeze had somehow managed to squeeze in through the cracks, causing the plastic that hung everywhere to move just the slightest bit.

She didn't see it. She heard it.

Her pulse sped up.

Instantly, her eyes went to the man who was at the center of it all. There was no way he could move and disturb the plastic that had been draped all around him, the plastic that was literally covering every square inch of the space. She'd seen to that.

Even so, she had to reassure herself that he wouldn't suddenly rise up and overpower her.

There was enough ketamine in her would-be lover to put down an oversize water buffalo, but still she watched him, watched his chest to see if it would rise and fall, signaling a man who was coming to.

It didn't.

The injection had done its trick.

She had done her trick, she thought with a small, tight smile.

"And now it's time for you to do your part," she whispered to the inert form.

With the precision of a surgeon, imitating the movements that Joel had shown her when the poor fool had tried to impress her all those years ago, she drove the thin boning knife in at just the right angle, just the right spot to end the life of this latest contributor to her thriving and ever expanding lifestyle.

Taking their money was only part of it. Avenging herself was far more important to her.

Blood spurted from the incision she had made onto the plastic that surrounded the man. She waited until it pooled around him, heralding the fact that his life had officially, and without fanfare, slipped away.

When she was satisfied that he was dead, she turned toward her knapsack where she kept the rest of her tools. It was time to separate John Kurtz from the parts of him that would facilitate his identification.

She had always liked tools, even as a child. They fascinated her. They could be used for so many things. People liked to build things with tools.

She liked to dismantle them.

Taking out the battery-powered saw, she switched it on. For a moment, she just listened to the high-pitched sound the saw made. The quiet, reassuring sound that promised to do its job and not fail her.

So many things had failed her. But the saw wouldn't.

She could feel the vibrations going through her arms.

She watched, almost mesmerized, as the gleaming, freshly polished blade sliced through the air like the sharp teeth of a tiger, straining to devour its prey. She always took care of her tools.

A person's work was only as good as the tools she used, she thought with a cynical smile.

Feeling almost giddy, she hummed a little song under her breath, a song from her childhood before horror had swallowed her up. It was a tune that kept haunting her.

She slowly lowered the saw blade and began to work.

One more down.

And tomorrow, tomorrow the hunt for a new, unwitting victim would begin all over again. Because this feeling, this satisfaction, lasted for only so long before it vanished.

Like her innocence.

But for now, she savored this part of her quest, savored it because she was victorious.

And that was all that counted.

Chapter 1

"Hey, Cavanaugh," a deep male voice called out. "There's somebody here asking to see you."

Detective MacKenzie Cavanaugh, currently assigned to the Missing Persons Division of the Aurora Police Department, looked up from her computer. She raised her intense blue eyes in time to see Detective Kyle Choi pointing toward her for the benefit of a distraught-looking older woman.

It took Kenzie a full minute to realize that the woman she was looking at *wasn't* really old, just incredibly beaten down and worn-out looking, like someone who had spent a great deal of time crying.

She actually *recognized* the dark-haired woman heading her way.

Kenzie rose from her chair, still trying to reconcile the woman coming toward her with the person she had once known.

Connie Kurtz.

She'd gone to college with Connie not all that many years ago. Ten to be precise. Something had obviously happened to the once upbeat young woman. Something that had stolen the light from her eyes. Connie looked as if she had aged drastically since the last time Kenzie had seen her. Connie had never been heavyset, but her face now had a sunken in appearance, like someone who hadn't slept or eaten in a while.

The Connie Kenzie remembered had the kind of figure that turned heads while the woman approaching her had lost a significant amount of weight. The clothes she wore hung on her body like they couldn't find a place for themselves.

"Connie?" Kenzie asked uncertainly, wanting to make sure that this wasn't ultimately a case of mistaken identity.

Connie offered a spasmodic smile of acknowledgment when she heard her name spoken, but the smile faded away before it had a chance to register.

The woman blew out a long, shaky breath. "When I asked the policeman downstairs for Detective Cavanaugh, he started to laugh and then he asked me, 'Which one?'" Connie appeared somewhat dazed and bewildered as she repeated the incident. "How many of your family members are there on the police force?"

"A lot," Kenzie answered, thinking it might be simpler just to leave it that. "Sit down, Connie. Please," she added when the other woman seemed disoriented.

Rather than taking her seat slowly, Connie dropped into the chair facing Kenzie as if the air had suddenly been let out of her.

Thinking to break the ice, Kenzie asked the haunted-looking young woman, "How long has it been?"

"A long time," Connie replied. She ran her tongue along her dry lips, as if they were stuck together, preventing her from saying anything further. It was as if she was afraid that if she did, something terrible would become a reality.

Silence hung between them.

Kenzie tried again. "Is there something I can do for you, Connie?" she asked.

She was unable to think of a single reason why someone she'd known from three classes when she was a college senior would deliberately seek her out now—unless it was for professional reasons.

"I hope so." The words came out slowly, like bullets fired cautiously and one at a time.

Since she'd begun working in the Missing Persons Division, Kenzie had become accustomed to talking to distraught family members, spouses and/or girlfriends and boyfriends. Getting any sort of viable information at times required a great deal of patience. Kenzie prided herself on being up to the job.

There were other times when interrogation was called for, and she was just as good at that as she was at displays of patience and employing kid-glove treatment with fragile people. It seemed to her that this situation called for use of the latter.

"Why don't you tell me why you're here, Connie," Kenzie coaxed, then told her, "Take your time."

Connie swallowed nervously. "You know, I'm probably just being paranoid," she said.

It was obvious that she was trying to talk herself into believing that. Kenzie could see that the woman was twisting her fingers together so hard, they looked as if they could just snap off at any moment.

Kenzie put her hand protectively over the other woman's hands with just enough pressure to make Connie stop twisting her fingers like that.

"Paranoid about what?" Kenzie asked gently.

Rather than answer, Connie said in a voice that almost broke, "He's probably sitting on some beach, or vacationing in the mountains—like I told him to." Connie looked at her, desperation once again entering her eyes. "You know, he used to talk about going to the mountains." Tears were sliding down her thin cheeks now.

Kenzie reached over on her desk and extracted tissues from a box she'd brought to the office to help her cope with her last cold. She offered the tissues to Connie, who took them after a beat, wiping away the telltale trail of tears from her face and dabbing at her eyes. She crumpled the tissues in her hand, as if holding them would somehow give her strength.

"Who's sitting on some beach or vacationing in the mountains, Connie? Who are you talking about?" Kenzie asked, thinking that Connie had to be talking about a boyfriend who had suddenly stopped returning her calls and pulled a disappearing act.

When they were in college together, Connie had had a social life that would have kept three other women on their toes and busy. Heaven knew that Connie had never wanted for company. More than once Connie had offered to "fix her up," but their taste in boyfriends were worlds apart. Back in those days, Connie was attracted to guys who easily came under the bad-boy heading.

On the other hand, if *she* had brought someone like that home, said "bad boy" would have been summarily threatened with bodily harm if he didn't vacate the premises voluntarily and immediately. She'd grown up with four brothers, a father and countless cousins, all of whom were incredibly protective.

Of course, that didn't keep her from making her own bad choice in the end, Kenzie thought ruefully. She forced herself to focus on the woman crying next to her desk.

More tears slid down Connie's face as she choked out, "John Kurtz. My father."

"Your father?" Kenzie repeated, confused. "You're talking about your father?" she asked again.

Connie wiped away the tears from her cheeks and then blew her nose, as well. She took in a deep breath and released it.

Kenzie pushed the box of tissues closer to her. "Why don't you begin at the beginning."

Connie swallowed, struggling to get hold of herself. "I guess that would be when my mother died."

Kenzie could remember a vivacious, lively redhead who had attended their graduation. They had that loss in common, she thought.

"I didn't know," she apologized. "I'm really sorry to hear that, Connie. When did your mother die?"

Connie closed her eyes, as if summoning the memory was painful. "A little over three years ago." Opening her eyes, she looked at Kenzie. "My father became almost a hermit after she died. It was understandable at first—" A sad smile punctuated her statement. "They'd been the classic high school sweethearts who got married right after graduation. My mother worshipped the ground my father walked on—and the feeling was mutual," she added with feeling.

Her voice cracked as she tried not to cry.

"Take your time," Kenzie told her again even though she really wanted to hurry the woman along and pull the words out of her throat. She tamped down her impatience. Kenzie was the type who always read the end of a book before she then turned to page one. She had *always* had an insatiable need to know how things turned out before she ever got to that part.

But in this case, she kept quiet, letting Connie tell her story at her own pace, in fits and starts.

Connie sighed again, as if that would somehow shield her from what she was talking about.

"Anyway, when she died, Dad just withdrew into himself. I thought he'd come around eventually, but when he didn't, I tried to get him to go out, to see people again. He thought I meant that he should start seeing other women—and maybe I did—but I told him he was wrong. And that it was also wrong just to sit home and brood day after day the way he was doing."

Connie sniffed and looked off, no doubt reliving the incident she was describing.

"And we got into a terrible argument, said some things we both regretted—at least I regretted them," the other woman said with a deep sigh. "Anyway, my father broke off all communication with me. I was angry, so I decided the hell with him." A sad smile curved the corners of her lips. "But, well, he's my father so I decided I should try to mend this breach between us. I called him—and called him—and I just couldn't reach him," she said with a note of desperation. "After a couple of days, I started to get this uneasy feeling that something was wrong so I went to his house. And he wasn't there," she cried, trying her best to keep her voice in check.

"Maybe your father did go on that vacation," Kenzie suggested.

But Connie shook her head from side to side. "My father's a very detail-oriented person. If he ever did decide to go on a vacation, he'd notify the post office to have them hold back mail delivery. Or, at the very least, he'd have his neighbor pick up his mail for him."

She looked at Kenzie with fresh tears in her eyes. "His mailbox is one of those large models—he used to get packages with kits in them," she explained. "Anyway, there was so much mail in the mailbox, it was overflowing. There's mail on his lawn, Kenzie," Connie cried, as if the sight of that mail had literally caused her pain. "So much mail that it's noticeable from the street." She let out another shaky breath before she could continue. "Anyway, that's when my father's neighbor called me."

"Your father's neighbor had your number?" Kenzie asked.

Connie nodded. "I gave Mr. Moore my cell number right after my mother died so he could call me in case my dad did…something stupid or got too sick to call or… You have to understand, my father wasn't himself after my mother died…" Her voice trailed off. And then she sat up a little straighter, her eyes holding Kenzie's prisoner. "Something's happened to him, Kenzie. I just *know* it."

"Not necessarily," Kenzie told her in a very calm voice. "Don't get ahead of yourself, Connie. You have to think positive," she advised the other woman. She kept her voice even, almost cheerful. "This could all be a just a misunderstanding or he just needed some time to himself, or—"

"Or he could be lying in some alley, bleeding or dead," Connie cried, interrupting Kenzie. "Tossed aside like so much garbage."

"You don't know that for a fact, Connie, and until you have reason to believe that's the case, I want you to focus on positive thoughts," Kenzie instructed, keeping her voice just stern enough to get the other woman's attention.

Connie covered her face with her hands, crying again. "I should have never yelled at him," she said, her voice hitching, "never told him that he was acting like an old man when he had so much of life to live still in front of him."

"Sometimes fathers need to be yelled at," Kenzie told the other woman with sympathy.

Connie raised her head, her eyes pleading for some sort of reassurance. "Have you ever yelled at yours?" she asked.

Kenzie laughed. "More times than I could even begin to count," she told Connie.

It wasn't true. At least she hadn't yelled at her father in years, but that wasn't what this woman needed to hear right now. She needed to be able to assuage her conscience in order to think clearly, so Kenzie told her what she wanted to hear.

Connie nodded, sniffling and once again struggling to get control of herself. "Then you'll look for my father?" she asked hopefully.

Kenzie nodded. "You just need to fill out this paperwork and we can get started on our end."

Kenzie opened up the large drawer to her right and took out a folder that was filled with official-looking forms. Beneath the folder she had another file folder filled with forms that were already filled out.

Those she had already input into the system over the last couple of years. Some of the people on those forms had been found, but there were still a great many who hadn't. Those people bothered Kenzie more than she could possibly say. Not because they represented opened cases that counted against her, but because they represented people who hadn't been reunited with their loved ones. People who might *never* be reunited with their distraught loved ones.

She didn't know what she would do if she ever found herself in that set of circumstances. Which was why, her Uncle Brian had told her when he'd assigned her to this department, she was the right person for the job.

Connie broke down and cried twice during what should have been a relatively short process of filling out the form.

The second time, Kenzie kindly suggested, "Do you want to go outside and clear your head?"

But Connie bit her lower lip and shook her head, refusing the offer. "No, I want to finish filling out the form. And then I want to help you find my father."

She could relate to that, Kenzie thought. But even so, she had to turn Connie down. She smiled patiently at the woman. "I'm afraid that it doesn't quite work that way."

Connie looked at her, confused. "How does it work? I don't mean to sound belligerent," Connie apologized. "I thought I could help, because I know all his habits. But I just want to know how you find someone."

"A lot of ways," Kenzie answered matter-of-factly. "We talk to people at your dad's place of work, to his neighbors, find out if he had a club he liked to frequent more than others—"

Connie cut her off quickly, shaking her head. "He didn't."

"All right," Kenzie said, continuing. "A favorite restaurant, then—"

Again Connie shook her head. "My father didn't like fancy food and he didn't believe in throwing his money away by having someone else cook for him when he could do a better job of it himself."

"How about his friends?" Kenzie asked. "Did he have anyone he was close to?" she asked, already doing a mental sketch of a man who had become a loner in his later years.

Connie shook her head just as Kenzie had expected her to. "My father stopped seeing his friends once Mom had died and after a while, his friends stopped trying to get him to come out." She sighed again. "I guess they all just gave up on him—like I did."

"It's not your fault," Kenzie underscored. "And I'd still like to have a list of his friends," she told Connie. "One or two of those friends might not have given up trying to get him to come out of his shell," she said to the other woman.

Connie looked almost wounded. "You mean the way I gave up?"

Part of her job, the way Kenzie saw it, was to comfort the grieving. Guilt was a heavy burden to bear. Kenzie did her best to help Connie cope.

"You had your own life to live, your own grief to deal with over the death of your mother," Kenzie insisted. "And you *didn't* give up on your dad. You just gave him a time-out so he could try to deal with the situation on his own."

Connie sighed. "When you say it that way, it doesn't sound so bad," she told Kenzie, a trace of gratitude in her voice.

"And it's not," Kenzie told her firmly. "Sometimes you can't drag a horse to water, you have to let him see the water and then clear a path for him so that he can go to it at his own leisurely pace."

Connie's mouth curved. "I never thought of my father as a horse," she commented.

"Maybe more like a mule?" Kenzie suggested with a smile.

Connie sighed. "He could be so stubborn, there was just no talking to him."

Kenzie nodded. "I know what you mean. I have a few relatives like that of my own," she told the woman. She saw a little of the color returning to Connie's thin cheeks. "Feel better?" she asked.

"A little," Connie admitted. "I'll feel a whole lot better once you find him," she said.

"So will I," Kenzie assured the other woman. When people came in to file a missing person report, she took great care in making those people feel as if this was a joint undertaking and that she was in this together with them.

It seemed to help them hang on. "Now, if you could give me as many names and addresses of your dad's friends, that would be a great help."

"I've got my mother's old address book at home. I kept it as a souvenir," Connie explained. "Will that help?" she asked.

"That will be perfect," Kenzie assured her.

"And you'll find my father?" Connie asked again, desperately needing to hear Kenzie make a promise to that effect.

"We'll do our very best to find your father," Kenzie told her.

Connie nodded, rising to her feet. "Okay. I'll get that address book to you today," she promised.

"That'll be great," Kenzie told her.

In her opinion, Connie looked a tiny bit better as she left the office.

Now all she had to do, Kenzie thought, was to deliver on her promise and everything would be fine.

Chapter 2

"Here, you look like you could use this."

Detective Jason Valdez placed a slightly misshapen container of coffee on the desk directly in front of his sometimes partner, Detective Hunter Brannigan.

Hunter raised his half-closed green eyes slowly from the container and fixed what passed for a penetrating look at the man who worked with him in the police department's Cold Case Division.

"You got this from the vending machine?" Hunter went through the motions of asking even though the answer was a foregone conclusion on his part.

"No, I had a carriage drawn by four matched unicorns deliver it. Yes, it's from the vending machine," Jason answered. "What do you think, I'm going to drive over to the closest coffee house to get you some overpriced coffee just because there's a fancy name embossed on the side of the container?"

Removing the lid, Hunter sniffed the inky-black coffee in the container and made a face. "This is swill," he pronounced.

Jason took no offense. Everyone knew that the coffee from the vending machine was strictly a last resort, to be consumed when nothing else was available.

"But it's swill that'll open up those bright green eyes

of yours," Jason told him, sitting down at the desk that butted up against Hunter's, "and I'm betting after the night you've had, you could use any help that you can get."

Hunter moved the container aside. "How do you know what kind of a night I had?"

"Because I'm a detective," Jason answered. "And because you *always* have that kind of a night, especially when it's on a weekend. For some reason, unbeknownst to me, women seem to gravitate to you, willingly buying whatever you're selling."

Hunter laughed. "You're just jealous because you're married and Melinda would skin you alive if she even saw you *looking* at another woman."

"Yeah, there's that, too," Jason agreed. He shook his dark head that recently sprouted a few gray hairs. He blamed that on his wife, as well. "I swear, ever since my wife got pregnant, she's turned into this fire-breathing, suspicious monster."

Hunter shook his head, suppressing a laugh. "There's no accounting for some people's taste, I guess." And then he grew more serious. "Just don't give her any reason to be suspicious."

"Any reason?" Jason questioned. "She's got me too busy running all these errands for her and going around in circles. Any free time I used to have now gets totally eaten up. I couldn't hook up with anyone else if I wanted to—*which I don't*," he emphasized in case that point had gotten lost in the conversation.

"Just hang in there, Valdez. Once the baby comes, Melinda will turn back into that sweet little woman you married."

Jason looked skeptically at the man sitting across from him. "You really believe that?"

Hunter lifted and then dropped his shoulders in a careless shrug. "Hey, it's good to have something to hang on to," he told Jason with a grin.

"I guess," Jason murmured. "It's for damn sure that these cold cases certainly don't fill that void," Valdez said. "Sometimes I wonder why we keep beating our heads against that brick wall."

Instead of a flippant remark the way he'd expected, his partner addressed his question seriously. "Because, every once in a while, there's a crack in that wall and we get to give someone some closure about a loved one. That, my friend, in case you've forgotten, is a good feeling," Hunter said.

Without thinking, he picked up the container Jason brought him and took a sip. Hunter made a face almost immediately, setting the container down again. This time he banished it to the far corner of his desk.

"I think the vending machine people have outdone themselves. This tastes like someone's boiled socks," Hunter declared in disgust.

"How would you know what boiled socks taste like?" Jason asked, apparently intrigued.

Hunter never hesitated. "I have a very vivid imagination," he answered.

James Wilson, a prematurely balding, heavyset man, peered into the squad room. Spotting whom he was looking for, he crossed the floor over to Hunter.

By the time he reached Hunter's desk, Wilson was breathing heavily, sucking in air noisily.

"You really should see a doctor, Wilson," Hunter said. It seemed to him that each time he saw the detective, the man just got heavier and heavier. There had to be a cutoff point.

"Yeah, yeah, you and my wife," Detective Wilson said

dismissively. He made an annoyed face. "You want to hear this or not?"

"Sure," Jason answered, speaking for both of them. "What brings you huffing and puffing into our corner of the world, Wilson?"

Wilson looked from one detective to the other, then answered with a single word. "Rain."

"You're a bit late, Wilson," Jason told the other man. "It rained yesterday. Unseasonably so," the detective added. "Ever notice how Californians drive in the rain? Like they've never seen the stuff before and just want to get home before they drown."

"Don't mind him, he's a transplant from New Mexico," Hunter told the detective. "I'm sure you didn't come all the way over here to talk about the unusual shift in the weather."

Wilson smiled, making Hunter think of a cat that had secretly swallowed a canary. "Indirectly, I am."

While Hunter claimed that his evenings out had no effect on him, last night had been particularly taxing. He'd gotten all of three hours' sleep, and it was beginning to catch up with him. Opening a drawer, he checked to see if he was out of aspirin. He was.

"Wilson," he said, closing the drawer again, "I've got a headache building behind my eyes and I'm not in the mood for twenty questions. Now, is this belated weather report going somewhere or not?" he asked.

Instead of answering the question, Wilson asked one of his own. "Mind if I sit?"

Hunter played along and gestured toward the chair next to his desk. "Now, what did you come all this way to tell me?"

James Wilson worked on another floor for another division, but what would have seemed close to another man was like a trek through the Himalayas to the man now sitting beside his desk. It had to have taken a lot to bring Wilson here, Hunter reasoned.

"You know that cold case you keep coming back to?" Wilson asked. When Hunter didn't respond, Wilson added, "That first one that you picked up?"

Hunter knew exactly which case the other detective was referring to. It was the one that really haunted him because he could never identify the victim for a very basic reason.

"You're talking about the man who was missing his hands and head," Hunter said.

Like a game show host, Wilson pointed toward Hunter, then touched the tip of his nose as if the other detective's answer was dead-on. "That's the one. You know that rain we had yesterday?" Wilson asked.

"The rain you led with?" Hunter asked. It was a rhetorical question. "What about it?"

Wilson enjoyed having other people listen to him and it was obvious that he was stretching this out. "Well, apparently it washed away some dirt."

"It was a torrential downpour," Jason recalled. "A *lot* of dirt was washed away."

"Yeah, but this dirt was covering up what turned out to be a shallow grave." Wilson paused, whether for dramatic effect or because he'd temporarily run out of breath wasn't clear.

In either case, both Hunter and Jason cried out, almost in unison: "What was in the grave?"

"Hands and a head," Wilson informed them almost smugly.

Hunter was on his feet immediately. "Where are those hands and that head now?" he asked.

"Where do you think? The ME's got them," Wilson answered.

Hunter started to hurry out of the squad room, then abruptly stopped. They were two men down today, bringing their total down to two. Jason and he couldn't both leave the squad room at the same time. He looked back at his partner, a quizzical look on his face.

The latter waved him on. "You go, Brannigan. This was your baby to begin with. I'll man the desk and answer the phones—not that they'll ring," Jason added.

"You sure?" It evolved into a joint case, although it was more his than Jason's since he had taken the case over from the retiring homicide detective who hadn't been able to close it.

"I'm sure." Jason grinned, looking at his friend. "Looks like the color came back to your cheeks, Brannigan. Both of our names might be on the report, but this is your case. I wouldn't deprive you of going down to see this latest piece of the puzzle," he told Hunter.

That was all Hunter needed.

"How did you happen to find out about this, anyway?" Hunter asked the other detective. He slowed down in order to allow Wilson to catch up.

"Heard two detectives talking in the snack room. Thought of that cold case you had," Wilson said with a touch of bravado. They got to the elevator and he pressed the down button. "What do you think are the odds that these hands and head are *your* cold case's head and hands?" Wilson asked.

"Well, given that this isn't a run-of-the-mill kind of kill," Hunter speculated as the elevator car arrived, "I'd say the odds are better than fifty-fifty."

Getting in and holding the door open for Wilson, he waited until the other detective got on, then pressed for the basement. Ordinarily, the medical examiner's offices were housed in a different building. However, in the interest of efficiency, in the last few months the office had been moved to the building that housed the police department. It now occupied the same floor as the CSI lab and the computer tech department.

The elevator arrived in the basement, but as the doors opened, Wilson remained where he was. When Hunter glanced at him, Wilson said, "I'll let you go the rest of the way yourself."

"You don't want to come with me?" Hunter asked.

He'd been surprised that the detective had accompanied him this far and had just assumed that Wilson would tag along to see if this was indeed connected to the cold case he'd taken over when he first came to the division.

However, Wilson looked more than a little pale as he hung back.

"I've seen enough things on this job to give me nightmares as it is. I don't need this to prey on my mind, too. Just wanted to bring you the 'good news,'" Wilson said, raising his voice just as the elevator doors closed again.

Hunter shook his head. "Takes all kinds," he murmured under his breath.

He wasn't particularly anxious to see a dismembered head either, but if it brought closure to the case he'd worked on over the last few years, it would be well worth it. Maybe now he could go through the database and put a name to the headless, handless person who had been his first case. Put a name to him and possibly bring closure to a family if the murder victim actually had one.

In any event, as long as the fingerprints weren't burnt off—and he really doubted that they would be, because why get rid of the hands if you could burn off the prints more easily—he stood a good chance of at least giving the victim a name.

The moment Hunter stepped into the medical examiner's room, he knew that the head and hands didn't belong to the man whose file was in his desk. The head and hands on the ME's table looked much too fresh, as if whoever had been dismembered and buried had suffered the indignities less than a week ago. Decomposition hadn't gone too far yet. The victim in his cold case file had been killed several years ago and his hands and feet—unless extraordinary measures had been taken to preserve those body parts—would have been badly decomposed.

Still, he was here so he might as well ask a few questions, Hunter thought.

"What do you have for me, Doc?" Hunter asked, walking in.

"Not all that much yet I'm afraid," Dr. Alexander Rayburn said, gesturing toward the three body parts on his table. "The crime lab techs just brought this lovely package to me about two hours ago."

The head he was looking at had gray hair and a very pale complexion. If nothing else, the victim hadn't been a sun worshipper, Hunter thought. "Can you tell me how long he's been dead?" he asked the ME.

"Well, all this is still preliminary, but my guess is that he's been dead for about a week, possibly less, maybe a little more. Judging from his face, I'd say that he's a man in his later fifties. A professional man," the doctor added.

Hunter looked at the ME, puzzled. "How can you tell that?"

"The hands," the doctor answered. He picked up one carefully in his gloved hand. "There are no calluses on his hands, no rough skin. He didn't work with his hands, he worked with his brain."

"Which it seems was generously delivered to you, as well," Hunter commented, looking at the victim's head. He circled the table slowly, looking at the three dismembered parts that were laid out on the table. "What kind of a person does this, Doc?"

"That's an easy one to answer," the ME said. "A sick person. A methodical person. And an extremely organized person." He looked at Hunter. "These cuts weren't made hastily, or haphazardly. The killer knew exactly where to cut for minimum damage and bone resistance. My guess is that the victim was anesthetized—or more likely, already dead—when he was cut up."

Hunter separated himself from the deed that the ME was describing. It was a coping mechanism he'd learned to use on his first case. Otherwise, he'd be spending every available moment in the men's room, throwing up his last meal.

"Anything else?" he asked the ME.

"Yes." The doctor looked up at Hunter and said with atypical passion, "I hope that the bastard who did this rots in hell."

"You and me both, Doc," Hunter agreed.

Well, he'd gotten what he came for. This didn't involve his cold case. Even so, Hunter remained in the room and continued to thoughtfully look at the body parts that were laid out on the ME's table.

"Something on your mind I can help you with, Detective?" the ME asked, glancing at Hunter over his shoulder. "You said these aren't the missing parts from your cold case."

"They're clearly not," Hunter agreed.

"Well, I know that it isn't my scintillating company that's keeping you here," the ME said, "so what's the problem?"

Hunter went on studying the dismembered parts on the table. He had an eerie feeling about them. About this whole thing.

"The problem is that I think my cold case might very well have been the first victim for whoever killed this man."

The doctor looked up from the notes he was taking and looked pointedly at the detective. "Are you saying what I think you're saying?"

Hunter nodded. "I think we've got a serial killer on our hands."

"Correct me if I'm wrong," the doctor said, pausing, "but doesn't it usually take three victims before someone can be declared to be a serial killer?"

Hunter nodded, but even as he did, he said, "I'm sure there's a third body out there somewhere. And possibly a fourth and a fifth. I'm going to take a cadaver dog out there with me and check that whole area where these hands and head were found," he informed the ME.

The ME sighed. The doctor had a very clear picture of what lay ahead if Hunter was successful in his "mission."

"I'd say 'good luck' but I'm not sure which way that would be," the ME told Hunter.

Just as Hunter was leaving the room, he almost walked right into MacKenzie Cavanaugh. Backing up, he inclined his head as he smiled at her. "Kenzie."

She nodded, as well, uttering a crisp, "Hunter."

"Suddenly there's a really cold chill in the room," the ME commented.

"Well, Brannigan's on his way out, so the chill'll be gone soon," Kenzie told the medical examiner.

The doctor looked in her direction. "What brings you down here?"

Kenzie wanted to make sure that she wasn't trying to

locate a man who was already dead, so starting out in the ME's office made sense. "I came to find out if you have any unclaimed bodies down here."

"Only mine," Hunter volunteered, speaking up from the doorway.

Kenzie chose to ignore him. Hunter Brannigan might be really close friends with two of her brothers, but she had no intention of encouraging the ladies' man to talk to her any more than absolutely necessary.

"Who are you looking for?" the ME asked Kenzie.

But at that moment, Kenzie had glanced down at the dismembered head on the table and her mouth dropped open.

"I'm looking for this man," she said, the words almost dribbling out of her mouth as she held up the photo that Connie had given her.

Chapter 3

The medical examiner looked briefly at the photograph that Kenzie had in her hand. There was no doubt about the match.

"Then I'd say you found him. Or what there is of him at the moment," the doctor amended.

Kenzie felt shell-shocked. This was so much worse than what she'd expected. Connie was going to be devastated when she broke the news to her.

"When—when did this happen?" Kenzie asked, trying not to let the scene get to her. It wasn't the gruesomeness of the crime so much as the crime itself that she found unnerving.

The medical examiner looked at her. "You're the second person to ask me that in the last few minutes. I'll tell you what I said to Detective Brannigan—" Dr. Rayburn got no further.

Kenzie looked at the ME sharply. "Detective Brannigan?" she echoed in surprise.

"That would be me," Hunter said, raising his hand as he walked back into the room.

She whirled around to look at the man who had managed to rub her the wrong way more times than she could possibly begin to remember.

"Why were *you* asking questions about John Kurtz?" she asked.

"I wasn't," he told her. "I was asking questions about the person whose body parts were spread out on the doc's table."

"John Kurtz," she repeated, as if to drill the name into his head.

"So it would seem, but I didn't know that at the time," Hunter pointed out.

Brannigan was just trying to confuse her, something he had always taken far too much enjoyment in doing, Kenzie thought. She deliberately turned her back on him as she addressed the medical examiner.

"You were about to tell me about John Kurtz's time of death, Doctor," she prodded.

"As I told Detective Brannigan here, I still have to run more tests," the doctor said, focusing on what he had on his table, "but my best guess is that your Mr. Kurtz has been dead for a week."

"Where was he found?" she asked. "Who brought him in?"

The interest in her voice was obvious. It in turn piqued Hunter's. He circled around Kenzie until he was facing her.

"Do you know him?" he asked.

"I know his daughter. She came in this morning to file a missing person report on him," Kenzie answered stiffly, addressing her words to the doctor, not Hunter. She deliberately avoided making eye contact with the detective. "Who found him?" she asked again.

The medical examiner told them what he knew. "From what I gather, he—or at least the parts that you see here—was in a shallow grave that yesterday's downpour washed up. A couple of kids playing in the mud made the discovery. Their rather hysterical mother called the police. The rest you know," the doctor concluded.

"Where was this?" Kenzie asked.

"Along the border of Aurora Park," the medical examiner answered.

"I'm taking a cadaver dog with me to the scene where the body parts were found," Hunter told her, speaking up. "Care to come with me?"

This time she did look at him.

The first time she had ever heard of Hunter Brannigan, two of her brothers, Murdoch and Finn, were talking about how Brannigan had a different woman on his arm every time he went out. To hear them say it, Hunter ran on batteries and Southern Comfort, although, amazingly enough, he was also considered a damn good detective who had risen rather quickly through the ranks on his own merit. He was assigned to the Cold Case Division because the thinking was, if anyone could clear the old cases, Brannigan could.

Maybe, in another lifetime, they could have even been friends, despite his confident swagger. But she had terminated a rather painful engagement a little over two years ago, the details of which she had kept to herself. Her fiancé, Billy Gibson, had been a tomcat who'd had a weakness for prowling around despite all his promises to reform and be faithful. After his third transgression, she'd given him his walking papers. She hadn't said anything to anyone because if her brothers had caught wind of why she'd broken the engagement off, they would have skinned Billy and proceeded to hang him from the highest flagpole.

Since then, Kenzie had been very leery of silver-tongued handsome men. That description fit Hunter Brannigan to a T.

"What interest do you have in John Kurtz?" Kenzie asked.

Hunter's shimmering green eyes skimmed over her from top to bottom before he answered. "I don't."

He could make her lose her patience faster than any human being she had ever encountered, and that included Billy. Kenzie struggled now to hold on to her temper as she asked, "Then why would you be going to the scene where he was found?"

He slowly smiled at Kenzie, knowing that it annoyed her. He couldn't explain why, but he really liked getting under her skin. "Let's just say I have a real interest in the person who did this to him."

"Why?" Kenzie demanded.

Hunter saw no reason to keep this a secret. Teasing Kenzie took a back seat to possibly solving a case—or at least getting one step closer to solving it.

"Because I think that my cold case might have been this guy's first murder," he told her.

"Why?" she repeated.

It was obvious to him that because of their past history, she was going to take some convincing. He had no problem with that.

"Because my cold case is missing his head and hands, too," he told her. "Now, you're welcome to come along, or you can stay here and I'll let you know what I find—if I remember."

He saw her eyes flash—just as he had expected them to. "This is *my* case, Brannigan," she insisted.

"That's not how I see it," Hunter replied mildly.

"Now, now, children, play nice," the medical examiner said. "I've got a feeling that there's plenty enough here for both of you to share."

Kenzie didn't want to admit it—since Hunter was

involved—but in all likelihood, the ME was right. But even so, she had no desire to team up with Hunter.

"I can take the dog," she told Hunter.

The same infuriating smile was back on Hunter's face. He dug in. "That's not happening."

She wasn't about to have this devolve into a shouting match—and she had no intentions of letting Brannigan go without her.

Kenzie frowned. "I have to let my partner know where I'm going."

"Go ahead and do that," Hunter told her. "I've got to go to the K-9 unit and secure a dog."

"They're not going to just *give* you a dog," she informed Hunter. "If nothing else, his handler has to come with the dog."

"Even better," Hunter commented. While he liked dogs, his involvement with canines ended with throwing a stick and having the dog chase it. Having someone along who knew what they were doing with canines was all good as far as he was concerned. "We'll meet you out back once I make arrangements with the K-9 unit."

A red flag went up in her head. Kenzie didn't trust Brannigan to wait for her.

"I've got a better idea," she told Hunter. "Why don't you come with me up to Missing Persons so I can tell Choi where I'll be and then I'll come with you to the K-9 unit."

She couldn't tell what he was thinking until his eyes washed over her again. "This isn't first grade, Cavanaugh. We really don't need to pair up to walk through the halls," he told her. "Although, I have to say that it does sound like it has potential."

"Listen to her, Brannigan," the ME advised. "She's a Cavanaugh. They tend to get things done."

"So do I, Doc," Hunter answered. "But in the spirit of détente, I'll bow to your wisdom," he said, inclining his head.

Kenzie left the morgue quickly. But although she moved fast, Hunter kept up with her pace as if it took no effort on his part at all.

They reached the elevator together. She had no intention of saying anything to Hunter, but the silence within the car once they got on became almost unnervingly deafening. She could all but *feel* his eyes on her, taking inventory. And when she turned to look at the man she'd heard some of her friends refer to as a dark blond Adonis, she saw that he was smiling at her.

A rather *wide* smile.

"Why are you grinning, Brannigan?" she demanded.

His shrug was careless and utterly infuriating. "I guess I'm just a happy person."

"Well, stop it," she ordered. "You might enjoy looking like a happy idiot, but I have to tell someone I know that her father's not coming home tonight." She set her mouth grimly. "Or ever."

"You want help with that?" he offered.

If she didn't know him, she would have said that his offer sounded genuine. But she *did* know Brannigan and she was convinced that he didn't possess a genuine bone in his body. "I don't need you to hit on her," Kenzie informed him.

"I wasn't planning to. Whatever else you might think of me, I *am* good at my job. Breaking bad news is never easy and I was just offering to help since you said you knew the victim's daughter. It might be easier on everyone all around if I handle this."

She resented his intrusion. Resented everything that

Brannigan represented. "I don't need *you* to handle anything for me," she informed him heatedly.

He raised his hands in the universal sign of surrender. "Point taken, Kenzie."

"Don't call me that," she snapped as they got off the elevator.

"What would you like me to call you?" he asked. "Your Majesty's a little formal, but I'm game if that's what you want."

Her eyes narrowed into blue slits of lightning. "Cavanaugh," she said. "Just call me by my last name, the way you would anyone else you work with."

"But you're not anyone else, are you?" He all but purred the question. Before she could work up a full head of steam by telling him what he could do with that obvious line of his, Hunter interjected, "You're Finn and Murdoch's sister and they're my friends."

Kenzie rolled her eyes. "Please, don't remind me." How her normally intelligent brothers could be friends with this egotist was beyond her. "C'mon," she urged. "Let's get this over with."

"Good detective work should never be rushed," he chided, knowing that saying that would just irritate her further. He couldn't really explain why, but he liked irritating Kenzie. Liked getting a reaction—any sort of reaction—out of her. Liked seeing the way her eyes blazed as she all but breathed fire.

When she walked ahead of him this time, he let her. She needed to work off her anger, he thought.

"I found our missing person," Kenzie told her partner when she walked back into the division's squad room.

Kyle Choi looked at her, a trace of bewilderment in his face.

"So soon? Where was the guy, hiding in a cabin, somewhere away from his daughter?" he asked with a chuckle.

"No, not exactly," Kenzie told him with a heavy voice. "John Kurtz is a homicide victim."

"Oh, damn," Kyle said with genuine regret. The detective glanced at Hunter, his bewilderment returning. "What's he doing here?" Choi asked. He addressed his question to Brannigan. "Thinking of switching departments?"

"It's a long story," Kenzie answered before Hunter could say anything to the other detective in response. She saw Hunter opening his mouth and spoke quickly. "But the short version is—no, he's not looking to switch departments. And even if he were, he certainly wouldn't be switching into ours," she concluded. There was no room for argument in her voice.

Rather than become annoyed, Hunter grinned—which in turn irritated Kenzie more.

"To hear you talk, someone would get the impression you don't like me, Kenzie," Hunter commented in an easygoing tone.

"And they'd be right," she retorted. Her eyes narrowed as she shot a look in his direction. "I told you not to call me that."

"It's your name, isn't it?" Hunter asked her innocently.

She decided that it would be better just to ignore him than to get into a verbal duel. So she spoke to Choi, telling her partner, "Parts of John Kurtz's body were found thanks to yesterday's monsoon and Brannigan—" she clenched her teeth "—is going to take me there."

Choi looked at Hunter quizzically and the latter lifted his broad shoulders in a shrug. "Not my idea of a romantic spot, but hey, different strokes for different folks, right?"

Kenzie saw her partner opening his mouth and quickly intervened. "Pay no attention to him, Kyle. It'll only encourage him to babble. We're going to see if we can find the rest of Mr. Kurtz in the general vicinity. I don't want to tell Connie about her father until we at least try to find the rest of him. Telling her that his head and hands were the only things that were found is just too gruesome for words," she told Choi. "I don't want her left with that memory."

Her partner nodded. As it was, he looked as if he was close to parting company with his breakfast burrito right about now.

"I've got plenty to keep me busy here," Choi told her.

Hunter looked over his shoulder at Kenzie's mild-mannered partner just before he followed her out of the squad room. "Wish me luck," he said to the detective.

He heard Choi laugh in response.

Kenzie glanced at Hunter disdainfully. "You do know where we're going once you get the dog and his handler, right?"

He knew she was trying to goad him into losing his temper, but he was having far too much fun for that. "I make it a point of always knowing where I'm going, Kenzie—sorry, Cavanaugh," he amended before she could say anything. "But in this case, I have the ME's report detailing where the body parts were uncovered. I am, however, open to suggestions if you have a different destination in mind," he told her cheerfully.

She blew out an annoyed breath. "Are you *always* on?" she asked.

The corners of his mouth curved until the smile on his face was a full thousand watts. "I do my best, Detective Cavanaugh."

Why did every word out of his mouth annoy her so much? "Trust me, your best isn't nearly good enough so fold up your little tent and just disappear into the night if you're going to continue with this juvenile act of yours."

He put his hand over his heart. "Why, Kenzie, I'm deeply wounded."

Once again, her eyes darkened until they looked positively stormy, glaring at him. "Brannigan, you don't know the meaning of the word *wounded*—but I can change that."

"Sorry, Cavanaugh, but someone already beat you to it," he told her and for just a second, she believed him. But then, she thought, that was just what he wanted. "I can show you the scars if you're interested."

"No, thanks," she told Hunter. "I'll pass."

They were outside now, heading for the kennels where the canines that were on duty were kept. "They're really phenomenal scars," he told her. "You don't know what you're missing."

"I know *exactly* what I'm missing—peace and quiet," she retorted, then regrouped. There was no point in talking to this man. It just somehow fed his ego. "Let's just do this and be done with it."

He nodded. "Sounds good—your place or mine?" he asked with what was probably the most wickedly sexy look she had ever seen in her life. Kenzie could almost see what women saw in this man—if he wasn't so transparent to her.

"You're never going to get that lucky, Brannigan," she informed him.

He grinned again. "Ah, a man's grasp should extend his reach, or what's a heaven for?"

She was not impressed. "Let me guess, you minored in English lit."

"No," Hunter told her. "But I once dated a girl who did."

"I'm sure you did." She wasn't in the mood to hear him spout off the list of women who had paraded through his life. "Put a lid on it, Brannigan. The less you talk, the less I'll be tempted to shoot you."

He laughed at that, tickled. "I bet you say that to all the guys."

"No," she responded, "only you."

If she meant to shut him down, she failed. That same wicked grin was back on his lips.

"I like being the first," he told her.

Kenzie decided that her best bet was to refrain from answering him when he talked.

With a toss of her head, she marched the rest of the way to the K-9 department, which was adjacent to the Animal Control Division.

A cacophony of animal sounds was heard as they passed by. Kenzie disregarded the noise in the same way she disregarded Brannigan.

She looked around to see if her cousin-in-law was anywhere around, but it looked like Brady wasn't there at the moment.

Officer Jake O'Reilly, a longtime veteran of the unit, came up behind them and asked, "Is there anything I can help you with, Detectives?"

"As a matter of fact, there is," Kenzie said, taking the lead. "We need a cadaver dog. A head and a pair of hands were found in the field around Aurora Park after yesterday's rain. We think there might be more buried in or around the area. We need help finding them."

"Got the dog for the job right here," O'Reilly said. "Come here, Jupiter. These nice detectives need your help." He opened the kennel door and a large German shepherd came bounding out.

Jupiter barked in response as if he understood what was expected of him. He excitedly shifted from paw to paw.

Chapter 4

They took Kenzie's vehicle to the area at the edge of Aurora Park where John Kurtz's head and hands had been found.

On the rather short trip over, O'Reilly sat in the back of the vehicle with his K-9 partner, Jupiter. The animal remained still until just before they arrived at their destination. Then he began moving about in the back seat.

Kenzie could feel herself growing tense with every passing minute, not because Hunter was sitting in the front passenger seat next to her, but because she had the very uneasy feeling that the detective could very well be right. If he was, that meant that they had a serial killer on their hands, and that was the last thing that *any* of them really wanted.

Except maybe for Hunter, she silently amended, slanting a look in his direction as she parked her car in the designated spot for park visitors. Finding out that this was the work of a serial killer could wind up being quite a feather in his cap, given that cold cases were called that for a reason.

One really didn't expect them to ever get warm.

"Is this the area where the body parts were first found?" O'Reilly asked Hunter as he got out of the vehicle.

Hunter glanced into the back seat that O'Reilly had

just vacated. Jupiter, still in the car, was moving from side to side, growing progressively more eager to be set free.

"Judging by the way your dog is acting, I'd say that's a firm yes," Hunter answered.

"I've got a really bad feeling about this," Kenzie said to the two men with her. "Or a good feeling," she added, glancing at Hunter, "depending on which point of view you take."

"Stay, Jupiter," O'Reilly ordered as he opened the rear door closest to him.

It was obvious that the shepherd wanted to leap out, but he remained where he was as his trainer reached in to get his leash and firmly wrapped it around his hand.

"Neat trick," Hunter commented to the handler. "Think you could teach it to me sometime?"

"Why?" Kenzie asked, looking at Hunter. "Are you having trouble keeping your girlfriends from bolting out of the car on you?"

Hunter grinned at her, amused rather than annoyed. "That's not the problem at all," he replied.

A sharp comeback rose to Kenzie's lips, but she bit it back. She'd started this round and if it played itself out, they'd wind up losing sight of why they were here to begin with. She couldn't afford to squabble with Hunter, at least not until she knew what they were up against.

"Truce," she declared grudgingly, looking in Hunter's direction.

"Fine by me," Hunter answered. He glanced toward the German shepherd straining at his leash. "O'Reilly, your dog looks really eager to show us his stuff. Why don't you let him?"

Jupiter was out of the vehicle now, all but dancing from side to side. It was easy to see that he was champing at the bit to get going.

O'Reilly, by no means a small man, looked as if he was having trouble holding on to the German shepherd. "I don't think I have much choice in the matter."

The words were no sooner out of O'Reilly's mouth than he slackened his hold on the leash. Jupiter suddenly began to tear through the area, all but dragging his handler in his wake.

"I guess that's our cue to get going," Hunter commented.

Because the rain had really come down heavily here, drenching the area, the ground was still very wet in a lot of spots. The resulting mud made the terrain extremely slippery.

Following Jupiter and O'Reilly wasn't nearly as easy as Kenzie had initially thought, no matter how carefully she tried. Trying to keep up, Kenzie slid twice. Both times she managed to catch herself at the last moment. The only thing that comforted her was that she saw Hunter having trouble keeping upright, as well.

But just as she was silently reveling in his narrowly avoiding making contact with the oozing mud beneath him, she suddenly felt her feet sliding out from under her. In a heartbeat, she braced herself for an undignified pratfall.

At the last possible moment, Kenzie felt a strong hand grip her arm, righting her and preventing her from making a face-plant in the mud.

The air whooshed out of her as first shock, and then an instant later relief, vibrated through her.

Her heart hammering wildly in her chest, she looked to her right, hoping against hope that O'Reilly had made a quick U-turn and was the one responsible for her last-moment save.

But it wasn't O'Reilly. It was Brannigan who was holding on to her arm.

Brannigan had been the one to save her face and her pride.

"Thanks." Kenzie uttered the word as if each letter cost her dearly.

Hunter smiled and graciously inclined his head. "I don't think I've ever heard gratitude so grudgingly dispensed," he told her.

She glanced at her arm. His hand was still wrapped around it. "You can let go of my arm now," she informed him icily.

"Are you sure?" he asked dubiously. "It's still pretty slippery here."

He was up to something, Kenzie thought. She just didn't trust this Boy Scout routine of his.

"I'm sure," she answered. She scowled when he went on holding her arm. "You're cutting off my circulation," she told him.

His smile widened. "From what I hear, according to your brothers *I'm* not the one cutting it off."

Kenzie shook off his hold. Striding after O'Reilly and Jupiter, she struggled to hold on to her temper. She did owe Hunter, aware that he could have very easily just let her fall. She still didn't understand why he didn't, but even so, that put her, at least temporarily, in his debt.

And she didn't like it.

"Can we please just stick to business?" Kenzie requested.

"Speaking of which," Hunter said, glancing over toward Jupiter. The dog had abruptly stopped in his tracks and was now suddenly digging eagerly. "I think we just might be in business now."

Hunter carefully made his way over toward the German shepherd as the dog furiously burrowed through the mud, oblivious to the fact that he was growing incredibly dirty as he dug.

"Looks like Jupiter found the rest of that body you were looking for," O'Reilly commented.

"Not quite," Kenzie said, squatting down to get a closer look at what the dog was digging up. She turned her head as more mud went flying at all of them. "O'Reilly, get him to stop for a minute," she requested.

"Jupiter, stay!" O'Reilly ordered gruffly.

Getting in closer again, Kenzie frowned. And then she turned her head slightly as she looked back at Hunter. He was a few inches away from her. "You don't need to breathe down my neck, Brannigan."

"I know. I thought that was a bonus," he told her innocently. Then, before she could speak up, Hunter said what they were both thinking. "That torso has been in the ground too long to belong to John Kurtz."

She frowned, hating the fact that she agreed with Brannigan's assessment. "And I'm thinking that it's also not decomposed enough to belong to your cold case," Kenzie added.

"This makes three," Hunter said quietly, as if saying the words too loudly would somehow make everything fall apart. "It's official," he told Kenzie and the officer. "Looks like we have ourselves a serial killer."

Kenzie felt her heart sink. Whether it was because she agreed with him, or because he was the one who put it into words first, she didn't know. Either way, she had her cell phone out. She hit a number on her speed dial.

"Who are you calling?" Hunter asked.

She held up her hand, silently requesting him to stop talking.

"Destiny?" she said, recognizing the voice of the person who had picked up on the other end. “Is the chief around?” she asked formally. “Thanks.”

“CSI?” Hunter guessed.

Kenzie nodded. Just then, the wind shifted. The next moment, Jupiter was off and running again. O’Reilly could barely keep up. In all probability he might have lost the dog had Jupiter not stopped in front of another mound. It was all dirt, not mud this time. Either way, the dog began digging furiously again.

Watching what Jupiter was doing, Kenzie came to attention as the phone was being picked up on the other end.

“Uncle Sean? This is Kenzie. Looks like I’ve got some unfinished business for your investigators. Detective Brannigan had the K-9 unit bring out a cadaver dog to go over the scene at Aurora Park where that head and hands were found today. The thinking was to find the rest of the body, but the dog dug up more bones. Old bones,” she emphasized. “How soon can you have someone from your team get here? Great. We’ll be here.”

Ending the call, she slid her phone back into her pocket. She looked over toward O’Reilly, who was having more trouble restraining Jupiter. The shepherd looked eager to take off again.

“The crime scene investigators will be here shortly,” she told the handler. She eyed the German shepherd. “Is he just excited, or—”

“I think it’s ‘or,’” O’Reilly replied with a heavy sigh.

Kenzie gestured toward the dog. “By all means, give him his lead,” she told O’Reilly.

Once again Jupiter was off and running, with O’Reilly not too far behind.

“Looks like that flash flood unleashed someone’s hidden graveyard,” Hunter observed. He made his way over to the third set of bones the dog had just dug up.

"Yes, but whose?" she questioned, saying it more to herself than to the detective standing near her. She surveyed the area with dismay. "This can't just be the work of one person—can it?" she asked him.

"There's no telling what one person is capable of," Hunter answered. "The Green River Killer racked up one hell of a large body count before they finally caught on to him."

Kenzie shivered. She remembered reading about the case. The man who was ultimately responsible for the killings broke all the previous rules that had, everyone believed, once been set in stone. The serial killer wasn't a withdrawn loner. Instead, he was a member of the community. A well-respected member who taught Sunday school on occasion, ran a youth group and was a man whom everyone liked. No one would have ever suspected him of doing anything wrong, let alone killing so many women.

With the playbook rendered completely null and void, that meant anything was possible and just about anyone could be a killer.

That unfortunately left the suspect pool wide-open, she thought.

"Looks like this means we're going to be keeping company for a little while longer, Kenzie," Hunter told her.

Kenzie jumped. For a minute, lost in thought, she had totally forgotten that he was there. Annoyed that Brannigan had managed to make her react like a skittish teenager, she asked him almost belligerently, "What makes you say that?"

"Isn't it obvious? My killer is your killer," Hunter pointed out simply. "It doesn't make any sense for us to pursue the guy separately."

From where she stood, pursuing the killer separately

made a lot of sense, Kenzie thought. Mainly because she didn't want to work alongside Brannigan any more than she had to. In her opinion, the man was as shallow as a raindrop and she was in no mood to be subjected to his feeble attempts to impress her or to dazzle her with his so-called detective skills.

"Why not?" she asked, challenging him. "This way, we can approach the crimes from two separate points of view."

"We can still do that, but together," Hunter countered stubbornly. "And it'll go faster if we don't have to stop and call each other every time a new idea hits one of us. All we'll have to do is look across the table—or however you intend to have your bull pen arranged," he told her.

Stunned, she realized just what he was getting at. "You're talking about getting a task force together," Kenzie cried, part of her still hoping that he would deny it.

But he didn't. Exactly.

"That all depends," Hunter answered loftily. "Do the two of us constitute a task force?"

Suddenly feeling cornered, she searched for a way to put Brannigan off. "I need permission to get a task force together," she told him.

Hunter looked totally unfazed by her excuse. "You're a Cavanaugh. Do you really *need* permission to do something?" he asked skeptically. It was obvious that the detective didn't think so.

So, he was one of those, was he? He thought she was privileged. Well, *she* didn't think she was privileged and she certainly didn't act as if she was, Kenzie thought, annoyed.

"It's *because* I'm a Cavanaugh that I need permission," Kenzie informed him, incensed that Brannigan had the gall to put her on the spot like this. "Just because I have that last name doesn't mean I'm privileged."

The smile on Hunter's face seemed to mock her and she would have given anything to physically wipe it off his lips—with her fist.

"The chief of Ds told you to say that, didn't he?" Brannigan guessed. His expression made it abundantly clear that he got a tremendous kick out of what Kenzie was saying.

She was *not* about to confirm Brannigan's guess, even though she grudgingly admitted that it was dead-on. As things stood between them, she would rather die than come out and say that.

Instead, she resorted to wordplay. "That doesn't alter the circumstances," she informed Brannigan with a toss of her head.

"All right," he obliged. "So go ahead, ask the chief for permission to put a task force together. The sooner you do, the sooner it'll be granted—" he glanced down at the body parts that Jupiter had just unearthed "—and the sooner we'll be on our way to finding the SOB who gets his jollies doing this sort of sick thing."

"SO*Bs*," Kenzie corrected pointedly.

Hunter looked at her, confused. "What?"

"You said there might be two of them, remember?" she reminded Brannigan. "I'm just trying to cover all our bases."

"Right," he agreed. He had said that, Hunter thought. But at the time he was just making guesses. "Hard to believe there're two people out there who are this depraved."

Kenzie looked at him, wondering if he was really on the level or if he was just pulling her leg, trying to get on the right side of her for his own reasons.

The look on his face didn't really give her a clue.

She had to ask him. "You're serious?"

Hunter nodded. Since they were apparently going to be working together, he shared a little of his basic philosophy with her.

"Gotta hang on to the light, or you wind up sinking into the darkness and before you know it, you wind up giving up."

That sounded deep, she thought. Too deep for Brannigan, she maintained. Kenzie was afraid to leave her defenses down, even for a moment.

"That's one way to look at it," Kenzie told him flippantly.

"Okay, so what's your way?" Brannigan asked her as they watched the shepherd begin to dig into the earth for yet one more time.

Kenzie looked at the detective. Sunlight was weaving through his hair. She did her best to ignore that, looking for his flaws.

"My way?" she repeated.

"Yeah," he answered. Jupiter was growing more agitated. "How do you look at what you do?"

She recited the mantra she liked to live by. "Catching the bad guys and making the world safer for everyone else."

Brannigan grinned at her and she was certain he was going to say something flippant or make fun of her. But instead, he surprised her by saying, "See, we're not that different after all, you and I."

She did *not* want to be likened to this man by anyone, least of all him.

"Oh, we're worlds apart, Brannigan. Worlds apart," she emphasized.

Hunter pointed over toward Jupiter, who apparently had unearthed still another would-be grave.

"I'd say that it looks like our worlds just got a little closer, Kenzie," he told her.

She clenched her teeth. "I told you not to call me that. Only my friends and family call me that."

"So how do I get to be part of your friends' club?" he asked.

"Simple," she told him. "You die and come back as someone else. *Anyone* else," she underscored.

He laughed, obviously getting a kick out of her—that was *not* what she had intended.

"I'll see what I can do about that," Hunter promised just before he made his way over to Jupiter's newest discovery.

Chapter 5

Chief Sean Cavanaugh, head of the crime scene investigation day crew, surveyed the very large area that had been cordoned off. Sporadic piles of dirt and mud pocked the entire terrain at this end of the park. Three investigators were moving around, documenting everything that could even remotely pass for evidence.

"The park officials are *not* going to be happy about this," Sean commented.

Vacation season had just begun and there were tourists to think of, not to mention regular residents who normally enjoyed utilizing the park's many attributes and were now prevented from doing so.

It looked as if there were miles of yellow tape designating the entire area off-limits. It was the police department's attempt to keep the public from accidentally trampling over any possible clues that hadn't surfaced yet.

Hunter nodded in agreement. This was his first professional interaction with the chief. "I'm not overly thrilled with this either, but I'm willing to bet it's most likely for a completely different reason," the cold case detective said.

Kenzie was standing close by and she looked at Brannigan in surprise. "I would have thought you'd be thrilled to death with this turn of events, Brannigan," she retorted.

"Thrilled?" Hunter echoed, puzzled. "Why?" he asked. "I'm not a ghoul—or bloodthirsty."

Hunter stopped himself before he could say anything further. He wasn't about to get into a possible shouting match with Kenzie in front of the chief. Instead, he turned toward Rayburn.

The medical examiner had arrived shortly after the chief and his team had. Rayburn was looking at the various piles of bones—torsos and arms and legs for the most part—and he was shaking his head.

"How many different people do you think Jupiter dug up today, Doc?" Hunter asked the man.

Dr. Rayburn frowned. "Hard to say before I get all these—these pieces to the morgue and see if I can match the right limbs to the right torsos," the medical examiner answered honestly. "Are you sure that the dog didn't accidentally stumble across some old, forgotten burial ground?" he asked. It was hard to miss the hopeful note in his voice.

"Way ahead of you, Doc," Kenzie told the medical examiner. "I already called Valri," she said, mentioning the name of the Aurora police department's most gifted computer tech, "and had her dig up the town's records for this area dating back almost a hundred and fifty years. There is no record of there being any cemetery or burial grounds in the vicinity."

Rayburn nodded. "I should have known." He glanced toward the chief, who was now busy instructing one of his investigators. "You people are nothing if not thorough. As for how many former citizens we have here," the medical examiner said, returning to Hunter's question, "I'll know more after I've had some time to examine all these different dismembered torsos and limbs." He looked thoughtful at the various pallets filled with headless bodies and unattached arms and legs that were being prepared to be taken into the two waiting vans. "This is going to be one for the books."

"Hopefully a solved one for the books," Brannigan murmured. It was almost numbing to look at all these body parts and realize that they represented lost lives and victims.

Kenzie looked at Hunter, mildly surprised to hear him express his thoughts. "Why, Detective Brannigan, is that doubt I hear in your voice?"

"There's always doubt," Hunter told her, refusing to rise to her bait. But then he allowed himself a smile. "Detective work is only as good as your weakest detective," he said, his gaze deliberately lingering over her for an extra beat.

Kenzie squared her shoulders. "Nobody asked you to be here, Brannigan," she informed him. Her implication was that he was free to go at any time. In fact, she would have preferred it that way.

"I always finish anything I start, Detective," Hunter told her.

Sean moved away from the investigator he was talking to and looked from Kenzie to Hunter. "Is there a problem here?" he asked.

"No, no problem, Chief," Hunter replied cheerfully. "As a matter of fact, I'm looking forward to working on this case. I cut my teeth on jigsaw puzzles when I was a kid," he told Sean.

A tall man, like the rest of his clan, Sean nodded and smiled at the detective. "Then you should be in seventh heaven here." Sean paused, his gaze sweeping over Kenzie, Hunter and O'Reilly. "There's not much more for any of you to do out here. Why don't you go back to the precinct and I'll let you know what we find once we finish processing the area."

Sean's smile deepened as he looked over toward Jupiter. Now that the dog had made his discoveries, the German shepherd seemed satisfied to just lie at his handler's feet, watching as Sean's team did their work. "Looks like Jupiter doesn't even have a clue as to the kind of far-reaching dust storm he just managed to kick up."

Kenzie couldn't resist glancing over in Hunter's direction.

"There's a lot of that going around," she commented. And then she asked her uncle, "Are you sure you don't need me to stay?"

"I'm sure," Sean answered. Seeing the skeptical look on her face, he added, "You know what they say about there being too many cooks, Kenzie." He could see that she was still undecided about leaving the scene. "My advice to the two of you is for you to save your strength for as long as you can. Something tells me that you're both going to be knocking on a lot of doors, asking a lot of questions before long."

Kenzie nodded, surrendering. In her experience, the chief was usually right. "Call me when you get back," she requested.

"Count on it," Sean told her. And then he looked at Hunter. "I'd stand back if I were you," he said, lowering his voice. "She has a tendency of steamrolling over people."

"Duly noted, Chief," Hunter told the older man, giving every indication that he intended to take the advice to heart.

Instead of saying anything to Brannigan, Kenzie walked away from what had at this point turned into an excavation site. Heading toward her car, she stopped to look around for O'Reilly. Finding him, she crossed to the handler and his dog.

"I'm heading back to the station, O'Reilly," she told him. "You two want a ride?" she asked, glancing at the dog as well as the handler.

"My mama taught me to always leave with the lady I came with," O'Reilly told her with a big sunny grin.

"I think that actually refers to bringing a date to a dance," Hunter told O'Reilly as he came up behind the handler and Kenzie.

Kenzie's eyes narrowed as she looked over her shoulder and glared at Hunter. "It refers to manners, something I'm sure you know next to nothing about, Brannigan."

"Ouch," O'Reilly said, wincing. "On second thought, I think it might be safer for Jupiter and me if we hitched a ride back to the station with the chief," the K-9 officer speculated. O'Reilly sounded as if he was only half kidding.

"Don't do that, O'Reilly. I know for a fact that Kenzie's had her necessary shots so you wouldn't be running the risk of getting rabies on the ride back," Hunter told the handler with a straight face.

Both men saw Kenzie's eyes flash. But there was no outburst of temper the way they might have expected. Instead, her voice was rather cold as she told Hunter, "I have no idea why my brothers find you amusing, but I certainly don't. I'm leaving now," she informed the two men. "You can either come with me or find your own way back."

As she began to walk, Jupiter fell into place next to her.

"Well, it looks like my partner's made his choice," O'Reilly noted with a laugh. He started to walk beside his dog. "I guess that's good enough for me."

Hunter joined them.

Officer O'Reilly raised a brow in his direction and

the cold case detective told him, "I decided that there's safety in numbers."

Without missing a beat Kenzie asked him, "Who says that the dog's on your side?"

O'Reilly's laugh was deep and rich. "She's got you there, Brannigan," he said as they reached Kenzie's vehicle.

Hunter merely smiled as he opened the door on the passenger side. And then he paused. "Okay if I sit up front?"

"I was thinking more along the lines of in the trunk or strapped to the roof," Kenzie said, buckling up. "But I guess I can put up with you sitting there for a few minutes."

"You weren't kidding about a few minutes," Hunter commented when they pulled up into the parking space several minutes later.

Kenzie had driven as if the car was on fire, squeezing through yellow lights just as they were about to turn red.

Hunter took a second to get the air back into his lungs. "I think I lost my stomach back there."

"Too bad you didn't lose your mouth," Kenzie retorted shortly. She slammed the driver's side door as she got out of the car. Her manner softened when she looked at O'Reilly and Jupiter as the duo climbed out of the back seat. "Thanks for all your help," Kenzie said to the handler.

"It's been an experience, Detective Cavanaugh," O'Reilly told her with a bemused smile. "It surely has. Be sure to let me know how the case goes."

O'Reilly's last request was addressed to both detectives but Kenzie acted as if the handler had said the words to her only.

"I'll be sure to do that," she promised Officer O'Reilly.

Hunter waited until the handler had taken Jupiter back

to the kennel and was out of earshot. Catching her arm to keep her from taking off, he asked, "What do you have against me, Kenzie?"

Kenzie shrugged his hand off. She seriously considered just walking away and ignoring the man and his question, but she knew that he wasn't going to drop it and she had no desire to be confronted in the squad room in front of people she worked with on a daily basis. He was capable of that.

So she turned around and faced Brannigan squarely as she replied, "Do you want that alphabetically, chronologically or in the order of magnitude?"

He whistled softly, as if impressed. "Wow, you've been saving that for a while now, haven't you?" Hunter asked. He saw Kenzie opening her mouth, but he acted quickly, beating her to the punch. "Tell me in any order you want to, *Detective Cavanaugh*," Hunter said, deliberately using her surname the way she had requested.

"I know your type, Brannigan."

He knew he was asking for trouble, but at the same time, he was rather curious what she had to say. "And just what type is that?"

"You're a narcissist who mistakenly believes that he is God's personal gift to women and despite your intelligence, you're not bright enough to know that you're not anything of the kind."

His eyes met hers. She expected him to back off. Instead, she saw that smile of his slowly curve the corners of his mouth.

"So," he said, his smile growing, "you think I'm intelligent."

She threw up her hands and started to walk away. "You're missing the whole point, Brannigan. Why am I not surprised?"

But he wouldn't let her walk away. This time, rather than take hold of her arm, he put himself in front of her, bodily blocking her path to the back entrance.

"Oh no, I don't think I am missing the point," he contradicted. "You had one bad experience with a Class A jerk a little over a year ago who didn't know how lucky he was and screwed up a really good thing. You let that color the way you view every other man who even comes *near* you and you judge them and shut them down before they ever have a chance to open their mouths."

Where the hell did he get off spouting all that at her? Did her brothers say anything to him? But how could they? She'd never said a single word to her brothers or anyone in the family about the way Billy had behaved or why she had dumped him. There was no way Brannigan could have known.

"Trust me, not opening your mouth is *not* your failing, Brannigan," she informed him. "Now, you might not have anything better to do than stand out here in the hot sun, flapping your gums, but I do."

And with that, Kenzie neatly turned on her heel and marched away from him and toward the rear steps of the police station.

She hurried up the steps quickly, intent on getting away from Brannigan as fast as she could. She needed to cool off before she slipped up and said something to confirm his assumption.

Hunter let Kenzie keep several feet ahead of him. It was really more prudent that way.

When he walked into the building a couple of minutes after Kenzie had, he wound up running into Murdoch, one of Kenzie's older brothers. He nodded a greeting at the detective and the other man crossed over to him.

Murdoch obviously had something on his mind. "I hear

your cold case just heated up and you're working with my sister," the homicide detective said.

The whole incident was less than a few hours old. There was a time not that long ago when Hunter would have been surprised that news about a potential "new" case could travel so fast.

But he had learned that there was an inside private line of communication within the departments, especially when it came to all matters concerning any of the Cavanaughs. It was almost as if at least some of them—if not all—were blessed with telepathy.

Hunter laughed at Murdoch's suggestion. "Not if she has anything to say about it," he told his friend.

"That cold case is yours, right? The guy without the head and hands," Murdoch specified just for the record as they walked over to the elevator bank.

"Right. That was my first case when I came into the Cold Case Division. I've managed to clear some of the other ones since then, but that one," Hunter told his friend, "it just kept going nowhere."

"Well, I heard that the case Kenzie just caught today looks as if it might be connected to your cold case," Murdoch repeated. "Both victims lost their heads."

Hunter shook his head, softly laughing to himself. "You Cavanaughs are just amazing, you know that? Somebody not knowing any better would say that you all seem to operate on the same mental wavelength."

Murdoch grinned. "Hey, who says that we don't?" he laughed. "Seriously, though, if Kenzie's case *is* somehow connected to yours, this could be the first big break you've had with it in a long while. I know how territorial she can be at times. Whatever you do, don't let her chase you away."

"Oh, I have no intentions of letting her do that," Hunter

assured the other detective. Belatedly, he pressed for the elevator. "I just plan on backing off for a minute or so to allow her to cool off and regroup. After that, I plan to go at this case again, this time full speed ahead. If there is a connection, I'm going to use it to my advantage. It's time this cold case was finally put to bed."

Murdoch nodded his approval. "Good for you. Kenzie's a good detective, one of the best, but she needs to know that she can't just boss people around whenever she wants to. You have every right to the information about this case as she does."

Hunter had to laugh at the simple statement. He bet that Kenzie didn't see it that way.

The elevator car arrived and he got on. Murdoch remained where he was, so Hunter put his hand up to keep the doors from closing just yet.

"You want to tell her that?" he asked Murdoch.

"Me? You kidding? Not on your life. Becoming a lion tamer might be easier. As a matter of fact," Murdoch said, "I'm damn sure of it. Good luck, though," he said to Hunter as the elevator door closed.

Hunter took the elevator up to his floor. He wanted to stop by his squad room long enough to let Valdez know what he was going to be doing for the next few days—or possibly longer.

As he got off the elevator, Hunter felt a rush of adrenaline, the way he always did whenever he felt he was closing in on a case. In his estimation, there was nothing else like it.

"We caught a break, Valdez," he told his partner as the latter was enjoying his third cup of inky-black, lukewarm coffee.

Valdez looked up. "You mean that lead that Wilson was

going on about actually panned out? That head that those kids found in Aurora Park belongs to your cold case?"

"No, but it looks like the killer might be the same guy who beheaded my guy. I think we're finally going to be getting some answers," Hunter told Valdez, trying his best not to sound too excited. "Looks like I'm going to be working with Kenzie Cavanaugh in Missing Persons for a week."

Valdez looked at him a bit doubtfully. "Does *she* know that?"

"Well, if she doesn't, she's about to find out now," Hunter said to his partner with an air of finality that left no room for doubt.

It was a known fact that Kenzie didn't welcome merging with other departments unless it was her idea. This didn't sound like it was that.

Valdez studied his partner for a long moment before finally asking, "Where would you like me to send your remains?"

Hunter suddenly found himself in the unique position of having to defend the very woman he knew would have been more than happy to see his head served on a platter.

"She's not all that bad," he told Valdez, doing his best to sound as if he believed what he was saying.

"Oh really? Well, I hear she's a spitfire," Valdez said, calling after his partner as Hunter walked out again. "Just don't say I didn't warn you. It's your funeral, Brannigan."

"Good thing my life insurance is paid up," Hunter shot back at his partner.

He left the squad room grinning with anticipation.

Chapter 6

Because he had heard stories from her brothers, as well as other family members on the force, about just how stubborn Kenzie could be, Hunter knew he was going to need significant backup if he wanted to be able to convince her that they needed to work together on this.

Appealing his case to her direct superior—or his—wasn't going to work. Neither one of their divisions focused on working homicides, but if the case one of them was working on turned out to be the result of a homicide, that could definitely add weight to the argument.

Hunter wasn't all that well acquainted with the lieutenant who headed cold cases. Lieutenant Wade Kilpatrick was a distant man whose main intent was getting promoted as quickly as possible. Hunter also had a strong feeling that whoever was in charge of the Missing Persons Division would be more inclined to listen to Kenzie than to him. And right now, he had a really strong gut feeling that Kenzie felt that there was no advantage in their joining forces—especially since he did. The woman was perverse that way.

What he needed to do was to present his case to a neutral third party, one who carried weight. Everyone, including him, felt that Brian Cavanaugh, the long-standing chief of detectives, was neutral, impartial and exceedingly fair. So when the elevator Brannigan was on stopped on Kenzie's floor, he changed his mind about his destination. He stayed in the elevator car and pressed the down button for the third floor, the floor that currently housed Brian Cavanaugh's office.

Arriving on the floor, he got out.

Proper procedure would have required that Hunter call to make an appointment, and under normal circumstances he would have. But he had an uneasy feeling that time was of the essence here, and the sooner he and Kenzie and whoever else they could get assigned to the task force got this investigation under way, the better their chances of finding the heinous killer out there.

"Is the chief in?" Hunter asked the attractive police lieutenant who sat at the desk that was just outside the chief of detectives' office.

Lieutenant Diane Bellamy looked up from her keyboard and the memo that she was inputting into the system. "Yes, he is, but he's—"

"This'll only take a minute," Hunter said, walking past the woman's desk.

Or three, Hunter added silently.

Knocking once on the closed door, he turned the doorknob and walked into the chief of detectives' brightly lit office.

The chief was not alone.

Lieutenant Bellamy popped up right behind Hunter. "I'm sorry, sir, he got by me," she apologized.

"It's not your fault, Lieutenant. Brannigan was born sneaky and pushy," Kenzie told the woman. She looked at Hunter. She didn't seem surprised to see him. "You actually took longer coming here than I thought you would."

"That's all right, Bellamy," Brian told the lieutenant kindly. "I'll take it from here." Turning his attention toward Hunter, he nodded toward the remaining empty chair that was facing his desk. "Sit down, Detective Brannigan. Detective Cavanaugh was just telling me about the possible odd connection and the coincidences between your two cases."

"She was?" Hunter asked. He was admittedly a little stunned that Kenzie had taken the lead on this and brought it to the chief's attention. He'd assumed that if anything, she would have attempted to keep him from getting the chief involved in this.

"I had a feeling you'd pull something like this, so I decided to beat you to the punch," Kenzie told him, as if reading the man's mind. She shifted back to face her uncle. "I thought I'd give the chief the details and then let *him* make up his mind whether he wanted us to work together on this or not."

"Detective Cavanaugh was thorough," Brian told Hunter, "but I'm open to anything you have to say from your point of view."

Since he didn't know what Kenzie had said to the chief—and added to that, she was related to the man—Hunter proceeded with caution and felt his way around.

"There isn't much to say, sir. My case is about six, seven years old and none of the leads that the Cold Case Division felt they had have wound up panning out. But the victim had the same sort of surgical cuts on his neck and his hands that were found on Detective Cavanaugh's missing person," he told Brian.

"So I take it that you believe the same person is responsible for killing both," Brian said, looking from one to the other for confirmation.

"He didn't just kill our two victims, sir. The cadaver dog we brought to the scene found several more headless torsos in that same field. Yesterday's torrential rain unearthed them," Hunter added for good measure.

"I'm aware that it rained yesterday, Detective, and that the city experienced some flash flooding as a result. Am I to understand that, besides the one head and those two hands that were found, the rest of the body parts that washed up turned out to be exclusively torsos?" the chief asked.

"That's right, sir," Hunter answered before Kenzie could.

"Why do you think that is?" Brian asked the two people facing him.

Again, Hunter spoke up before Kenzie had the chance to render speculation. "Maybe he panicked, got confused between where he buried the bodies and where he disposed of the heads and hands. That had to be the guy's system, otherwise why would he go through all the trouble of sawing off those particular body parts?"

"I'll tell you why. Because he's a sick man," Kenzie interjected.

Brian nodded in agreement. "Well, that goes without saying," he said. "At least the sick part."

Kenzie stared in disbelief at the man she held in the highest esteem. Was he saying what she thought he was saying?

"Do you think that this could be the work of a woman, Chief?" she asked Brian uncertainly.

"After you've been at this job for as long as I have, you realize that nothing is exactly what it looks like and that anything might be possible." With that, he gave them his ruling. "I think you're right. There might very well be a connection between the cases. We'll know more after the medical examiner examines the body parts that were discovered in Aurora Park, but I trust your instincts." The comment was made to both the detectives sitting before him. "So I'm pretty sure that Dr. Rayburn will find that the cuts were made using the same kind of instrument. I want the two of you to put a task force together. Start with two, three other people. Add more if you need them. Since we apparently have the identity of the last victim," he said, looking at Kenzie, "start there.

"Maybe if you find his killer, you'll find *the* killer. And keep me apprised of your progress."

The chief's tone indicated that the meeting was officially over. He noticed that while Hunter was on his feet, Kenzie was still seated and she was hesitating about something.

"Is there anything else, Detective Cavanaugh?" Brian asked.

Kenzie avoided looking in Brannigan's direction. Instead, she nodded in response to Brian's question. "There's just one thing, sir."

Brian inclined his head. "Go ahead."

"Who's in charge of the task force?" she asked.

Brian smiled as his eyes swept over Kenzie's clenched hands as she leaned against the desk. He knew that she wouldn't welcome having Brannigan in charge even though his case was the older one. But putting her in charge might lead to a communication problem. He was well aware that she could be headstrong and not the easiest person to work with. However, he also knew that didn't detract from her abilities as a detective.

This was going to be challenging.

"Well, tell you what. Since you came across those bodies together, and technically neither department handles homicides as a rule unless homicide is a direct result of one of your cases, I'm going to make this a joint task force."

"Joint?" Kenzie questioned, saying the single word as if it pained her.

"That means you're both in charge—and need to check with one another before charging ahead. Is that understood?" he asked, looking pointedly at Kenzie and then at Hunter.

"Understood, sir," Hunter said.

They both looked at Kenzie, who exhaled a loud sigh as she got to her feet. "Understood, sir," she replied formally.

"Good, then we're clear. Now, go find this damn SOB before he—or she—finds another victim to carve up."

"Yes, sir," Kenzie replied.

"Yes, sir," Hunter echoed.

Turning on her heel, Kenzie walked out of the office with Hunter following closely behind her.

"I'm surprised you went to your uncle about our working together," Hunter said, still following behind Kenzie.

She was striding ahead of him but had to come to a stop at the elevator.

"Like I said, I had a feeling you were going to see if you could get Uncle Brian on your side and I wasn't sure just what agenda you'd be pushing, so I wanted to present my findings first." She pushed the button for the elevator.

"With the idea that we'd be working together?" he questioned, surprised that she would actually be willing to do that.

"Just because I find you to be an egotistical peacock doesn't mean I wouldn't work with you if I needed to," she informed him. "Hell, I'd work with the devil himself if it'd help me find this killer."

Hunter laughed softly under his breath. "I'm not sure if I should be insulted or flattered," he told Kenzie.

"Just be useful and we'll call it even," Kenzie answered. The elevator arrived and they got on, then she hit the button for her floor. "We'll work in my squad room," she told Hunter. "And before you say anything, it's because your division has a squad room that's the size of a tiny walk-in pantry."

"It's bigger than that," Hunter felt obligated to protest.

Kenzie frowned at him. "All right, it's bigger than a walk-in pantry—but not by much."

Hunter really couldn't argue with that, not in all honesty at any rate. "The chief said we each get a person to start out with."

"No, what he said," Kenzie corrected, "was that we get two people for the task force and we can get more if we find we need them."

"Well, it's only fair if I get someone from my division and you get one from yours," Hunter told her pointedly.

Getting out of the elevator on her floor, Kenzie frowned at the simplistic way he put that. "This isn't a game of war, Brannigan."

He followed her out. "Isn't it?" he asked, looking at her with barely suppressed amusement.

She was acutely aware that they were gathering attention from the people who were walking by them. "All right. In the interest of not standing out here in the hallway arguing, fine, you get your partner and I'll bring mine aboard—unless you want someone special from your division," she said. Turning around, she walked down the hallway toward her squad room.

"Nope, my partner will be fine," Hunter answered. "We work well together."

She took that to mean only one thing. That his partner was a carbon copy of Brannigan. "Great, that's all I need. Two playboys to deal with," she murmured under her breath. One of whom, she thought, was much too handsome for her own good.

He debated letting her labor under that assumption but decided that it wouldn't be fair to his partner. So he set her straight.

"You'll be happy to know that Jason Valdez is married and he has a kid on the way. He's the complete antithesis of me."

She looked at him doubtfully, then decided that he was telling the truth. "Then there's hope for the man. Good to know."

"How about you use that sharp mind—and tongue—of yours and apply it to the case instead of using it on me?" he suggested.

Kenzie stopped walking for a second and smiled up at him. He didn't trust that smile of hers. For one thing, it was way too distracting,. "I fully intend to, Brannigan. We're on the clock on this, so much as I like telling you what I think of you, I'm going to have to put that on a back burner until this killer is caught." She saw the look of mild surprise on Hunter's face and took that to mean that he was wondering why she would put a clock to their case. "This is the first time the chief of Ds personally put his seal of approval on my task force. I am not about to disappoint the man and come up empty."

"In case you missed it, it's not *your* task force. The chief gave it to both of us," Hunter reminded her.

She surprised him by saying, "Exactly. So if you have any thoughts of dragging me down so that I fail, just forget it," she ordered. "You'll wind up burning yourself, as well. It's not happening."

"Is that how you think?" Hunter marveled. "That this is all just a big case of one-upmanship to you and that I'm going to be looking for ways to trip you up?" One look at the expression on her face told him that he had guessed correctly. "I don't know who you've been dealing with, but I'm not that kind of cop."

"Actions speak louder than words," she said before adding, "Prove it. Now, you go and get your 'second in command.' We'll meet back in my squad room. I've got something to take care of first."

He wasn't about to be sent off like a schoolboy. Instead, he caught hold of her shoulder to keep her in place as he said, "What?"

Anger clouded her eyes. "Being in command jointly doesn't mean that you get to keep track of my every move, Brannigan."

He disagreed and he wasn't about to back off until he had his answer. "What is it you need to take care of?" he asked again.

Kenzie's eyes narrowed.

It was obvious to anyone who passed by at that moment that she didn't like having to tell him anything, but she also knew that if she didn't tell him what she was about to do, he would just follow her.

The words felt bitter in her mouth as she told him. "I don't have any excuse to put it off," Kenzie said. "CSI unearthed those body parts. In all likelihood, Mr. Kurtz's torso and legs were among that batch that was found. I have to go tell Connie that her missing father isn't missing anymore."

He knew for a fact that being the one to deliver that sort of bad news was wearing on the soul. He didn't need to have anything else put her in an even worse mood. "I'll come with you."

He'd made the offer earlier and she'd already turned him down. She took his insistence to mean that he thought she needed to lean on someone. Even if she did, it wouldn't be him.

"I don't need you to come and hold my hand, Brannigan," she told him.

"I'm not coming to hold your hand," Hunter informed her.

"Then why would you come along?"

"To find out everything the victim's daughter can tell us about who her father interacted with in his last month or so," he answered.

Okay, so he did have a reason. But she still wasn't going to have him come with her. "Connie already told me that she and her father were estranged. That means she hadn't seen him."

"I know the meaning of the word *estranged.* I do crossword puzzles," Hunter told her glibly. "But the funny thing about people is that sometimes they don't know what they know. While you're comforting your friend, it'll be my job to delve into that."

Okay, it was time that she took a stand, Kenzie thought. Hands on hips, she glared at him. "You can't come with me."

He remained unfazed. "You know, the nice thing about being joint partners on a task force is that you really can't order me around any more than I can order you around. That being said—" he gestured ahead of him "—let's go."

She mumbled a few choice words under her breath as she walked in front of him back to the elevator.

Chapter 7

The eight-mile drive to the newly built Spectrum Apartment Homes, located on the south side of Aurora, felt like one of the longest drives that Kenzie had ever undertaken. At the same time, part of her was wishing for a sudden traffic jam that would impede her route, but there really weren't any.

Kenzie reached her destination a great deal faster than she was happy about. She could feel her heart pounding hard in anticipation of what she was about to experience.

Pulling up into the underground parking area that housed guest parking, Kenzie turned toward the man who had silently occupied the front passenger seat next to her. He hadn't said a word since they had left the precinct, which in itself was a huge surprise. It wasn't like him.

"You're awfully quiet, Brannigan. Regret coming?" she asked. "You can stay in the car if you've changed your mind about this."

Hunter noticed that although she'd released her seat belt, she hadn't gotten out yet. It told him that he had read her correctly. Despite all of her bravado about not wanting or needing anyone to hold her hand, it was obvious to him that Kenzie was dreading having to tell her friend about the woman's father.

It looked like Kenzie was human after all, he concluded.

"No, I don't regret coming," he told her, unbuckling his seat belt. "I just felt that maybe you needed the quiet to help you pull your thoughts together."

Kenzie opened her mouth to say something flippant about always welcoming a break from his steady stream of unwanted opinions, but then she abruptly shut her mouth again. She realized that it might seem like she was protesting too much, which might get Brannigan thinking that she was hiding the way she actually felt about him. It was better not to say anything at all.

So instead of a wisecrack, Kenzie said, "Thanks," then got out of the vehicle.

Hunter's feet were on the ground a second later. The fact that Kenzie had been polite to him had left Hunter momentarily speechless. He had a feeling, though, that if he made any sort of response, the truce would be over in an instant, so he merely nodded and fell into place beside her.

Thinking it was safe to say something about where they were, he commented, "This is a pretty big complex. It's more like its own little city." He looked at her. "Do you know the woman's apartment number?"

Kenzie blew out an exasperated breath. "No, I'm just going to ring doorbells, yelling out her name, until I find her. Yes, I know her apartment number," she told the detective.

And she's back, Hunter thought.

Out loud, he asked, "What is it?"

"Number 730," she answered as she scanned the parking structure where they were.

He made a guess as to what she was looking for. "The

elevator's over there," he told Kenzie, pointing to the far wall on the left.

"How do you know that?" she asked, then immediately answered her own question. "You've been here before, haven't you?" Most likely with one of the scores of women Brannigan escorted to those clubs she'd heard that he frequented, she thought.

"Nope," he answered in an easy voice. "But I can read and there's a sign pointing to the elevator." He indicated it now.

Kenzie frowned, annoyed with herself that she hadn't seen that herself. She made her way over to it. Brannigan easily kept up with her. She practically punched the button. The elevator arrived quickly. It was empty as they got on.

Reaching around her, Hunter pressed "7." She shifted to get farther away from him.

"Offer still stands," he told Kenzie, settling back.

"Offer for what?" she asked. "For you to withdraw from the investigation?"

She knew that wasn't what he meant and that she was back to being flippant, but right now, flippant answers temporarily got her mind off what she was about to do.

"No," he answered patiently, "for me to break the news to John Kurtz's daughter so you don't have to go through that."

Kenzie slanted her eyes in his direction. "My case, my responsibility," she answered stoically.

He shrugged as if her answer was what he'd expected. "Just so you know that I'm here."

She laughed shortly. "Trust me, Brannigan, I *know* you're here."

The elevator reached the seventh floor all too quickly

and the door opened. They got out. But once off the elevator, Kenzie stopped walking.

"Something wrong?" Hunter asked her, quietly adding, "Other than the obvious."

She needed to say this quickly before she changed her mind and didn't say it at all. "Look, I'm sorry. I didn't mean to snap like that. I know you're trying to be decent about this and I haven't made it easy—"

Taking pity on her, he stopped Kenzie before she could get any further. "Look, I get it. This isn't easy and everyone deals with having to break this kind of news in their own way."

He was being decent about it, even providing her with excuses, and it just made her feel that much worse. Kenzie opened up before she could think better of it. "I just know how I'd feel if someone came to tell me that my father had been hacked to pieces."

"Then don't focus on that," he told Kenzie. "Get her to focus on finding who did this to him." He saw the doubt on her face and assured Kenzie, "Revenge can be a surprisingly galvanizing feeling."

Kenzie blew out a breath as she squared her shoulders. "I suppose that it is," she agreed.

Hunter let out a low whistle. "Well, this is certainly a red-letter day for me."

Kenzie stared at the cold case detective, confused. "What are you talking about?"

"You apologized to me and said I might be right all in the space of a few minutes. That deserves to be noted down in my book," he told her.

"Don't get used to it," Kenzie warned him as she started walking again, but Hunter noticed that one of the corners of her mouth curved just a little bit. She was definitely softening, he thought.

"I don't plan to," he told her easily, "but I can still savor the moment."

"Savor fast," she ordered. "The apartment's right here." Kenzie pointed to the apartment that was two doors down.

Taking a deep breath and bracing herself, Kenzie pressed the doorbell.

The door swung open before she even had a chance to remove her finger.

Connie Kurtz stood in the doorway. The woman looked even worse than she had when she had come down to the precinct to file a missing person report on her father. Her eyes darted back and forth between the two people standing on her doorstep.

"This is bad, isn't it?" she said in a quavering voice.

"What makes you say that?" Hunter asked the woman kindly.

Connie looked as if she was having trouble breathing. "Because Kenzie brought backup with her."

Kenzie realized that she hadn't made the proper introduction. "Connie, this is Detective Brannigan," she said.

She was stalling. As long as she didn't say those awful words, *Your father's been murdered*, Connie could go on believing that her father was alive, at least for one more minute.

Connie's eyes darted from the woman she'd known in better days to the detective Kenzie had brought with her. Her breath turned raspy, as if it had just stopped moving in her lungs.

Connie licked her dry lips, afraid that the words would stick to them.

"He's dead, isn't he?" she asked Kenzie in a frightened voice.

There were words Kenzie wanted to say, words to prepare her friend for the shock of what she was about to hear.

But faced with Connie's blunt question, Kenzie had no recourse except to answer, "Yes."

The moment the word was out, Connie's eyes rolled back in her head and her knees just gave way, sending her crumbling.

Hunter caught the woman before she could hit the floor, scooping her up. Holding the unconscious woman in his arms, he made his way to the first place where he could lay her down, a turquoise-and-white flowered sofa that seemed to be the main piece of furniture in the living room.

He pulled aside a pillow and tucked it under her torso rather than her head.

"What are you doing?" Kenzie asked him. Connie looked contorted.

"Trying to get the blood to flow back into her head—unless you've got smelling salts on you." He said the last part as if it could be a possibility.

The next second he knew that it wasn't. He tucked a second cushion under Connie's torso.

Kenzie looked around the apartment to orient herself, then suddenly hurried off to the kitchen. She was back a second later carrying a wet towel in her hands.

"No smelling salts," she told him. "But this might help." Kenzie indicated the wet towel.

"Well, it can't hurt," he told her, taking the towel and placing it on Connie's forehead.

The woman stirred ever so slightly, moaning. It was another few seconds before she opened her eyes. When she did, there was a haunted, horrified look in them.

"How?" she asked Kenzie in a raspy voice.

"You don't want to hear the details now," Kenzie told her in a firm voice.

Pulling off the wet towel, Connie sat up, then wavered

slightly before getting hold of herself. She was struggling for control over herself, if not the situation.

"Are you sure it was my father?" she asked, her voice sounding a tiny bit stronger now.

Hunter intervened, taking the burden of answering that from Kenzie.

"I'm afraid that we're sure," he told Connie in the kindest tone he could manage. "Do you know if your father was seeing any new people, doing anything different these days than he normally did?"

Connie covered her mouth. "I don't know," she cried. The color was slowly returning to her face, but she still looked pale. "I don't know," she repeated, frustrated and helpless.

"Connie and her father were estranged," Kenzie explained to Hunter so that the young woman didn't have to suffer through having to say the words that seemed so much more hurtful now than they had initially. There would be no healing the rift, no words of forgiveness in the offing now.

There would only be guilt.

"Can you tell us where your father lived?" Hunter asked.

She looked up at him. "In the house where he always lived. In the house where I grew up," she whispered, then asked, "Why?"

"Connie," Kenzie said in a gentler voice than Hunter could recall ever hearing her use, "we need your permission to go through his things."

"Why?" the woman asked, looking from Kenzie to Hunter. "What are you looking for?" An expression of total horror came over Connie's face. "Did—did someone kill my father?"

"I'm afraid that someone definitely killed your father,"

Hunter told Connie, thinking that the response would be too painful for Kenzie to have to tell her friend at this moment.

Connie stared at him, her face a mask of incredulous disbelief. "You think my father *knew* who killed him?" she cried.

"We really don't know right now," Kenzie admitted. "But we have to start somewhere. Maybe he saw people that you don't know about, or they saw something that made them think he was a danger to them," she suggested, jumping around from subject to subject.

But Connie shook her head. "My father wasn't the kind of man who made friends easily. I told you, after my mother died, he just withdrew into himself. Like a hermit."

"Still, if there's anything in his home that could possibly give us a clue about how he spent his last few days, it would really be a great help," Kenzie told the grieving woman.

Connie was crying now, tears spilling down her cheeks. She kept wiping them away, but they refused to stop flowing. Swallowing, she nodded her head. "Of course. I'll take you there."

But Hunter put his hand on the woman's arm, stopping her movement. "Why don't you just give us the address and we'll take it from there," he told her gently. "You don't need to put yourself through this."

"I have keys," Connie told him. She was breathing hard, desperately trying to stop crying, but it took more than a few minutes to get under control. She wiped the back of her hand across her cheeks, trying to dry them. "I'll let you in."

"Are you sure you're up to this?" Kenzie asked her, concerned. "Why don't you stay here?" The woman looked so lost, so incredibly stricken. "Is there anyone I can call for you?" Kenzie asked. "I promise that I'll bring your keys back, Connie. I just don't think you're in any shape to go over there right now."

Connie pressed her lips together, holding back another sob. She nodded, struggling to collect herself. "Maybe you're right."

Doing her best to get hold of herself, Connie gave them the name and number of a friend. Kenzie called the number and quickly explained the situation to the woman who answered. Sherry Peters promised to be right over.

Kenzie and Hunter stayed with Connie until her friend arrived.

"You know, in college Connie was this warm, friendly social butterfly who was always throwing parties and organizing get-togethers. I never saw her look this lost and lonely before," Kenzie confided as she drove her vehicle to John Kurtz's house.

"Growing up is no picnic," Hunter agreed. He glanced in Kenzie's direction. "You know, she still doesn't have a clue how her father was murdered."

"I know." She'd stopped herself from volunteering any details. "I don't think she's going to get much rest tonight. I didn't want her having nightmares on top of that." She slanted a quick glance in Hunter's direction. "I'd rather keep the details between us until we have something a little more concrete to go on. Might as well give it to her all at once instead of in dribbles and drabs."

He nodded. "Good call," he told Kenzie. And then he smiled to himself.

She caught his expression out of the corner of her eye. "What?"

"You realize that we seem to be getting along," Hunter pointed out.

Kenzie blew out a breath. "It'll pass," she responded.

"Yeah, you're probably right," Hunter agreed. And then he smiled again. "But I have to say that it's nice while it lasts."

Kenzie found herself shaking her head as she made a left turn. "You know, I really don't know what to make of you, Brannigan."

"Why do you have to try to make anything at all out of me?" he asked.

"Because if I'm not careful, I'll get caught with my guard down, and I don't like being caught with my guard down," she answered.

"Tell you what," he proposed. "Why don't we focus on finding out who killed your friend's father and why they killed him so we can figure out what sort of crazy person we have on our hands right now. Once we do that, *then* we can sort out the small stuff like what to make of me," Hunter told her. "At least you know that I'm not going to be hacking anyone to pieces, so that should be a comfort to you."

"Yes, I suppose that there's that," she agreed. Pausing, she suddenly said, "That was a nice catch back there." She looked at Hunter. "How did you know she was going to faint?"

"I didn't," he admitted. "I just have really quick reflexes," he told her. And then he grinned. "See, aren't you glad you brought me along?"

"Right now, the jury's still out on that," she informed him glibly. "And even if it wasn't, I'd say that the word *glad* is really stretching the sentiment a bit."

"Wow, tough crowd," Hunter commented.

"You better believe it," Kenzie responded.

A couple of minutes later, Kenzie pulled up in the driveway of the single-story stucco house where, until recently, John Kurtz had lived his life.

Putting the vehicle into Park, she pulled up the hand brake and then looked over toward the detective beside her.

"Okay, you ready to look for a needle in a haystack, Brannigan?" she asked.

"More than ready," he answered, getting out of the car.

He just hoped it wasn't going to turn out to be a wild-goose chase.

Chapter 8

John Kurtz's house was close to fifty years old and was one of the original houses in the second development that was built when Aurora was still only a vague idea in the minds of the family who were the founders of the city. Since then, the boundaries of Aurora had grown and spread out, but no one would have felt that way if all they saw was the small development where John Kurtz had lived.

The faded light gray stucco was badly in need of not just a fresh coat or two of paint but some serious repairs, as well. There were large chips visible along one of the lower edges of the stucco. And when Kenzie looked up at the roof, she was willing to bet that it leaked during the rainy season. Badly. There were more than a few tiles missing from her vantage point and probably more that she couldn't see.

Hunter noticed the pensive look on Kenzie's face and guessed what was at the center of it.

"Doesn't exactly look like a cozy cottage, does it?" he asked.

"It probably was once," Kenzie answered, trying to picture it when the house was new.

Taking out the key that Connie had given her, Kenzie put it into the lock and turned it.

"He's not home."

Kenzie and Hunter turned around to see a thin, wiry older man of medium height wearing jeans that sagged against his body and a plaid shirt. The man was glaring at them from beneath wispy gray eyebrows that resembled angry caterpillars engaged in battle.

He looked at them as if he thought they were intruders and he had taken it upon himself to foil a robbery attempt.

Hunter immediately engaged the man he took to be a self-appointed neighborhood watchman. "Have you seen anyone suspicious hanging around?"

"I seen you two. Now back off or I'll call the police." He pulled out a flip phone from his pocket and held it up like a cross meant to ward off vampires. "My grandson gave me this and I know how to use it. I can have the police department here faster than you can blink. The police chief's a personal friend of mine," the man boasted.

Kenzie played along and looked impressed. "Really?"

"Yeah, 'really,'" the man shot back.

"You know my uncle?" Kenzie asked, keeping a straight face.

The old man's bravado faded a shade or two. "Um, yeah, sure. Who are you again?" the man asked. He stepped forward and squinted at their faces to get a better look at them.

"I'm Detective Cavanaugh and this is Detective Brannigan," Kenzie told him. They both held up their shields and IDs for the man's benefit.

The neighbor studied both carefully, then stepped back. "Detectives, huh?" His protective, defensive ardor faded a little more. But curiosity immediately took over. "You here about John? He's missing, you know. His daughter's been looking for him."

"Yes, we know," Kenzie answered. "Would you know

where he might have gone, Mr...?" Kenzie's voice trailed off as she looked at the man, waiting for him to fill in the blank.

The man raised his head proudly, introducing himself. "McGinty. Franklin McGinty," he said, leaning over and shaking each of their hands in turn. The leathery hand lingered over Kenzie's a shade longer than it had with Hunter's. "His daughter asked me the same question. I told her I didn't know."

Hunter looked at McGinty and made a calculated guess. "But you do know, don't you, Mr. McGinty?"

Thin shoulders moved up and then fell in a vague shrug. "Not exactly. But if I was to guess—and I didn't want to tell his daughter this because fathers don't admit these things to their daughters—" he confided to the pair in a lowered voice, "but if I was to guess," McGinty repeated, "I'd guess that he went off with that lady friend of his."

Instantly alert, Kenzie and Hunter exchanged looks. Was this a break, or just the idle speculations of an old man with too much time on his hands?

"What lady friend?" she asked McGinty.

"The one I seen coming here a couple of times about three weeks ago." McGinty pressed his lips together, as if he realized that he was being judgmental, but it was his civic duty to tell these detectives everything. "If you ask me, she seemed like she was too young for him. Yes, sir, I'd say that old John was out of his league with that one." He leaned in closer again. "But men do foolish things when they lose the love of their lives after all those years."

Having unlocked the door, Kenzie opened it farther and gestured for McGinty to come inside with them.

"You're talking about his wife, Edith, aren't you?" she asked.

McGinty nodded, pleased that she knew the woman's name. "That I am. Fine lady, Edith," he pronounced. "John just kind of fell apart when she died. He kept on hoping right until the very end that she was going to come around. You know, recover," he confided. "But she didn't," McGinty told them sadly. "We all figured he'd be one of those people who died right after they lost their partner. But old John, I guess he turned out to be too darn ornery to die."

"We?" Hunter questioned, picking up on the word the other man had used. "Who's 'we'?"

"The people in the neighborhood," McGinty said. "What's left of them." The man went into another narrative. "This was a tight neighborhood once upon a time. But people sold their houses and moved away. Or they died. Either way, there's only a few of us old originals left." His voice trailed off for a moment.

"Could you describe this woman?" Kenzie asked.

"I only seen her from across the street a couple of times, and my eyes, they're not what they used to be," McGinty admitted. And then he launched into a detailed description. "But she was a blonde with what they used to call an hourglass figure." He paused to smile to himself. "She was a little taller than John, but that's 'cause she wore those fancy high heels. And she wasn't real friendly either," McGinty added.

"What makes you say that?" Hunter asked, curious what had prompted that opinion.

"Well, I yelled 'hi' to her when I saw her, but she didn't say anything back." He frowned. "Just acted like she didn't even hear me, and I know she did. I'm not the shy, retiring type, you know?"

No, he certainly wasn't, Kenzie thought. "What was Mr. Kurtz like around her?" she asked the talkative neighbor.

"Funny you should ask that," McGinty commented.

"John acted like someone had put a spell on him. You know, kinda like a teenager or something. But like I said, I only saw her a couple of times. For all I know, he didn't go off with her at all. But I never seen anyone else here, so my final guess is that he did," McGinty concluded proudly, looking at the detectives to see if the pair went along with his opinion.

"Well, you've been a tremendous help, Mr. McGinty," Kenzie said, subtly ushering the man toward the door. "If you think of anything else, anything at all," she emphasized, "please don't hesitate to call." She took a card out of her pocket and handed it to the neighbor. "Anything at all," she repeated.

The old man squinted at the writing on the card, trying to get the letters into focus.

"I'll be sure to do that." He slipped the card into his breast pocket, then continued on his way toward the door. "I sure hope that old John didn't just become a cliché."

"How's that again?" Hunter asked, unclear as to what McGinty was saying.

"You know that old saying, Detective." McGinty paused dramatically, then said, "'There's no fool like an old fool.' Let me know if you find John," McGinty said, crossing the threshold.

Hunter could see by her expression that Kenzie was debating telling the man the truth about his missing neighbor.

"I promise that we'll let you know," Hunter called after the departing figure, speaking up before Kenzie could.

"I'll just close the door behind me, Detectives," McGinty volunteered.

"Thanks," Hunter replied, still raising his voice to be heard. He turned toward Kenzie once the door was closed. "You were going to tell him, weren't you?"

"Just as a warning," she responded. "There might be someone out there preying on defenseless old men who live in the area."

Hunter grinned. "Why, Detective Cavanaugh, is that a conclusion you just jumped to?" he asked. "I thought that was against your religion."

She frowned. It looked as if their truce was over. "The only thing 'against my religion' is putting up with smart-mouthed detectives." She glared at him pointedly before beginning to rifle through the drawers of Kurtz's desk.

"Then I guess we're both out of luck, Detective, aren't we?" Hunter asked her, his grin settling into a smile.

"Not necessarily," Kenzie answered. "Despite, according to Connie, her father's total resistance when it came to looking for female companionship, Mr. Kurtz was obviously 'keeping company' with a member of the opposite sex, as they used to say."

"Wonder if that 'company' was what caused him to lose his head," Hunter mused.

Kenzie winced. "Do me a favor. Try not to be so graphic, please."

"Sorry, just trying to lighten up what has all the markings of a very dark situation," he told her.

Kenzie nodded absently as she tried to think. "If you were a lonely widower, how would you go about finding a potential romantic partner?"

As she continued searching through a desk full of papers, Kenzie threw the question out on the floor, not really expecting Hunter to answer. Certainly not expecting him to laugh at her.

But he did.

Hunter looked at her in disbelief. "You're kidding, right?"

She knew where he was going with this, but in her mind she had already ruled out the internet.

"This is an older man, Brannigan," she reminded the detective. "Not some kid born attached to a keyboard."

But Hunter wasn't buying her dismissal. "Doesn't matter," he told her as he rifled through cabinet drawers in the kitchen. There seemed to be endless clippings shoved into one drawer. The edges were all curling and turning a darker color. "You heard McGinty. He was proud of the fact that he knew how to use his cell phone."

"Maybe," Kenzie allowed. "But he's probably an exception to the rule. Connie told me that her father absolutely *hated* technology. He wasn't patient enough to pick it up."

"Maybe he developed patience," Hunter speculated. "Maybe he got so bored with feeling empty that he took a class so he could learn how to open up 'the wonderful world of the internet.' If not a class, maybe a book. There are hundreds of illustrated how-to books to show even someone who can't read how to find their way around a computer and, consequently, eventually stumble their way onto the internet. From there it's only a short hop, skip and a jump away from finding dating sites."

Kenzie shook her head, still resisting the idea. Connie had said that her father was dedicated to the memory of his late wife. They had fought about her even suggesting that he go onto a dating site. "I don't think that—"

But Hunter was certain that he was right about this. "There are dating sites for all ages, all backgrounds these days. Hell, there's probably a dating site that helps lonely dolphins swimming in Hawaii to connect. There's certainly a site designed to help the discerning over-seventies club connect."

"What makes you say that?" she asked.

"This."

She turned around from the papers she was sifting through and saw that he was holding out a page that had been carefully printed out. It was a profile page that had the words *Second Time Around* written across the top of it. She grabbed the paper from him.

"You might have led with that," she told him, taking the page from him.

There was a glimmer of mischief in his eyes. "What's the fun in that?"

She looked at the man, exasperated. Was everything just a huge game to him? Didn't the man have any principles?

"We're not here to have fun, Brannigan," she told him. "We're here to solve a murder, possibly more than just one."

"Some of us consider *that* to be fun," Hunter told her.

She looked at the URL across the bottom of the page that Hunter had discovered and typed that into her phone. A webpage popped up.

"Son of a gun, there it is. Now all we have to figure out is whose profile he accessed—or who accessed his profile," she added.

"I'd say that the first order of business is to see if Kurtz had a computer hidden away somewhere in the house," Hunter told her.

A quick search of the orderly house showed that there was no desktop computer.

Disappointed when they came up empty, Kenzie sighed, "Nothing."

Hunter looked at her. "Who says he had to have a desktop computer?"

It just stood to reason to her. "If the man was going

to spend time typing, he'd need a desktop with a large screen."

Hunter shook his head. "Not if the old boy wanted to keep this 'vice' of his hidden in case his daughter suddenly popped over. Think about it. If she saw a desktop, that would have forced him to admit that she was right."

He'd forgotten one key piece of information, Kenzie thought. "But John and his daughter were estranged, remember?"

Hunter discarded the argument. "Estranged people come around all the time," he told her. He could have pointed out several incidents involving former girlfriends, but he decided it was wiser to focus on her instead. "You always play by the rules, Detective?"

Because she believed in being truthful, she couldn't say yes.

"Not always," Kenzie admitted. She felt as if he was talking down to her.

"I'm willing to bet that neither did Connie's father. See if he's got a laptop hidden in one of his closets or under his bed."

Kenzie felt it was a losing battle, but she was nothing if not thorough. She was determined to prove Brannigan wrong.

She didn't.

There was a laptop under the bed in John's guest room. Pulling it out, she placed it on top of the bed. "I really hate it when you're right," she grumbled.

"Cheer up. I promise to be wrong the next time," Hunter told her.

He took the laptop into the kitchen, placed it on the table, plugged it in and turned it on. Less than a minute later, a home screen popped up. As did a request to log in.

"Son of a gun, the old boy had a password," Hunter

marveled, impressed despite himself. "Who would have thought it?"

She slanted a glance at Hunter, but he wasn't rubbing it in when he could have. "I guess he was more devious than his daughter thought." The other detective began to type, hitting Enter each time. "What are you doing?" she asked.

"Trying out a few of the obvious passwords," he answered.

Kenzie frowned. "Do you have any idea how many of them there are?"

"Some astronomical number that's beyond my ability to count," he responded. Hunter blew out a breath after the fifth attempt. "This could take forever."

"It could take *you* forever," Kenzie corrected.

Hunter gave her an exasperated look. "But not you," he guessed.

"No," she answered glibly, stretching the game out a second longer, "not me."

Hunter went along with her. He'd accept any port in a storm, he thought. "I take it you're some kind of computer wizard."

She thought of saying yes, then decided to go with the truth. "No, but I am related to a computer wizard. We're taking this to Valri," she told him. "If she can't break the password, then it can't be broken."

"Valri," he repeated. Something in his brain clicked. "Valri Cavanaugh," he remembered. "I've heard that she's good."

"Good?" she echoed, then all but laughed at his assessment. "Mint chip ice cream is *good.* Apple pie is *good,*" she said dismissively. "Valri is *fantastic.*"

Hunter thought of a problem. "If she's that fantastic, isn't she swamped with work?"

She'd never approached her cousin with anything, but

her brothers had and she knew Hunter's concern was legitimate. "She is, but she's also family."

"So are all the other Cavanaughs who work at the police department." His point was that they might all be converging on this computer wunderkind.

Kenzie got his meaning. "You know, Brannigan, you can be a real downer sometimes. Actually, most of the time," she amended. "We just made some headway. We had no clues when we got here. Now we have clues," she declared as if they had just discovered a brand-new world. "Focus on that for a while."

He gave her a properly subdued expression. "Yes, ma'am."

Her eyes narrowed as they walked out of the house with the laptop. "You're not fooling me with that 'ma'am' business."

Hunter looked at her, the complete picture of innocence. "I wouldn't dream of trying to fool you, Kenzie."

He was getting under her skin. "If you call me Kenzie one more time, I'm going to leave you here and you can walk to the station."

"No, you won't," he said knowingly.

He was right, damn him. She didn't want to waste time by leaving him here. The man had proved he had a head on his shoulders and they needed all the help they could get. She tried to focus on what he added to the investigation and not how distracting being so close to him was turning out to be. Where were these thoughts coming from and for pity sake, why now?

"Just shut up and get in the car," Kenzie retorted.

"Yes—" Kenzie looked at him sharply and he concluded his sentence with an obedient "—Detective Cavanaugh."

"That's better," she told him, getting into her vehicle.

"That's a matter of opinion," Hunter murmured under his breath as he got in on his side. He tried his best not to be aware of her presence just inches away. When did the inside of the car get so small? Did it shrink?

Kemzie glanccd in his direction. "Excuse me?"

Hunter pretended to be preoccupied with buckling his seat belt. When it slid into its slot and clicked, he answered, "Nothing."

Kenzie started up the car, keeping her eyes forward. "I didn't think so."

She turned up the radio, temporarily blocking out the need for any conversation.

It helped.

A little.

Chapter 9

Detective Valri Cavanaugh was the police department's go-to computer wizard. Mentored by the chief of detectives' daughter-in-law, Brenda, in an incredibly short amount of time, Valri had managed to surpass her teacher.

So much so that Brenda felt free to reduce her huge amount of hours down to the size belonging to regular highly skilled computer technologists. These days Brenda even took occasional vacations.

Valri, on the other hand, hardly ever left her desk during the week and there were times when she came in on weekends. She had also transformed from a soft-spoken young woman who accepted any and all assignments to a woman who knew how to stand up for herself and to say no if the situation warranted it.

So when she saw Kenzie carrying a laptop and walking in with another detective she vaguely recognized, Valri braced herself for battle.

She allowed her cousin to state her case quickly, heard her out and then shook her head.

"No."

Stunned because her brothers had told her that Valri was a godsend who had helped them whenever they asked for her assistance, Kenzie momentarily found herself speechless.

And then, finding her tongue, she said, "Valri, please."

Valri didn't even look up from her keyboard as her fingers flew across the keys, summoning a database. "Then take a number," she murmured.

Kenzie held up the laptop, using it as a visual aid, but her cousin ignored it, never even looking up.

Kenzie tried again. "This computer belonged to a man who was recently murdered," she told Valri with a sense of urgency.

Valri swept her hand around the immediate area surrounding her desk, the movement taking it all in. There were scores of laptops, phones and tablets on every flat surface near her.

"Like I said," Valri repeated, "take a number."

But Kenzie wasn't about to give up so easily. "The guy could have been a victim of a serial killer, Valri," she told her cousin, trying to arouse Valri's interest. "You wouldn't be helping to solve just one murder but several—maybe dozens."

This time Valri did raise her deep blue eyes and she looked at Kenzie. "And this is different how?" she asked. Serial killers were apparently more common than had once been thought and the police department had seen more than its fair share. "Look, I'm not heartless, I'm just really overworked. I haven't seen the top of my desk in weeks—maybe months," Valri complained.

Before Kenzie could say anything further, Hunter spoke up. "We didn't mean to put any pressure on you," he told the computer tech. "It's just that we're stumped and we didn't want to waste any more time trying to figure out the password when you could do something like that blindfolded—literally. But we didn't realize how swamped you were." Hunter picked up the laptop from the edge of her desk. "We'll just find a way to figure it out," he told her as he started to walk away.

Valri sighed deeply and held out her hand. She knew she was being played, but at the same time, she couldn't just ignore a plea for help either.

"All right, give the laptop to me," Valri told Hunter.

But Hunter continued to hold on to it and he shook his head. "No, you've got all these other things to get to. We can—"

Valri's eyebrows drew together in a formidable V.

"Give it to me," she repeated, sounding sterner this time.

Looking properly grateful as well as contrite, Hunter relinquished the laptop and placed it next to Valri, making sure to turn the screen toward her.

She glanced at the dormant screen for a moment, thinking. "Can you give me any information about the owner—other than he's dead?" Valri qualified.

Kenzie produced the form that Connie had filled out when she had come in to the Missing Persons Division, hoping to have the police locate her father.

"This is all I have right now. His daughter filed this when she was worried that he was missing," Kenzie explained.

"Good instincts," Valri commented grimly. Glancing at the form, she folded the papers and put them on the side of her desk. "I'll see what I can do. No promises," she added.

"Understood," Hunter responded. He smiled at her warmly. "Thanks for doing this."

"Yeah, yeah," Valri answered, waving the two detectives away.

Taking her cue, Kenzie thanked her cousin and then withdrew. She walked ahead of Hunter back to the elevator bank.

When he caught up to her, Kenzie slanted a look at him that he couldn't quite read.

She pressed for the elevator before speaking what was on her mind. "So, that's you turning on the charm?"

"No, that's me being my charming self," he told her. "I just wanted your cousin to know that we understood the pressure she was under and that we didn't want to add to that load."

Yeah, right. Kenzie eyed him skeptically. "Knowing full well that by playing the understanding detective-in-need, Valri wouldn't turn you down, is that it?" she asked as the elevator arrived and its door opened.

Kenzie looked at him before stepping into the elevator. His expression was the very picture of innocence.

"I'm sure I don't know what you're talking about, Detective," Hunter answered.

Kenzie sighed. This was pointless, she thought as she pressed for her floor. The steel door slid closed. She focused on the plus side.

"Well, at least it got Valri to take a look at the laptop," she said.

Kenzie could almost *feel* the other detective's smile as it curved the corners of his rather sensuous mouth and made its way up into his eyes.

"Yes, it did, didn't it?" Hunter asked.

The man was proud of himself. She resisted the urge to pummel him. "Are you expecting me to say thank you?" she asked.

"No, I'm just expecting to make a little headway on the case," he answered innocently as he looked up into the air. The floors between the basement and Kenzie's squad room seemed to go by in slow motion. "But if you feel compelled to say thank you—"

"I don't," she retorted.

He shrugged as if he'd been expecting that answer. "Then problem's solved, isn't it?" he asked. The door opened and they walked out.

They had no sooner turned the corner, about to walk into the Missing Persons squad room, than Kenzie felt her cell phone ringing. Digging it out of her pocket, she announced, "Cavanaugh."

"Kenzie, it's Valri," the voice on the other end of her cell said. "I unlocked that laptop you and Mr. Tall-Not-so-Dark-and-Handsome brought in."

Kenzie stopped walking. She knew that Valri was quick, but this was fast even for her cousin.

"Already?" she cried incredulously. "We haven't even reached the squad room yet."

Hunter made no pretense of not hearing her. "She got in, didn't she?" he asked her, grinning.

Kenzie waved him away as if he were no more than an annoying gnat. "We'll be right there," she told her cousin.

"You're the best, Valri," Hunter praised, leaning in and saying the words into Kenzie's phone.

Hearing him, Valri responded, "That's why you brought it to me," before she terminated the call.

Kenzie had no idea if Valri's response was to her or to Hunter, but she had her suspicions. Putting her cell phone back in her pocket, she realized that Hunter had turned on his heel and was already on his way back to the elevator they had just vacated.

She quickened her pace, managing to catch up to him at the bank of elevators. A sense of triumph blended with the desire to fillet the detective. She glared at Brannigan.

"You're pretty proud of yourself, aren't you?" she said.

He looked at her and asked in seemingly all innocence, "Should I be?"

Kenzie frowned. They'd gotten this far this quickly

in part due to Hunter flexing his very obvious sexuality. She knew that, but she didn't want to condone his behavior—exactly.

"Ask me again when we catch Kurtz's killer," she told him.

He smiled broadly at her. "I'll do that," he said, getting back into the elevator.

She'd never wanted to strangle someone this much before. She tried to sublimate her reaction by being cryptic.

"Careful, your insecurity is showing," Kenzie told the detective.

Hunter merely grinned in response.

She'd always believed in being fair no matter how much it cost her to do it. "All right, you did good," Kenzie said reluctantly between clenched teeth.

He looked at her as if he was surprised to hear her speak. "Excuse me?"

Her eyebrows drew together. "You heard me."

"I did," he confessed, unable to suppress the twinkle in his eyes. "I just wanted to hear it again."

She closed her eyes, searching for strength. "You are a *very* difficult person to work with," she finally told Hunter. *For more reasons than one*, she added silently.

He was completely unfazed by her declaration. "Don't worry, I'll grow on you."

That was exactly what she was afraid of. "Ha!" she deliberately laughed. "So do warts and fungus and I wouldn't look forward to experiencing either—or you," she added pointedly.

"We'll see," was all Hunter said to her in response.

The elevator door yawned open. Getting out, they headed back to the computer lab. Kenzie was surprised when instead of letting her enter first, Hunter walked into the computer lab ahead of her and went straight to Valri's desk.

"Valri," he said warmly, "we can't thank you enough for unlocking the laptop for us. You saved us an awful lot of effort and time."

Surprised by the enthusiasm in the handsome detective's voice, it took Valri a second to respond. "It was basically very simple," she told the duo. "Mr. Kurtz used his late wife's birthday."

Kenzie looked at her in surprise. "How did you know her birthday?" she asked. "Or that John Kurtz even had a late wife?" she added now that she thought about it.

Valri smiled at her cousin. It was the same sort of tolerant smile that an indulgent mother bestows on a very young, very slow child. "The internet is a wonderful source of information if you know how to use it," she told Kenzie glibly.

"I know that," Kenzie responded, trying not to sound impatient or insulted. "I just meant that I didn't think you had enough time to find all that out."

Valri gave her a knowing look. Kenzie wasn't serious, was she? "You came to me because you knew I was quick and thorough, right?" she asked.

That *was* why they had come to Valri in the first place, Kenzie thought. Because she was the quickest computer tech anyone had ever encountered.

"Right," Kenzie granted. "And it's not that I don't appreciate this, really—"

Valri cut her off. She didn't have time to listen to accolades. "If you want to show me how appreciative you are, just take the laptop and go so I can get to the rest of all this," she said, nodding at the paraphernalia on her desk, paraphernalia that Kenzie could have sworn had somehow managed to get even higher in the last ten minutes.

Hunter took possession of the laptop. Kenzie began to

edge out of the room, but Hunter stood where he was, assessing the situation.

"You need help," he told her.

"I have help," Valri responded, smiling her gratitude at Hunter. It wasn't lost on Kenzie. "He's been out sick for the last couple of days. Now please go—and shut the door behind you."

Kenzie jerked her thumb at Hunter. "I could leave him posted at your door to keep the riffraff out," she volunteered.

Valri was already working on her next challenge and just waved them both out of the room.

"That woman is amazing," Hunter commented as they walked down the hallway back to the elevator for a second time within a few minutes. "Is there any way that the department can clone her?"

Kenzie shook her head. "She's in a league by herself—and they've probably tried," she added regarding his cloning comment.

Hunter glanced down at the laptop he had tucked under his arm. "I just hope this turns out to be worth her effort and has something other than videos of cute animals falling all over themselves in their race to get to the dinner dish."

"Not much chance of that," Kenzie responded. "The description Connie gave me of her father doesn't make me feel that he was the type to spend his time watching videos of kittens no matter how cute or what they were doing."

"According to Connie, Kurtz wasn't the type to get caught up in dating again either," Hunter reminded Kenzie, looking at her pointedly.

Kenzie inclined her head. "Point taken." Out of the corner of her eye, she saw him grinning at her as they got back on the elevator. "What?" she asked in barely concealed exasperation.

"You just agreed that I had a point," Hunter answered. "You know, you and I might just wind up having a decent working relationship yet."

She pressed her lips together, refusing to smile at the optimistic comment. "Don't let it go to your head," Kenzie warned.

Amusement curved his lips. "Does that mean I should be braced for disappointment?"

"At the very least," she answered.

Arriving at her floor, she led the way into the squad room. Kyle Choi was on his feet the moment he saw her walking in.

"We've been given the back room," he told her. He nodded a greeting at Hunter.

"Just like that?" Kenzie asked, surprised.

"It might have had something to do with the chief of Ds calling the lieutenant to make the arrangements," Choi confided, deliberately dropping his voice.

"That reminds me," Hunter suddenly said. "I still get to ask Valdez to work with us, right?"

He asked her the question out of a sense of courtesy, not wanting Kenzie to feel that he was steamrolling over her.

But it was Choi who answered him. "He's already here. He looked like a guy who had been sprung from a trap. Just how dead are things up in the Cold Case unit?" he asked Hunter.

"Very," Hunter answered without a second's hesitation.

"Let's get cracking on this," Kenzie told the two men, taking hold of the laptop and sliding it away from Hunter before he could tighten his grip on it.

"After you," Hunter told her, gesturing toward what he assumed was the back room.

Holding the laptop almost defensively against her chest, Kenzie led the way into the back room.

Jason Valdez was seated at the rectangular table. The only other furniture in the small room, other than the six chairs that were around the table, two on each side facing one another, one at each end, was a large rolling bulletin board. The bulletin board sported a row of silver tacks along the upper edge, waiting to be pressed into service.

"I guess our cold case isn't so cold anymore, is it, Brannigan?" Valdez happily asked his partner.

"That's the working theory," Hunter responded. Realizing that introductions might be in order, he said to his partner, "Detective Jason Valdez, meet Detective McKenzie Cavanaugh. I take it you two have already met," he said, nodding at Choi.

Valdez glanced over his shoulder at the other man. He grinned broadly at Hunter. "Hell, we're best buddies," Valdez cracked.

"You two really are lonely up there, aren't you?" Choi observed. He looked at his partner and pointed to the laptop she had in her hands. "What's that?"

"This is the laptop that Connie Kurtz didn't know her father had, and hopefully, it's also the key to unlocking the mystery of how a lonely old widower wound up losing his head in the middle of Aurora Park," Kenzie told her partner. "Literally."

At that moment, Hunter's cell rang, emitting a jarring noise that sounded like an old-fashioned dial phone.

Kenzie frowned, thinking it was one of the detective's many girlfriends.

Her mood didn't improve when he held up his hand to prevent her from talking while he listened to whatever it was that the person on the other end of the call was saying to him.

Chapter 10

By the time Hunter put his cell phone away, Kenzie was more than mildly annoyed. She had just started thinking of him as a decent detective, but the call she'd just witnessed had instantly demoted him back to useless playboy status.

She could barely keep her temper in check. "You need to tell your girlfriends that you can't accept their calls until you're off duty, Brannigan," Kenzie informed him briskly.

"Girlfriends?" Hunter repeated, his handsome brow wrinkling with a touch of confusion.

"Don't act so innocent, Brannigan. I'm talking about whoever just called you." Exasperated, she waved her hand at the pocket where he'd tucked away his cell.

"Oh." And then he grinned at Kenzie as if he'd just realized what she had mistakenly thought. "Sorry." And then he told her, "But the ME's really not my type."

"The ME?" It was Kenzie's turn to be confused by the subject of their conversation. "You mean Doc Rayburn?"

"Yes," Hunter told her. "That was who called just now. You remember the ME, don't you?" he asked. "The poor guy who was on the receiving end of all those body parts that we just dumped in his morgue."

Kenzie's partner glanced at her and it was obvious

that Choi thought this wasn't going to end well, so he ran interference.

"Why was the ME calling?" Choi asked, tactfully.

"Glad you asked," Hunter said. "It seems that even though the doc is dealing with headless torsos, he was able to make an ID."

Kenzie's brow furrowed. "How's that possible?"

Hunter turned in her direction. "Apparently our serial killer should have been lopping off his victims' legs, as well, because one of the bodies the dog found had an artificial hip put in," he told the other three detectives.

For the first time since he'd become part of the task force, Hunter saw Kenzie really smile. He caught himself thinking that she really could light up a room and he wondered if she was even aware of that.

"And artificial hips come with serial numbers that are registered in databanks," Kenzie cried excitedly.

"Nice to know that if my uncle Oscar ever turns up dead during one of his many 'global excursions,' they'll be able to identify him and ship him back to my aunt Rosa," Valdez commented.

"The wonders of medicine," Kenzie commented to Hunter's partner. She did her best to tamp down her eagerness as she asked Hunter, "So what's the victim's name?"

"I don't know," Hunter admitted.

"What do you mean you don't know?" Kenzie demanded. "He just called you."

"The ME wants to tell us in person," Hunter told her, his tone a great deal calmer than Kenzie's was.

Kenzie took a deep breath, managing to get a grip on herself.

"Fair enough," she allowed. And then, she asked sarcastically, "Mind if I come along since you and Rayburn seem to be such good buddies?"

"Sure," Hunter answered. Then, unable to resist, he said as they left the back room, "Aw, Kenzie. Don't be jealous. I'm just less intimidating to the poor guy than you are."

He watched in fascination as storm clouds gathered in her eyes.

"I am *not* intimidating," Kenzie informed him as she strode ahead of him and out of the squad room again.

Tickled, Hunter began to laugh in response to the sound of her annoyed tone.

Kenzie glared at the man who was swiftly becoming her nemesis.

"What's so funny?" she asked. And then she answered her own question. "You think I'm intimidating, is that it?"

He didn't have to fake surprise. Was that a serious question? "Have you *met* you?" he asked.

Intimidating? How could he say such a thing? "I don't intimidate you," she pointed out.

No, she didn't, he thought. But there was a reason for that.

"When I was a kid, for a time I was raised by a tough old grandmother," he told her as they got on the elevator again. "She buried three husbands—I'm assuming they were dead at the time but I'm not a hundred percent positive of that," he added with a chuckle. "Grandma took no garbage from anyone and if she's still out there somewhere, I'm sure that woman can *still* drink any five guys under the table. She also had a mouth like a sailor, so no, you don't intimidate me—but then, I'm a unique case."

She sighed. He would think that, she thought. "You *are* a case all right," she told Hunter.

The elevator went straight down to the basement without any stops.

"You know," she said as she watched the numbers become lower, "I'm beginning to think we should just relocate to the basement to save ourselves the travel time."

"And deprive me of our cozy few minutes together?" Hunter asked, indicating the elevator car.

"You're not funny," Kenzie informed him.

"I wasn't trying for funny," he told her in a low voice that seemed to seductively skim along her skin before it faded away.

Walking out of the elevator, Kenzie did her best to shake off the lingering effects the sound of his sexy voice had created. She was well aware of his reputation and she was not about to buy into the man's act.

"Focus on the case, Brannigan. Amateur hour is over," she informed him just before she pushed open the door to the morgue with the flat of her hand.

"Amateur hour, eh?" he repeated with a very unsettling laugh. Leaning in, he promised, "To be picked up later."

"Not if I can help it," she murmured under her breath. Raising her voice as she walked toward the medical examiner, Kenzie asked, "So what's so special that you had to tell us in person instead of over the phone, Doc?"

"Something to knock your socks off—if you had on socks," Rayburn amended, glancing at Kenzie's long, bare legs before continuing. "Either one of you familiar with the name Anthony Pagliotti?" he asked, looking from one to the other.

The name meant nothing to her. "Should we be?" Kenzie asked.

"He's the opera singer who fell off the face of the earth after he lost his voice, isn't he?" Hunter asked the doctor.

"Looks like Detective Brannigan gets the gold star," Rayburn announced with a flourish, pleased as well as duly impressed.

Kenzie stared at the man next to her. "How would you know who he is?" she questioned Hunter.

"My grandmother had a cultured side," the detective said matter-of-factly. "It was small, but it was loud," he added.

She was getting to know a lot more about her new temporary partner than she'd thought she would. Kenzie wasn't sure she was happy about that state of affairs. As long as she thought of him as a walking egotist, she could ignore him. But the more human he became, the harder he would be to write off.

Turning away from Hunter, she addressed the ME. "Okay, so what about this opera singer?"

"As Brannigan said," Rayburn said, starting over, "he went missing." The medical examiner paused, then said almost like a game show announcer, "Until now."

Hunter looked down at the skeletal remains on the ME's table. "This is him?"

Rayburn nodded. "What's left of him after a decade. Looks like he ran afoul of your serial killer," the doctor pronounced.

"Are you sure that this opera singer was killed by the same person?" Kenzie asked. She looked dubiously at the remains.

Rayburn reviewed his findings. "Same MO, same kind of cuts made to separate the man's head from his torso, so yes, I'd say this is the work of the same suspect—whoever that might be," the medical examiner interjected.

Kenzie's eyes were almost sparkling as she appraised the torso laid out on Rayburn's table. "This is really helpful, Doc. The more information we have, the more chances we'll have to find the killer." Her mind was already racing ahead. "We'll start interviewing the people Pagliotti knew," she said as she began to leave.

"He was a recluse," Hunter told her, putting a pin in her balloon.

Another reclusive victim, Kenzie thought. "I'm sensing a pattern here. Still, there's got to be *someone* we can talk to about this man," she insisted. "You just said he was once famous, so maybe he had die-hard fans, or maybe—"

"Um, Detectives?" Rayburn called after them as they were about to walk out the door. When they turned around to face him, the medical examiner said, "I haven't quite finished being helpful yet."

Kenzie immediately strode back to the doctor. Hunter was just behind her.

"There's something else about our reclusive opera singer?" she asked Rayburn, thinking that the man was doling out evidence for dramatic effect.

"No. This is about another one of the bodies," Rayburn answered.

"Another victim with an artificial hip?" Hunter guessed.

The medical examiner scrunched up his face. "Not quite as definitive," he told them. Since he had no other way to identify the incomplete bodies, he gave them each a number. "Torso number five isn't nearly as badly decomposed as the others. Number five has tattoos all over his chest. Very unique tattoos," Rayburn specified.

Leading the pair over to one of the metal drawers, he opened it to illustrate his point. "I doubt if there are too many places that have tattoo artists who can do renditions of Madonna and Child of this impressive quality," he told them.

Hunter looked down at the decorated torso. Most of it was still in rather good condition. "This one hasn't been dead all that long, has he?"

"No. A month, tops, would be my educated guess," Rayburn told them. "I'm still waiting for some results to come back from the lab, but while we wait, I'd say that you stand a good chance of putting a name to this one, as well."

Hunter exchanged looks with Kenzie and nodded at what the doctor had just told them. "Anything else?" he asked the medical examiner.

"Just that all the victims you brought me have one thing in common," Rayburn replied. "They are all men," Rayburn told them, then said with emphasis, "older Caucasian men."

There was silence for a moment, and then Hunter put into words what they were all thinking. "Looks like our serial killer might have some very serious 'daddy' issues."

Kenzie bit her lower lip, mulling the theory over in her head. On the surface, it fit the preponderance of victims to a T. But maybe the matter was even simpler than that.

"Either that or it's just that older men offer a great deal less resistance, aren't as quick to flee, can be easily overpowered and, in general, they put up less of a fight," Kenzie concluded. She looked at Hunter, waiting for him to counter her theory.

Rayburn listened to what she had to say thoughtfully. "You just might have a point there," the doctor agreed.

"I'll send someone from the task force to take photos of that tattoo—" she pointed toward the work of art on the torso "—and make the rounds of the tattoo parlors with them, see if they can turn up something," Kenzie told the medical examiner.

His attention had been captured by her first sentence. "A task force," Rayburn repeated with a nod of approval. "Is this your first one, Kenzie?" he asked.

She was about to say yes, but that would have been misleading. The last thing that she wanted to do was say something that Brannigan could wind up holding over her head, taunting her with.

"Not exactly," she answered. "It's a joint task force."

"Joint?" Rayburn echoed, his eyes darting toward the detective standing next to her.

Hunter confirmed the doctor's unspoken question. "I'm her better half," he said.

Kenzie was quick to clarify the statement. "Euphemistically speaking."

Rayburn nodded in response and chuckled. "I'll keep that in mind," he told her, and Kenzie had the uneasy feeling that the ME was politely saying that he didn't believe her protestations.

"Let us know if you come up with anything else," Hunter told the doctor.

Because the medical examiner had called Brannigan and not her, she assumed he had misplaced her cell number. She took the proper precaution. Taking out a card, she pressed it into Rayburn's hand.

"Call me if you find anything else. Day or night. The time doesn't matter. Call me," Kenzie instructed.

Rayburn looked down at the card and then at Hunter, as if silently asking for his thoughts on the matter.

"What she said," Hunter told the medical examiner, adding, "Call her or I'll never hear the end of it." And then he grinned.

Why did she constantly feel that he was having fun at her expense? She'd never met anyone who made her feel so undermined in her life.

"Stop grinning, Brannigan, or someone's going to mistake you for a hyena," she retorted.

"I doubt it," Hunter answered and went right on grinning. He couldn't help getting a kick out of how hard she was trying to keep the barriers up between them.

* * *

"Choi, take your camera and go down to the morgue," Kenzie said the moment she walked into the back room the task force had been given.

Choi was momentarily caught off guard. Recovering, he said, "I don't know what you heard, but I'm not into that kind of kinky stuff."

"This isn't kinky stuff," she informed her partner, ignoring Hunter, who was stifling a laugh. "I need you to take pictures of one of the victim's tattoos. It's a distinct one. The doc will show you which victim. Once you have a good set of photographs, I want you to hit all the local tattoo parlors to see if you can find the artist who did them. Maybe we'll get lucky and get a third name for our list."

Resigned, Choi rose from the table. "And when I got up this morning, I thought it was going to be just another day in paradise."

"Instead, you get to earn your keep," Kenzie told the thin, dark-haired detective with a tight smile. When she turned toward the other two men who were left in the room, she saw that Hunter was wearing the same smile he had been earlier. "What?" she asked, bracing herself.

Hunter's eyes met hers. "Like I said before. Intimidating."

Mentally, she counted to ten, then informed Hunter, "Choi went because I'm in charge, not because he's afraid of me."

"Sure," Hunter agreed. "That sounds good, too."

She knew Brannigan was humoring her, but she didn't have any time to butt heads or argue with the infuriating man. There was a serial killer loose out there, preying on old, lonely men from the looks of it, and she was determined to find and stop him.

She turned toward Brannigan's partner. "Valdez, why don't you see what you can find out about Anthony Pagliotti—if he adhered to a schedule, who saw him last, if anyone ever declared him to be missing or filed a report to that effect."

Valdez slanted a look toward Hunter, waiting for the latter to say the same thing to him. He wasn't disappointed.

"You heard the detective," Hunter said. "Start digging."

"Okay," Valdez said, backing out of the room. "I'll just go find a computer to log on to."

Once Valdez had left the room, Hunter turned around to look at Kenzie. His eyes slowly and carefully washed over her face and body before he finally spoke.

"Okay, now that you've got me alone, just what did you have in mind for us to do?" he asked in a low, particularly seductive voice.

"You must be the only person alive who can make detective work sound like a proposition," she told him, shaking her head.

"What can I tell you? It's a gift." Hunter glanced over toward the laptop that Valri had unlocked for them. "Want me to troll through the sites that Kurtz visited?"

"See if he has a profile on the Second Time Around website," she said.

"Think he used his own name?"

"He probably wasn't creative enough to come up with anything on his own. Just doing this was a big step for him. He probably didn't even think that there were people who made things up to put down in their profiles." She paused for a moment, then decided to ask Brannigan the question that occurred to her. "You ever go to one of these sites?"

"Nope. I like face-to-face better," he said honestly.

"That way you know if you have any chemistry. You can't experience chemistry through a website."

"Some people do," she pointed out.

Actually, she thought, more than a few, considering the stories that she had heard over the last few years. The idea of filling out a form online in order to meet her perfect soul mate never even remotely appealed to Kenzie. People could lie on the internet just as easily as they could lie in person.

Hunter watched her with piqued interest. "Do you?" he asked.

Kenzie drew herself up indignantly, as if he had just insulted her.

"I don't have time to spend on those kinds of websites. If I have any extra time, I'll spend it reading a good book."

His mouth curved as he looked at her. That, he thought, would be a colossal waste on her part. "Yeah, me, too."

Chapter 11

"You know, I kind of missed the days when if you needed something or wanted something, you had to physically *go* to a brick-and-mortar building to get it," Kenzie said as she pulled up in an industrial parking lot. This particular parking lot was located in the next county. The building that was the focus of their attention had taken them the better part of two hours to pinpoint and find.

"You mean like groceries?" Hunter asked, curious as he came around to her side of the vehicle.

"I mean like *anything*," Kenzie stressed. She looked up at the twelve-story office building that housed a variety of businesses, including the one that ran the dating website they were about to investigate. "There was a time when you could look up a place in the phone book, jot down the address and, armed with a trusty, well-worn map, *find* that place."

"'Trusty, well-worn map?'" Hunter echoed. "Just how old *are* you, Kenzie?" he asked her, amused as well as surprised by the sentiment she had just expressed.

She gave Hunter a withering look. "I have an old soul," she informed him.

"Apparently," he commented, following her up the front steps to the building's entrance. "But I actually kind of get what you mean. The internet has managed to bring us closer together and further apart at the same time," he observed. "Human interaction isn't a priority—unless you want it to be."

Kenzie raised an eyebrow, surprised at his comment. "That's deep—for you," she added. Turning on her heel, she pulled open the entrance door. "Well, let's go 'interact' with the CEO of Second Time Around," she said.

Once inside, they headed for the three elevators that were standing side by side. She glanced at the directory to double-check that the office hadn't been moved to another floor. It hadn't. The office that contained the dating service was on the ninth floor. Room number 905.

Hunter pressed for the elevator. The one to their extreme right was already there, and it opened its door the moment Hunter had pushed the up button.

"Maybe they can help you find the woman of your dreams," Kenzie said as they got on.

"The woman of my dreams wouldn't be wasting her time filling out forms online," Hunter told her. He slanted a glance in her direction.

Kevin Campbell looked much too young to be able to empathize with the people who turned to his "over fifty" dating service for help in finding companionship. He also looked none too friendly when he came to the glass door in response to their repeated knocking.

Opening the door only a crack when they wouldn't go away despite his gestures for them to do just that, he informed them coldly, "I'm sorry, we're not hiring just now."

"That's good because we're not here about a job opportunity," Hunter told the preppy-looking CEO.

"We don't take walk-ins either," Campbell told them. "You'll have to fill out a profile online like everyone else." He paused, actually looking at them for the first time. "You two are rather young-looking for Second Time Around. You looking into this for one of your parents?" Campbell asked, his almost black eyes moving like restless pinballs from one person in his doorway to the other. "Same rules apply. Do the profile online."

He began to close the door, but Hunter pushed his shoulder against it, making it immobile.

"What the—"

In response, Kenzie and Hunter took out their IDs and badges simultaneously, holding them up for Campbell's benefit.

"We'd like to get some information about someone who did just that," Kenzie told the man.

Campbell sighed, then stepped away from the door.

Because they were out in the open with a dozen pairs of eyes looking their way, Campbell motioned for them to follow him. "Come into my office."

"Sure thing," Hunter said amicably, following behind Campbell. Kenzie was right at his side.

Campbell's inner office was a glorified cubbyhole with little more charm. Closing his door to separate them from the outer office, he told his new visitors, "I'm afraid I can't release any information. It's all private and privileged," he informed them like a highly paid lawyer.

Kenzie frowned and gave it another try. "How about if we tell you that we believe that someone who filled out one of those online profiles was killed by someone else who had filled out one of your online profiles. Does that make it less private now?" she asked. Her voice grew stern. "We *need* to take a look at your files."

Kevin crossed his arms before his chest, digging his heels in. "Do you have a warrant?" he challenged. His smug manner indicated that he knew they didn't.

"No," Hunter answered. "But we have something better

than that. We have word of mouth as well as contact with several very popular bloggers. If you make us go back for a warrant, I can *guarantee* that your little dating service will go the way of the dial phone and Myspace faster than you can say the word *archaic*."

Campbell puffed up his rather small chest. "You're bluffing."

Kenzie added her voice to Hunter's. "Only one way to find out," she told the dating site CEO with a frosty smile.

Campbell's face clouded over. "Whose profile are you looking for?" he asked grudgingly, dropping his voice as he sat down behind the computer on his desk.

"John Kurtz and anyone who responded to his profile," Kenzie told him.

The scowl on Campbell's face only intensified. "This might take time," he told them belligerently.

"Lucky for us, we've got nowhere else to be," Hunter cheerfully assured the angry CEO.

Looking like a man who was struggling to hang on to his temper and keep from saying things that would only make the situation worse, Campbell began to type. A few moments later, he turned his monitor around so that it faced the two detectives.

"This the guy?" he asked.

Kenzie leaned in to get a better look. The photograph on the website matched the one that Kurtz's daughter had brought in. Obviously the man hadn't taken many pictures, she thought.

Nodding, Kenzie said, "That's him."

"Now we need you to print all the information you have on everyone whom he connected with online through your website," Hunter instructed.

"I have no way of knowing that," Campbell protested vehemently.

Hunter wasn't buying it. "Sure you do," he contradicted. "This is the internet age. Every keystroke struck using your website is out there somewhere and you're aware of it." Hunter took a step closer and loomed over the CEO. "So stop wasting our time by playing dumb and get us those profiles—or we'll be forced to shut down your business and confiscate your computers so that our own computer wizard can access the information you're attempting to withhold."

Campbell glared at the two police detectives invading his business, but after a second, he angrily began typing again, almost pounding on the keys.

Not trusting him, Hunter circled around the man in order to watch what came on the screen.

Campbell stopped typing. "I can't think with you looking over my shoulder," he complained.

Hunter wasn't about to back off. "Sure you can," he told the belligerent CEO. "Just think of it as showing off for an audience."

Campbell muttered something unintelligible under his breath, but his fingers began moving across the keyboard again.

A couple of minutes later, the printer against the back wall in the corner came to life. Pages connected to the profiles that Campbell was pulling up began to materialize.

Kenzie was on her feet in an instant, crossing over to the printer. She gathered together the pages that the printer was spitting out. After several more minutes went by, the printer went silent.

Kenzie looked over toward Campbell. "That's it?" she asked.

"What do you want me to tell you?" Campbell asked, raising his angular shoulders in a frustrated shrug. "The guy's shy."

"He's also dead," Hunter informed the arrogant CEO.

"Then you weren't just kidding when you tried to get me to give you the files?" Campbell cried.

"Nope. He's dead," Hunter repeated. "As in no longer about to access *anything* online."

Campbell jumped up from his desk, his entire manner defensive. "You're not saying that you think my website has something to do with this Kurtz guy being dead, are you?"

"We're looking into all possibilities," Hunter replied, sounding as calm as Campbell was agitated.

"We want to talk to anyone who had contact with Mr. Kurtz before he was killed," Kenzie added.

The added information only managed to horrify the CEO further. "Now he's not just dead, he was killed?" Campbell cried, his voice going up a full octave at the end of his question.

Kenzie took out her phone and searched for the picture of the victim's head and hands as they appeared on Rayburn's table. Because arrogant people like Campbell irritated her no end, she held the photo up for him to view.

"You tell me," she said to Campbell.

The color drained from Campbell's face. The next second, Campbell covered his mouth with both hands like a man struggling not to throw up.

His face was even paler when he finally managed to get control over himself. Taking in a deep breath, Campbell dropped his hands from his mouth. When he stared at the two detectives, his eyes were watery.

"There has to be some other explanation," he insisted, his voice cracking.

"We're open to suggestions," Kenzie told him magnanimously.

Campbell's breathing had grown shallower. "You're

the police. You're supposed to have the suggestions," he retorted desperately.

Hunter exchanged glances with Kenzie. It was obvious that he thought it was time to go.

"Thanks for your help. We'll be back if we think of anything else," Hunter told the trembling CEO.

"Don't worry, we'll let ourselves out," Kenzie said to Campbell.

Glancing back at the website CEO, she saw the man reaching into his bottom drawer and taking out a bottle of what looked like Scotch. She almost felt sorry for Campbell.

Almost.

When they got back into Kenzie's car, it was growing dark. They had put in a very long day.

"It's getting late," Hunter said. "Why don't we pick this up in the morning."

Kenzie pointed her vehicle back toward the precinct. "Hot date tonight?" she asked him.

Hunter refused to rise to the bait. "Yeah. With my shower. It's been an exceptionally long day and I'd kind of like to wash the stench off—if it's okay with you," he added, glancing in her direction.

Kenzie wasn't oblivious to the sarcasm and she supposed she had it coming.

"Sure, wash away," she told him. Pausing, she waited a beat, then said, "You did a good job back there, getting Campbell to cooperate."

A flippant response rose to Hunter's lips, but then he thought better of it and accepted the olive branch Kenzie was extending to him.

"Thanks." Hunter waited a couple of minutes, then decided that if she was behaving like a human being, he had nothing to lose by asking, "After we clock out, you want to stop somewhere for dinner?"

Kenzie could feel herself tensing. "I've got dinner waiting for me in my refrigerator."

Hunter laughed softly. "Of course you do," he commented matter-of-factly, then shrugged. "I'll take a rain check, then."

She felt as if Brannigan was attempting to corner her. "I didn't offer one," she said as she pulled up into the police station.

"I know," Hunter said cheerfully. "It was implied," he told her.

Kenzie got out of the car and stared at him. The man was unbelievable.

"In what universe?" she asked.

But Hunter merely smiled at her. "You know the answer to that one," he said. Turning on his heel, he began walking toward the police station.

"No, I don't," she protested.

She found herself walking behind him as they went up the stairs. The man really could move quickly when he wanted to, she thought grudgingly.

"You sleep here last night?" Hunter asked when he walked into the back room the following morning.

He would have bet that he had beaten everyone else in, but apparently not, he mused, setting the paper tray with its four covered containers of coffee down on the table.

Kenzie was already at the table, her laptop opened. She was reviewing the three profiles that Campbell had been forced to surrender to them, along with the one that John Kurtz had filled out.

She'd made notations on each of the pages. Something new had struck her every time she went over the profiles. When Brannigan walked in, she looked up briefly, then deliberately went back to what she was doing.

She also ignored his question.

"No," Hunter said, pretending to reconsider his question, "that's a change of clothes you have on so I guess you didn't sleep here after all. But you were still here when I left last night and you're here now—and this is early for me," he emphasized. He waited for Kenzie to say something. When she still didn't, he asked another question. "Did you get *any* sleep at all?"

She finally glanced up at Brannigan. She didn't like being questioned. "I don't need much sleep to get by," she replied.

"Even that mechanical rabbit in those commercials needs new batteries put in every once in a while," Hunter pointed out.

She frowned, setting the pages down on the table in front of her. "I don't need any batteries put in," she told him.

"Maybe you'd feel better if you did," Hunter quipped, then asked, "Did you get up on the wrong side of the bed today, Kenzie?"

It was like he had pushed a button. She didn't like him using her name. It made him sound as if they were on intimate footing and they weren't. And she *certainly* didn't like him getting personal.

"I *told* you not to call me that, Brannigan," she snapped.

"What's wrong—Cavanaugh?" he asked, inserting her last name as an afterthought.

Aggravated, Kenzie threw the printouts that Campbell had given them on the floor in disgust. "What makes you think that there's something wrong?"

"I'm a detective. I pick up on these things," he said dryly. "Now, why do you look like someone who's about to throw a fit?"

Kenzie blew out a breath. "See these profiles?" she asked, gesturing to the papers.

He forced himself to look at the papers on the floor and not the increasingly gorgeous woman in front of him. This was not the time to allow his hormones to get carried away. It might never be. "What about them?"

"They're fake," she accused.

He shrugged in response, which didn't improve her mood. "So somebody padded their profile. I hear people do that—"

"No," she interrupted, then repeated more adamantly, "They're fake. These three women *don't exist*."

That got his attention. He bent down and picked up one of the sheets. He looked it over. "What do you mean they don't exist?"

"All their pictures were lifted from one of those general photo pools you can find online. I looked up each of these women's names, and if they have a social media page—and only two did—the photographs don't match the names. Someone used their names to create different personae."

"Why?"

She shook her head. "As bait. To fulfill a fantasy, to lure an unsuspecting male into their web, to boost their egos. I don't know. But whatever correspondence that John Kurtz had with these three so-called women has been erased. It could all be innocent or it could be part of a more intricate plot, but without anything else to go on, we might never find out."

Hunter gathered up the remaining pages and rose to his feet. "Let me take these down to Valri and see if she can piece something together."

She had to admit that she was surprised by his initiative. She was also surprised at his suggestion.

"You have a death wish?" she asked Hunter.

"No," he freely denied, "but I do have this overwhelming

need to find out if any of these so-called women is somehow involved in John Kurtz's death and dismemberment."

Kenzie rose from her chair and he looked at her quizzically. He had the impression that she had settled in. "Where are you going?"

"I'm going with you to Valri's lab. I am *not* about to allow you to waltz into the lion's den by yourself," she informed him.

Hunter grinned at her in response.

"Now what?"

Hunter's eyes crinkled as his smile widened. "I knew I'd get you to care."

She rolled her eyes at his response. "Don't push it, Brannigan," she warned.

Hunter raised one hand as if he was about to take a pledge.

"This is me, not pushing it." And then he nodded at the coffee containers. "Don't forget to take your coffee with you—maybe you can use it as a peace offering," he suggested.

"Valri's overworked and underpaid. It'll take more than coffee," Kenzie told him as they left the back room, headed for the computer lab. "You have any extra money on you?"

The sound of his responding throaty laugh shimmied up and down her spine.

Chapter 12

Valri looked only mildly surprised when she saw Hunter and her cousin coming into the computer lab.

"I have *got* to get them to put up a no-trespassing sign on the door," Valri murmured almost more to herself than to them.

"This won't take long," Hunter promised her, then, to sweeten the deal, he added, "We'll be out of your hair before you know it."

"You already *were* out of my hair, remember?" Valri pointed out.

"This time for sure," Kenzie told her cousin, adding weight to Hunter's promise. "We just need a little bit more help."

"'Said Noah to his sons after they brought in all the lumber to build the ark,'" Valri quipped. She sighed, as if resigned to the situation. "Go ahead. Tell me what you need."

As succinctly as possible, Hunter told her of the roadblock their investigation had encountered. The photographs were fakes, as were the profiles. Someone, presumably the same person, was behind creating all of them. Was there a way to find out who that was?

Valri pressed her lips together as she shook her head. "Sorry, not possible," she told the two detectives at her desk.

Kenzie felt the same sense of letdown she'd experienced at six when she'd discovered that there was no Santa Claus.

"I thought you specialized in the impossible," she said to her cousin.

"The impossible, yes," Valri replied. "This, however, would take sorcery, and computer technology doesn't cover black magic," she told them. Kenzie could see that Valri was just as frustrated as they were. "I'm really sorry, but my energies are better spent focusing on things I *can* do. So unless you have a fingerprint or some trace of DNA we could use as a first step, I'm afraid I can't help you with this."

Resigned, Hunter nodded. "Thanks for trying," he told her.

"Talk to the crime scene investigators," Valri suggested as her cousin and the cold case detective began to leave the lab. "They might have dug up something when they found the victim's head and hands."

"Yeah," Kenzie answered unhappily. "Mud. They dug up mud. And, more than likely, the killer probably wore gloves when he handled the body parts before he buried them."

Valri was already back to typing on her keyboard. "Well, you know where to find me if something does turn up." She nodded at her desktop as she typed. "Chained to my computer."

"I was really hoping that Valri could come up with something," Kenzie said as they went back to her floor together.

Hunter was already searching for another avenue to steer the investigation.

"Well, like she said, she can't just conjure up answers for

us," he told Kenzie. "Maybe we'll have better luck trying to find and talk to Anthony Pagliotti's family or friends."

Just then, Kenzie's phone began to vibrate. It had to be angled inside her pocket in an odd way because her whole pocket began to move.

"Is that your phone," Hunter asked, nodding at her side, "or are you just excited by my idea?"

"Don't get carried away," Kenzie told him sharply as she took out her phone. Swiping it open, she said, "Cavanaugh." The moment she responded, the person on the other end began talking. Loudly.

"Wait, slow down. I can't understand what you're saying." Kenzie saw Hunter raise an eyebrow as if to silently ask her who was on the other end of the line. The next word out of her mouth, he had his answer. "Connie, please, stop crying. We'll be right there." Closing her phone, she looked up at Brannigan. "That was Connie Kurtz."

"I figured that part out," he answered drolly. "Why is she crying and why do we need to be right there?" he asked.

"It seems that Connie just went to her father's bank to notify them of her father's death," Kenzie told him. "They in turn notified *her* that he had closed out his accounts over two weeks ago."

"Accounts?" Hunter questioned. Things began to fall into place. "He had more than one?"

"Just a checking account and a regular savings account," Kenzie answered. "And before you ask, the accounts weren't anything overwhelming. They just represented a lifetime of frugality."

"Could the bank have made some kind of a mistake about his accounts being closed out?" Hunter asked her. "Confused them with someone else's accounts?"

Connie had provided an answer to that question in her

rather disjointed narrative. "Connie did say that her father had been banking at the same bank for the last thirty years. They knew him there. There was no mistake made," she concluded.

Resigned, the pair made a U-turn just in front of the squad room and headed back on the elevator. Again.

"I wonder if the elevator gives out frequent flier miles," Hunter cracked as they got into the elevator car and pressed for the first floor.

"If it doesn't, considering all the time we've spent riding up and down on it in the last couple of days, it should," she commented.

"Was he alone?" Hunter asked her out of the blue as they got back into Kenzie's vehicle.

She started up the car and then looked at Brannigan, confused.

"Was *who* alone?" she asked.

"Kurtz. The victim," Hunter specified. "Was he alone when he made his bank withdrawal?"

She eased into the flow of traffic, narrowly avoiding one car that had come flying into their lane, then zipped into the next lane at the last moment. People were still going to work at this hour and this driver was apparently late.

Swallowing a curse, Kenzie said, "I have no idea. Why? What are you getting at?"

"Maybe Kurtz's mystery woman accompanied him. Or hung around outside, waiting for him to close out his accounts," Hunter said.

The light was changing to red. Kenzie gunned her way through it, making it through the intersection by just a hair.

Glancing at Hunter, she smiled. "You're thinking surveillance camera," she suddenly realized.

Hunter nodded, hopeful. "That would make life a lot easier for Valri. She might be able to actually match a face to someone in the facial recognition database."

"You're assuming that this woman's face is actually *in* some database," Kenzie said.

He didn't bother to deny it. "That I am."

"That's a stretch, Brannigan," she told him.

He chose to see it differently. "It's called taking a leap of faith. Sometimes in our business, that's about all we have to hang on to—faith."

And that way, she thought, led to disappointment. "Well, let's not get ahead of ourselves," she told him. "Maybe Mr. Kurtz went alone to make the withdrawal."

"If you were this mystery femme fatale, would *you* trust your mark enough to send him off on his own to get your future nest egg?" Hunter asked.

"Femme fatale?" she questioned.

He shrugged. "I was watching an old film festival last weekend," he told her.

"Well, to answer your question, *I* wouldn't, but then I've been told that I'm not the average woman," Kenzie answered.

He considered the description an apt one. There was nothing average about the vivacious detective. "No, that you are not," he agreed.

Just for the tiniest second Kenzie felt as if there was some sort of veiled communication going on between Brannigan and her. The next second, she discarded the thought. This was not the time to allow her imagination to run wild, she thought.

"But let's just say for the sake of argument that some things are just universal—like greed. At the very least, we can get the bank's security tech to look through that day's surveillance tape for us." Hunter looked around at the passing scenery and realized that he had no idea where they were headed. "Not that I mind going on a joy ride with you, but just where are we going?"

"To meet Connie at her house. She's about fifteen minutes away from the bank where her father usually conducted his transactions," she said, once again flying through another intersection as the light began to turn red.

That brought up another matter. Hunter realized that he didn't know all that much about the victim. "Was he retired?"

"From what I found out, he was planning to be by the end of the year," she answered.

"Retired from what?"

"From engineering," she said. And then she frowned. "You would think an engineer would be more careful than that."

Hunter laughed dryly. "A high IQ has nothing to do with matters of the heart—or knowing how to cope with loneliness, for that matter," he told her. "From what you told me about your friend's father, he was a one-woman man. When he lost that woman, he kind of got lost himself." Hunter sighed as he looked straight ahead. "Lost men do desperate, stupid things."

Something in his voice caught her attention. So much so that she slowed down at the next intersection and for once didn't fly through a changing light.

"Are you speaking from experience?" she asked.

He frowned at the woman next to him. "Why do you do that?"

Kenzie had no idea what he was talking about. "Do what?"

She was playing dumb, Hunter thought. She knew damn well what he meant.

But to move things along, he explained, "Turn everything I say into some sort of indictment against me?"

"I don't do that," Kenzie protested a little too quickly and heatedly.

"Yeah, you do," was all he said and for once, the gregarious detective allowed silence to mushroom through the interior of the vehicle.

Just before they pulled up in front of Connie Kurtz's house, Kenzie made an impulsive decision and parked at the curb two houses away.

Pulling up the hand brake, she forced herself to look at Hunter. The words felt like cotton in her mouth, but she pushed them out.

"I'm sorry," she told him. "You have a reputation and some of the things you say just remind me of—"

"Of?" he asked, waiting for her to complete her sentence.

Kenzie took a breath. At the last second, she lost her nerve and didn't say what she'd intended. Instead, she said, "Of the kind of guy who doesn't play by the rules and who just thinks that the world revolves around him."

Hunter looked at her for a long moment. He made a calculated guess. "That wasn't what you were going to say, was it?"

Her back went up. "So now you're a mind reader?" she accused, her eyes flashing.

He made a mental note to talk with Finn or Murdoch about Kenzie's former engagement the first chance he got. All he knew was that she'd been engaged—and then she wasn't.

"Let's just go in there and see if we can find out something we can work with from Kurtz's daughter," Hunter said.

Not waiting for Kenzie to pull her car up into Connie's driveway, he got out and started to walk to the woman's front door.

Kenzie pulled her car up into her former friend's driveway, getting there at the same time and coming within a hairbreadth of clipping her temporary partner in the leg.

He jumped back out of the way. "Hey!"

Getting out, Kenzie slammed the driver's side door and then hurried to catch up. "You're supposed to wait for me," she shouted at him.

To which he rejoined, "You're supposed to make me *want* to wait for you, not run for my life to keep from becoming a hood ornament."

Kenzie was about to make a scathing retort when the front door flew open. It was obvious that Connie had been standing there, waiting for them.

The victim's daughter didn't even bother with a greeting.

"All of it," Connie cried. "She took all of it. How could my father have been so blind? It's like I never even knew him," she lamented.

The next moment, Connie dissolved into tears, draping her arms around the first available person in front of her, which right now turned out to be Hunter.

Holding her for a moment, Hunter told the grieving daughter, "If it's any comfort to you, he probably didn't even know himself. Grief makes people do strange, impulsive things just to be able to feel like their old selves again. Your dad missed your mother, missed having a partner to love and to care about him. It sounds like this woman took advantage of that."

Fresh tears came to Connie's eyes as she nodded her

agreement with his assessment. "I should have been there. Why didn't he come to me? Why did he turn away like that?" she cried.

Very carefully, Hunter turned her around and coaxed her back into the house. He kept his arm comfortingly around the sobbing woman.

"Sometimes strangers are easier to talk to than family members or friends. It wasn't your fault. It wasn't his fault," Hunter told her. "It just *was*."

Observing him with her old college friend, Kenzie kept quiet. It was obvious that what he was saying was comforting to Connie. It seemed to be helping her regain her composure and to put a small distance between herself and the grief and shock she was experiencing.

Swallowing her tears, Connie nodded. "I guess you're right."

"Why don't you sit down for a second," Hunter told her, leading her to the sofa. "Pull yourself together." Once she sat down, he sat down next to her, taking her hand in his in a further act of comfort. "This is going to keep hitting you in waves," he told her. "You think you've got it under control and then suddenly, bam, there it is again, washing right over you like an unexpected huge tidal wave, sucking away your very air. But it'll get better," he told her.

Connie looked at him with huge, watery eyes. "Will it?"

He acted totally convinced of what he was saying. "Given time, it will. You just have to give yourself permission to hurt at first," he said.

She nodded like a child who was promising to do better.

Thinking that she would never get a better opportunity to ask than now, Kenzie inserted herself into the conversation. "Connie, when you called me, you said something about your father closing out his accounts," Kenzie prompted.

Connie pressed her lips together. "Every last penny," she whispered. "When I called the bank, I never expected to hear anything like that."

"Nobody does," Hunter assured her comfortingly.

Connie wiped the back of her hand across her wet cheeks as she sniffled. Taking out his handkerchief, Hunter leaned over and gave it to the sobbing woman without a word.

"Thank you," Connie murmured.

Kenzie felt almost single-mindedly cruel, trying to urge the conversation along in the right direction. But she felt that they were on the clock. She couldn't shake the feeling that the killer was even now looking for another victim to rob and kill.

"Could you tell us the name of the bank and where it's located?" Kenzie pressed. "We'd like to question the bank president."

Connie took a deep breath, as if she was struggling to collect her thoughts.

"No hurry, Ms. Kurtz," Hunter told her. "Take your time."

Responding to Hunter's words and his tone, Connie seemed to pull herself together right in front of their eyes.

"It's First Interstate National," she told him. "Dad does—did," she corrected painfully, her voice nearly cracking, "all his banking at the branch on Alton and Yale," she told them. After taking in another shaky breath, she offered, "I can come with you."

"No, we'll take it from here," Kenzie assured her. "You've been more than helpful. You need to try to pull yourself together."

"Do you have someone staying with you the way Kenzie suggested?" Hunter asked.

Kenzie looked at him in surprise. The fact that he said it was her idea stunned her.

Connie nodded. "My cousin Rachel. She just stepped out to get some lunch for us when I made that phone call to the bank."

As if on cue, a petite redheaded woman walked into the house, carrying a large pizza box.

"Connie?" she asked quizzically. Her attention was focused on the two people who hadn't been there when she had gone out.

"We were just leaving," Hunter told the redhead. "I'd say you came just in time," he added, nodding at the pizza box in her hands. "Looks like it's hot. You'd better put it down before your fingers start to feel the heat," he told her.

Connie's cousin stared at the good-looking man leaving the premises. She looked like a woman whose mouth was watering.

"I will," she said. Belatedly, she put the box on the coffee table, still staring after the departing stranger.

Her reaction was not lost on Kenzie as she followed in Hunter's wake. He really did need to beat them off with a stick, she thought.

Chapter 13

Kenzie searched for a way to give Hunter a compliment. She wanted to be fair—he'd been kind to the bereaved woman and that seemed to comfort her—but she didn't want what she said going to his head. In her opinion, the man's ego was already large enough.

"What you said back there to Connie," Kenzie began, and then paused, trying to find the right words.

Hunter suppressed a sigh as he got into the car. There was undoubtedly a lecture coming on. "What'd I do wrong?" he asked.

"Nothing," she said, starting up the vehicle. It rumbled to life. She could feel his eyes on her, probably waiting for her to say "but." She glanced in his direction before pulling out. "That's just it. You were very nice and understanding."

He laughed softly. *About time*, he thought. Out loud he said, "You act surprised."

"I am," Kenzie answered honestly, then decided to go a little further. "It doesn't go with your swaggering image."

He considered her response. "Maybe my 'swaggering image' doesn't really go with the person I am."

She was going to need a lot more evidence before she was convinced of that, Kenzie thought. Merging into the far lane on the right, she made a turn at the end of the block.

"Yeah, well, we'll see," she told Hunter, backing away

from the subject. She had only one final thing to say. "One robin doesn't make a spring."

Hunter congratulated himself for not laughing out loud. "Very clever," he told her. "I'll have to remember that."

"Why do I even bother?" Kenzie cried, figuratively throwing up her hands as they arrived at the bank, pulling up in front of it.

"Because," he told her as they parked, "in my case you've already played judge, jury and executioner and now you're having second thoughts that maybe you were just a little bit too hasty passing the sentence." He looked at her for a moment before getting out of the car.

She didn't answer Hunter, mainly because she felt he *did* have a point and she hated admitting that she was wrong, especially to *him*. Besides, the man *did* act as if he was God's bonus prize to all women—just like Billy had, she thought, setting her jaw hard.

Granted, Brannigan was better-looking and, in the grand assessment of things, he had at least a few redeeming qualities, but that still didn't change things—or make her any less on her guard against any sudden moves on the detective's part.

Holding the glass entrance door open for her, Hunter nodded at Kenzie as she walked through.

"Thanks," she responded, her lips barely moving.

"That's pretty good," he told her, following her in as he let the door go. "With a little bit of practice, you could become a world-class ventriloquist," he told her. When she shot him a withering look, he said innocently, "What? I just gave you a compliment."

She didn't answer him.

Instead, Kenzie looked around and approached the first banker she saw in one of the cubbyholes that were scattered throughout the floor. "Detectives Cavanaugh and

Brannigan," she said, identifying herself and Hunter for the banker's benefit as she held up her ID. His nameplate said his name was Aaron Jacobs. "We'd like to speak to the branch manager."

The man stood partially up from his chair and pointed toward the enclosed office at the far end. It was slightly larger than the others in the room.

"That would be Ms. Murphy," the banker told them. He pulled his shoulders back a little, a soldier ready to go into battle. "Is there anything I can help you with?" he asked.

Kenzie offered him a hint of a smile before turning him down. "I'm afraid not," she replied.

The click of her heels against the beige travertine floors sounded like the rapid fire of a discharging rifle as she made her way over to the person who had been pointed out to them.

Jacobs had apparently had a change of heart and decided to precede them.

"Ms. Murphy, these two detectives would like to speak to you," the young man announced, looking a little uneasy as he spoke.

Kenzie tried to figure out if Jacobs was intimidated by them, or by the woman he was talking to.

Ana Murphy was impeccably dressed, wearing a light gray jacket and matching straight skirt that flirted with her knee line when she rose ever so slightly from behind her desk. Her jet-black hair was pulled back from her face and her makeup looked perfect. Kenzie had a feeling that Ana Murphy was one of those women who would look exactly the way she did right now even in the middle of an unexpected tornado.

The branch manager limply extended her hand to them. Kenzie thought the woman's hand felt cold to the touch as she shook it.

"Please, sit down," Ana Murphy requested. She waited until they did, then asked in a measured tone, "How may I help you?"

"We're interested in viewing any surveillance tapes you have from August 7. Especially the tapes that you have giving a view of the street directly in front of the bank," Kenzie told her.

The term *Ice Princess* came to mind as Hunter sat observing the branch manager. There seemed to be no sign of any emotion registering on the woman's face or evident in her behavior.

"That sounds very specific, Detective," the woman noted. "May I ask *why* you want to see tapes from that day?" she asked.

This was not going to be easy, Kenzie thought. "According to what one of your tellers told Connie Kurtz, Mr. Kurtz's daughter, that was the day her father closed his accounts and withdrew all his money," Kenzie told the woman.

Something flickered in the woman's dark eyes. Murphy was protecting her territory. The next words out of the woman's mouth convinced Kenzie she was right.

"Our customers are perfectly free to close their accounts at any time," the branch manager informed the two people at her desk.

"We're not trying to dispute that, Ms. Murphy," Hunter informed the woman in a sterner tone than Kenzie could recall hearing him use. "We just need to view the tapes."

Ana Murphy raised her chin. "Do you have a warrant?" the woman asked. "Our clients rely on this bank to maintain their privacy and we—"

"Mr. Kurtz is dead," Hunter told her shortly.

There was no sign of surprise in her behavior. "I am aware of that, Detective, but—"

"And are you also aware of what it means to be charged with obstruction of justice?" Kenzie asked. "In case you didn't know, it can be applied to anyone interfering with a murder investigation, so unless you are prepared for some really bad publicity for your bank in general and your branch in particular, I suggest you let us review those tapes."

Long, carefully manicured nails clutched at the edge of her desk as Ana Murphy thought and then made up her mind.

"Very well," Ms. Murphy replied coldly. Picking up the phone on her desk, she pressed a button on it. Someone on the other end picked up instantly. "Matthew, I need you to come in here."

She'd no sooner hung up than Matthew materialized in her doorway.

Matthew was a beanpole who looked as if he was barely out of high school but apparently he was currently taking college courses and interning at the bank. That meant that he was at the branch manager's beck and call, ready to do whatever needed doing.

"Matthew can help you get what you need," the woman informed them. Her tone indicated that the interview was over and she wanted them to leave her office.

Kenzie and Hunter were more than happy to leave the woman's presence.

"We need to see the surveillance tapes from August 7," Hunter told the young intern as they walked out of the woman's office.

Away from the branch manager, Matthew was gregarious and eager to help.

"I can't let you take them, but you can definitely see them here," the young intern said.

He took the two detectives into a back room equipped

with multiple monitors. The monitors viewed not only every angle of the bank's interior, but the parking lot and ATM machine that faced it, as well.

"Wait here," Matthew told them. "I'll be right back. You're lucky you came early. The tapes are only kept on-site for ninety days."

"What happens to them then?" Kenzie asked. "Do you tape over them?"

"Oh no," Matthew assured her. "They get batched. The really old ones get archived."

"But you do hang on to them?" Kenzie asked, wanting to be sure that they would be able to view the tapes.

Matthew laughed. "One way or another, we've got every single tape ever made since the bank started keeping an eye on its clients to make sure they were safe."

That was a very rosy way of saying that the cameras were spying on people. Although, she reminded herself, if there were no surveillance monitors, there would be that much less of a chance of finding whoever stole John Kurtz's money, perhaps even his life.

Kenzie made herself comfortable at one of the viewing monitors.

"How do you want to do this?" Matthew asked a few minutes later as he returned with a box of SD cards. "You want to split these up? Or do you want to view these together because, you know, two sets of eyes don't always see the same thing," Matthew cheerfully told them. The friendly young intern was prepared for them to make either choice.

Hunter looked into the rectangular box. "That's an awful lot of SD cards," he commented.

Matthew's head bobbed up and down. "We've got a lot of cameras at the bank, taking multiple views." He reached into the box to pluck an SD card as a visual aid. "Each of the cameras has an SD card."

Hunter glanced at Kenzie. There was no other way to do this except to do this. "Then I guess we'd better get started."

He then took a seat in front of one of the monitors and inserted the first SD card.

Two hours later, Kenzie felt as if her eyes were becoming crossed. *Crossed* could also aptly describe her disposition, she thought, rubbing her hand along the back of her aching neck.

"I don't think I'm ever going to watch anything on TV ever again," Kenzie complained. She also had an uneasy feeling about the search they were conducting. "Maybe Connie got the date wrong," she said to Hunter. "Maybe it wasn't August 7. Maybe it was some other date and she got confused."

Hunter briefly raised his eyes from the monitor's screen. "You wouldn't last a day in the Cold Case Division," he told her.

Kenzie swallowed a retort. She just shot Hunter a dirty look.

"Is that supposed to get me angry enough to buckle down and go on screening this grainy tape?" she asked.

His mouth curved just the tiniest bit as he turned his head in her direction. "So, did it work?" he asked Kenzie.

Actually, it did, but she wasn't about to admit that to him. What she did say was, "If you can do it, I can do it."

The corners of his mouth curved further. "I figured as much," he said under his breath, although just loud enough for his voice to carry.

"What you 'figured,' Brannigan, is of no interest to

me— Hold it!" Kenzie suddenly cried, her whole body becoming rigid.

Stopping the tape, she leaned forward for a closer look at the frozen screen. Unfortunately, closer didn't make the photo appear less grainy. It made it more so.

Instantly alert, Hunter shifted in his chair, physically moving it in closer to hers.

"Did you see something?" he asked, already scanning the screen.

"I don't know. You tell me," Kenzie answered.

She turned the monitor so that he had a better view of the screen. Once she had it in position, she pressed Play.

Hunter watched the screen intently. There was a tall blonde in the distance across from the ATM machine. The woman appeared to match the description that Kurtz's neighbor had given them. The blonde was restlessly moving around and then she walked closer to the entrance. She seemed to be debating something with herself, then she appeared to have made up her mind and came inside.

Another camera picked the woman up as she opened the front door, walking inside the bank.

At no time did she approach Kurtz while he was inside the bank. But it was obvious that she was watching his every move intently.

"Watch her body language when he finishes his transaction," Hunter told Kenzie. He rewound the tape, playing the last ten seconds again. "For just a second there, she looks like she's beaming, like someone who had just won the lottery."

"Maybe, as far as she was concerned, she had," Kenzie told him.

Playing one tape to another in sequence, they watched Kurtz finish filling out all the required paperwork the banker had given him. The banker took the forms, disappeared for a couple of minutes, presumably to have the forms okayed, and then returned with a rectangular piece of paper. He handed it to Kurtz. The latter's hand seemed to be shaking ever so slightly as he accepted it.

"That has to be his life's savings," Kenzie said.

"That would be my guess," Hunter agreed.

"And there's the vulture," Kenzie commented, "swooping in to get at the check."

As they watched, the blonde rejoined Kurtz just before he exited the bank. When they walked out through the entrance, the woman immediately wrapped both her arms around one of his like a schoolgirl welcoming her boyfriend home after a long vacation spent apart.

"Wait, that's not John Kurtz's car," Kenzie realized, watching Connie's father and the woman who had completely bewitched him getting into a vehicle she didn't recognize. "Connie said he drove a ten-year-old Honda Civic."

"Well, if I don't miss my guess, that's an all-terrain vehicle," Hunter told her.

"Being a little modest here, aren't we?" Kenzie asked with a laugh.

One of the first things her brothers told her about Hunter Brannigan was that he was into cars. He could identify a variety of different makes and models and, according to Finn, Hunter was an absolute wizard when it came to taking those cars apart and putting them back together.

"I thought you might like that," Hunter told her with a grin, "given that you think I have a swelled head."

"I never said that," she denied. Then, when he continued to look at her, she added, "Exactly."

He let that slide. "But you thought it."

"Are you back to mind reading again?" Kenzie asked with a touch of exasperation.

"Nope, not me," he denied, his eyes sparkling as if he already had her number.

"Because if you have mind reading powers, why don't you put them to good use and see if you can make out a license plate number on that car." She tapped the screen with the tip of her nail.

"We'd probably have better luck trying to see if there's another view of the vehicle on any of the other tapes," Hunter said.

Twenty minutes later, after reviewing every possible shot of the parking lot and that particular vehicle, they managed to piece together only three of the numbers out of seven.

"Three is better than none," Hunter said, trying to make the best of it.

"And seven would be better than three, but maybe we'll get lucky," she said, not sounding very optimistic.

"Well, it's worth a shot," he said. "As it happens, 'Lucky' is my middle name."

"I just bet it is," she said under her breath as she took out her cell phone and proceeded to make copies of the pertinent videos they had found.

Chapter 14

They brought both the partial license number and a copy of the video of the woman who had accompanied the slain victim to empty out his life savings to Valri. Swamped as usual, the computer tech still looked as if she had expected to see them coming in again.

"What do you have for me this time?" she asked patiently, putting her hand out.

"How does a partial license plate and a surveillance video of the mystery woman sound?" Hunter asked.

"Like work," Valri answered crisply. But she stopped what she was doing to look at the video, moving it frame by frame in an attempt to get a better look at the woman's face. "If she was ever arrested, her likeness is probably in the database, but matching it can get a little tricky. I'm making no promises," she told them, looking back at the video and continuing to advance it one frame at a time.

Kenzie did her best not to sound impatient. Offering Valri a pained smile, she told her cousin, "We understand."

With a nod, Valri got back to work, her fingers once again flying across the keyboard.

"Well, if we don't hear from you," Hunter said to the computer tech as he edged out of the lab, "see you at the party next Sunday."

"Sure," Valri answered without looking up.

Kenzie's head shot up. "What party next Sunday?" she asked as she walked out with Hunter.

Hunter appeared mildly surprised by her question. "The one the chief's giving to celebrate his son Shaw being made chief of police."

"I know who Shaw is," Kenzie retorted between gritted teeth. "And Shaw was appointed chief a while ago," she reminded the man walking next to her.

Reaching the elevator bank, she hit the button for the elevator with the flat of her hand.

"Yeah, I know," he agreed. "But this is the first opportunity that everyone's had to get together to celebrate that fact," Hunter told her.

The fact that Brannigan knew and she didn't annoyed Kenzie more than she could possibly put into words. "How is it you know more about what my family's doing than I do?"

He had a simple explanation for that. "Maybe I just pay more attention. I don't have a huge family to distract me," he added. The fact was all he had these days were memories. Both his father and his younger brother were gone. "You are going, aren't you?" Hunter asked. "I'm only asking because you've missed the last few gatherings and I think it would mean a lot to your uncle if you showed up for this one, especially given the reason why he is throwing it."

Getting into the elevator, she stared straight ahead at the closing door, her back up. "You realize that this is none of your business, don't you?"

If she was expecting him to say yes, she was disappointed.

"Well, the Cavanaughs are a large part of the police

department," Hunter said, "and the police department is my business, so in a way, yes, it is."

"Wow, talk about double-talk," she marveled. "I'm not going to bother trying to unscramble that. I've got enough on my mind trying to find whoever is killing men, chopping them up and scattering them in parts unknown." Kenzie could feel Brannigan's eyes on her and she knew he was waiting for an answer to his question. So, finally, as the door opened on her floor, she sighed and said, "Yes, if there is a celebration—"

"There is," he interjected.

"—then I'll be there." Walking toward the squad room, she deliberately didn't look at Brannigan. "Now, let's see if your man was successful in turning up any of Anthony Pagliotti's relatives to talk to."

Hunter laughed quietly. "I don't think Valdez will like being referred to as 'my man,'" he commented.

"I'll refer to him any way he wants me to as long as he's come up with some kind of a lead," Kenzie answered.

Crossing the threshold into the Missing Persons squad room, she made her way toward the small back room they'd been allocated.

"You've made progress," Hunter commented as he and Kenzie walked in. His eyes were immediately drawn to the bulletin board. There were photographs on it now. "Either that, or you've decided to liven the place up with illustrations."

There were a few photographs lined up in a row at the top of the board depicting the victims who had been identified. John Kurtz was first. Next to him was a somewhat faded, blurring photograph of Anthony Pagliotti—in and out of costume. There were also a couple of pictures beneath the deceased opera singer.

Next to the two victims who had been identified was a third photograph on the board.

"Who's this?" Kenzie asked, making her way over to it. It was of a man whose hair was cut so short, it almost looked nonexistent. It was so blond that it looked practically white. He had spent way too much time in the sun and it had left its mark on his skin, turning it into tanned leather. His face was a mass of wrinkles.

"Meet William Kelly," Choi told her. "That picture was taken just prior to his tattoo phase."

Kenzie smiled at her partner, pleased. "You identified the guy with the Madonna and Child tattoo?" she asked.

"Yes. Well, I didn't," Choi modestly backtracked, "the database did. Did you know that the FBI has a very extensive database listing people who have unusual or interesting tattoos on their bodies? They did it to help them identify criminals and terrorists," Choi added, pleased with the result of all his digging.

"How did you get access to that?" Hunter asked, curious.

Choi's dark eyes slid over Kenzie and returned to Hunter. "The less you know, the better," Choi told them. "Let's just say I have friends who would rather remain anonymous who are also willing to share certain pieces of information."

"Okay." She was willing to let that go. She wasn't a stickler for staying on the straight and narrow as long as it got her what she needed. What mattered right now was identifying the man, not how that identification was accomplished. She assumed that Choi didn't stop digging when he learned the man's name. "What do we know about William Kelly?"

Choi thought for a minute, organizing the information he'd managed to find. "He went missing around last

December. His brother filed a missing person report on him, then withdrew it, saying Kelly probably took off for Vegas."

"What made him say that?" Hunter asked.

"Well, it was what he assumed when he found out that Kelly had emptied his bank account," Choi said. "The bank forwarded a notification that the account was officially closed. His brother found it in Kelly's mail when the landlord called to say he was evicting Kelly because he hadn't paid his rent for a couple of months."

"Hold it," Kenzie said. "Back up. Kelly emptied his bank account?"

"That's what the brother said," Choi told them. "Why?" Choi looked from Kenzie to Hunter. The latter two detectives had the same expression on their faces. "Does that mean something to you?"

"Might mean there's a pattern," Hunter speculated. He turned toward Valdez. "Valdez, why don't you see if you can look into Pagliotti's finances. Find out what opera company used his services. See if you can find out where they might have sent his checks. If we can find out what bank he used—"

"You're thinking that maybe he emptied out his bank account before he died, too?" Valdez guessed.

Hunter inclined his head. "I'd say that from what we've seen, there might be more than a fifty-fifty possibility that he did, yes."

A fragment of an old saying crossed Kenzie's mind. "You're thinking this is a case of a fool and his money being soon parted, aren't you?" Kenzie asked, rewording the old phrase.

"I think in this case," Hunter said grimly, "a fool and his head were soon parted. Whoever is doing this is obviously doing it for the money and then eliminating the main witness." He looked soberly at the three people in the room. "Let's see if we can find some names for these other victims." He turned toward Kenzie but the instruction was for all of them, including himself. "Why don't we pull all the unsolved missing person cases from the last ten years. Narrow the candidates down to just single or widowed men fifty or older."

He looked around to see if there were any objections or other suggestions. For now, there weren't.

"It looks like we just might have ourselves a real black widow," he said. "Except that it doesn't look as if she marries her victims. But she does kill them like a black widow."

Kenzie looked at him. "So you *do* think a woman did this?" she asked, wanting to get a clear understanding of what he was thinking.

"What is that old saying?" Hunter asked, his eyes meeting hers. "Something about the female being deadlier than the male?"

Choi appeared unconvinced. "Still, she would have to kill them, cut them up and then haul them away to bury them. That's a lot of work and effort, don't you think?"

"It's a lot of work, but it's not impossible. And our 'black widow' could be working with someone else. She lures the victim, entices him and then her partner kills them. Or," Hunter continued, "she could be doing it all on her own. There've been female serial killers," Hunter reminded the team. "And that woman we saw on the surveillance tapes from the bank," he said to Kenzie, "she looked as if she could more than hold her own if the occasion arose." Hunter looked at her for a long moment. "Some women are not the delicate, helpless creatures that they pretend to be."

Her eyes met his. "Keep that in mind," Kenzie told him.

But it was obvious that his comment amused her more than it goaded her. She considered the task ahead of them for a second. "I'd say we've got our work cut out for us. The chief of Ds said we could get more help if we needed it and going through those open missing person files is going to take time. I say we get help," she told Hunter.

"Great. You have anyone in mind?" he asked Kenzie. She knew the people who worked in her group far better than he did.

"Dylan O'Hara just closed a case yesterday," Choi reminded Kenzie.

"O'Hara works well under pressure," she commented. "Get him before someone else does," she told her partner. Turning toward Hunter, she asked, "Do you want anyone else?"

"Let's see how much headway we make with an extra set of hands," Hunter suggested, and then asked her, "That okay with you?"

She liked the fact that Brannigan asked her for an opinion, that he hadn't just forged ahead and taken over the team the way another detective might have. She decided that Brannigan was really making an effort, even after she'd been less than congenial toward him from the onset of this joint task force.

Kenzie supposed that she owed the man an apology. She had allowed her past relationship with Billy to affect the way she looked at everything—and specifically the way that she had treated Brannigan.

She was going to make more of an effort to be fair to the man, Kenzie silently promised herself.

Although, she thought as they got started after they had recruited O'Hara into their group and filled him in on what was happening, it wasn't going to be easy. There was just something about Hunter Brannigan that made her want to shout "No" whenever he said "Yes."

No doubt about it, Kenzie grudgingly thought. The man had skills. Valuable police skills that definitely proved to be an asset in this joint effort of theirs. She had to keep that in mind and not allow her prejudices—specifically inspired by Billy—to make her see things in a negative way.

Things, she thought, that she should be viewing in a positive light.

Kenzie sighed. "I never realized that there were this many men in the state who went missing and just never turned up again," she commented to the detectives she was working with. They had all been going through the open cases well into the next day.

Kenzie was still relatively new to the Missing Persons Division.

She had been transferred from Robbery approximately two years ago because the Missing Persons Division had lost two people because of retirement as well as losing one because he had moved to another state. The division had been seriously shorthanded when the request had been put to her.

Kenzie willingly went wherever she was needed and could do the most good. At the time she was still getting over the breakup that she had initiated and welcomed the diversion of learning something new.

In a way, she was still getting the hang of it, although that was something she wouldn't admit to anyone except herself—and even that not so readily.

But trolling through the various reports, searching for missing males who fit the profile, had suddenly made her keenly aware that there were a startling number of men who went missing and stayed that way.

It didn't seem right somehow.

It was another two days before they finally got through all the reports that were currently on file within not just the Aurora database, but the one for the state of California, as well.

"Okay, I'm done," Hunter declared like a marathon runner who had finally made it across the finish line. "This is assuming that our black widow and her possible accomplice haven't branched out to include any other states," he added, taking in a deep breath.

"There's a chilling thought," Kenzie commented, shivering. She leaned back, having just finished herself. "Okay, Brannigan, how many did you come up with?"

He glanced at the total files he'd pulled. "A hundred and ten."

"I've got a few more to review, but so far it's eighty-three for me," Choi answered.

"I've got almost two hundred in my bunch," Valdez said. "Does that make me some kind of winner?" he asked grimly.

"Only in a backward world," Kenzie answered. "I've got seventy-four unaccounted-for missing men," she announced, then looked at the newest member who had joined their task force. "O'Hara? How many open missing person cases do you have?"

O'Hara frowned, looking up. "I only found sixty-eight."

"Only," she repeated. In this context, it was a distasteful word. "You add up all those numbers and there is no *only* about it," Kenzie said. "That's a hell of a lot of missing men. I really hope that our black widow didn't cross most of their paths."

"Well, she had to have crossed at least ten of them because that's the number unidentified of what we found," Hunter reminded her, thinking of what the medical examiner had told them. "A total of twelve headless torsos."

"And one man without a body," she added.

That honor belonged to Connie's father. The crime scene investigators had gone back to the site twice but no more body parts had been found and it appeared that of the torsos that were found, none belonged to John Kurtz.

"That is one sick person if you ask me," O'Hara told the other people seated at the table with him.

"Nobody here is going to argue with you about that," Hunter assured him. "Okay, everyone here worked hard to put together this list. Now, let's try to narrow it down a little."

"How do you propose that we do that?" Valdez asked.

Hunter took out a manila envelope and deposited its contents on the table. A bizarre collage comprising four-by-six photographs of headless torsos rained down onto the table.

"I had one of the crime scene investigators take photos of the torsos they found. We're going to try to match the descriptions of the missing men we came up with to the torsos in the morgue."

Choi winced. "Do you have any idea how gruesome that sounds?"

"Well, gruesome or not," Kenzie said, speaking up, "that's what we're going to have to do. If we had fingerprints, it would be a hell of a lot easier. But these men have no fingers, so we're out of luck. We owe it to these victims not to let our personal feelings get in the way of trying to find out who they are so that they—and their families—can have some kind of closure…or at least something close to that."

O'Hara sighed, surrendering. "You're right. This is the job. It's not always all glamour," he quipped.

Laughter followed, mercifully relieving some of the tension.

"Anyone hungry?" Kenzie asked. "I thought I'd order up some food."

"Food?" Valdez repeated as if it was a foreign word. "What's that?"

"I hear that it involves chewing," Hunter told his partner.

"Then I guess I'm in," Valdez answered.

"Me, too," Choi said.

"And me," O'Hara chimed in, holding up his hand as if there was a head count being taken.

"Looks like you found a way to lift their spirits," Hunter commented to Kenzie with an engaging smile. "Nice work."

It took her a moment to look away and place her call. It took her longer to bury the warm feeling that had popped up in response to his smile and started to spread out within her chest.

Chapter 15

Progress was painfully slow.

Implementing a process of elimination, which took almost another four slow-moving days, the task force managed to whittle down the all-but-overpowering list of names from 531 possible victims to a hundred.

A hundred missing person files that were hiding the identities of the ten unidentified of twelve torsos that had been uncovered in the park.

"Damn," Valdez complained, still undecided whether or not to eliminate the person in the form he had just spent the last twenty-five minutes reviewing. "This just doesn't get any better, does it?"

"Nobody said this was going to be easy," Hunter reminded his partner.

Choi met his statement with a moan that seemed to come from his gut. "Yeah, but nobody said it was going to be like looking for a needle in a stack of needles either."

Hunter looked across the length of the table at the other detective. "You want to quit?"

"No, I just want better vision care when the time comes," he grumbled.

"Don't worry, I'll spring for a pair of contact lenses for you if it comes down to that," he told Kenzie's partner.

Turning toward Kenzie, who seemed totally absorbed

in carefully reviewing the stack of possible matches that still remained, Hunter raised another point.

"Have we heard anything from your cousin about a match using that facial recognition database?" he wanted to know.

"No," she answered, then added, "And to be quite honest, I've been afraid of calling her because I just am not up to hearing any negative news."

Nodding, Hunter rose from the table. He was going cross-eyed himself and could definitely use the break. "I'll go and pay her a visit."

"No," Kenzie said, on her feet instantly. "She's my cousin. I'll go. Besides, if I sit here another hour I'm going to wind up growing roots into the floor." She shifted her shoulders and had to stop herself from wincing. "How can a person get so stiff doing nothing?" she marveled.

"That's one of the age-old mysteries of life," Hunter replied with a laugh.

Kenzie began to walk out and saw that he was coming with her. She wanted him to stay here, working with the others.

"You don't have to come with me," she told him. "It doesn't take two of us to ask Valri if she's found a match."

The elevator was right there and Hunter got on behind Kenzie. "Just think of me as your moral support," he told her.

"Well, there's a first," she quipped. "I don't think that *anyone* has ever thought of you in that light before, Brannigan."

He grinned at her and for the first time, she became aware of the fact that he had a dimple in his cheek. "You'd be surprised," he told her.

The elevator door opened and she hurried out ahead of

him, but there was no outpacing the man. "Yes, I would be," Kenzie answered honestly.

Anxious now, Kenzie forced herself to wait until she was practically on top of Valri's desk before hopefully asking her cousin, "Any luck?"

Valri glanced up to see who was talking to her. "Lots of luck," she told Kenzie. "Some good, some bad."

"We're talking about matching the woman in the video's face to someone in your database," Hunter specified.

Just then, the printer in the far corner came to life, methodically spitting out one page after another. Valri smiled at the two detectives at her desk.

"Funny you should ask about that," she said. She got up from her main desk and walked over to another computer, the one that was currently running the facial recognition program. The results of that search were still coming out of the printer. "I think we might have some answers for you." Valri quickly scanned the pages that had been printed. "Looks like your suspect really led a very full life and liked to get around."

Neatly putting the pages together in a uniform pile, Valri returned to her desk. "The woman in your video has been arrested and charged with a number of felonies under a whole array of different names. You're either dealing with someone with a serious case of multiple personality disorder or a very creative criminal."

Kenzie thought of the grief that Connie was going through. "I vote for the latter."

"Is there a last known address?" Hunter asked, although he didn't really hold out much hope.

Valri raised her eyes to his, then doubled-checked the printout. "What do you think?"

Hunter frowned. He hated being right. "I think that

we'd have a better chance of tracking down the tooth fairy."

"At least the tooth fairy leaves something on your pillow before taking your tooth," Kenzie commented, suppressing a sigh as she looked at the printout that Valri had handed to her. "Thanks for this," she told her cousin, holding the pages up.

"I live to serve," Valri cracked. "Now, if you'll excuse me, I need to go serve someone else."

"Bye," Hunter said to the woman as he and Kenzie began to leave.

Already back at work, Valri murmured, "Until next time," in response.

"Was that your cousin's way of saying we're like a bad penny?" Hunter asked Kenzie as they walked down the corridor.

"You mean because we always keep turning up? Yeah, probably." Kenzie stopped in front of the elevator bank, looking through the list of aliases ascribed to their suspect. "Just look at all these names," Kenzie marveled. "How does she manage to keep them all straight? Forget about the last names," she added with a hollow laugh.

"I'm sure she doesn't forget about them," Hunter told her. "There's a strong possibility that her life just might depend on her remembering them."

Kenzie frowned as she looked at the woman's photograph and the names that Valri had uncovered for them. For all they knew, this was only a partial list. There could be more names—and more victims. The very thought of there being even more victims than they'd already found made Kenzie sick to her stomach.

The elevator arrived and they got on. "Do you have any street people?" she asked Hunter suddenly as they rode back up to the squad room.

The question had come out of the blue, apropos of nothing. "Excuse me?" Hunter asked.

"You know, people on the street." Kenzie's voice grew more agitated as the idea gelled in her head. "Sources. People who could help us locate this woman. We *really* need to talk to her."

"That probably is a lot harder than it sounds," Hunter told her.

All Kenzie wanted was a chance to be left in a room alone with this horrid woman. "I know, I know, but best case, she's guilty of stealing John Kurtz's money. Worst case, she killed him or set him up to be killed. In either case," Kenzie stressed, "we need to talk to her to see what she can tell us."

"And in order to do that," Hunter pointed out, "we need to find her."

"That's where the street people come in. Finn has sources if you don't," she said, referring to one of her older brothers. "I'll have him put the word out, see what he can find out."

Hunter nodded. "How about Murdoch?" he asked. He knew for a fact that Murdoch had developed a rather well-connected network of sources.

"Sure," Kenzie answered with an all-inclusive shrug. "The more the merrier—just as long as we get this damn black widow to stop killing and get off the street."

Walking into the back room, Kenzie and Hunter were all ready to report to the others that, thanks to Valri, they had managed to secure another piece of the puzzle. But before they could say a word, O'Hara, Choi and Valdez announced that they had news of their own.

Choi was the first to speak up. "We found that the three victims we've managed to identify so far have something else in common," he announced. "All three of them had profiles on that fifty-plus dating website."

"It's called the Second Time Around. Or Second Chances," Valdez told them.

"Second Time Around," O'Hara corrected. "Even that opera singer is on it," he added.

The investigation was moving painfully slowly, but it *was* finally coming together, Kenzie thought.

"Run all the names on the list we compiled from Missing Persons," she told the others. "See how many of them turn up on the website."

"But we still don't know if those names belong to any of those torsos that the ME has in the morgue," Valdez protested.

"No, but maybe this website is how the black widow found her victims. It might be a roundabout way of making identifications. Without any more information," Kenzie reasoned, "this is all we've got to go on right now."

"Okay," Choi said, resigning himself to the new task. And then he sighed, a balloon that was losing the last of its air. "I don't know about the rest of you, but I've never been so happy to see the weekend approaching in my life. It's going to be a hell of a huge relief to be able to kick back and do something normal just for a couple of days."

"Yeah, I know what you mean," Valdez agreed. "Even the idea of going out shopping with my wife sounds pretty good right about now—and we all know how much I *love* shopping." Valdez glanced over toward his partner. "What about you, Brannigan?" he asked. "Got anything special planned?"

The expression on Valdez's face clearly said that he thought his partner was going to be spending the weekend enjoying the company of yet another blazing-hot woman.

"As a matter of fact, I do," Hunter answered in a measured cadence. He deliberately looked at Kenzie, waiting until she looked up.

The moment that she did, she realized what Hunter was referring to. The party that the old chief of police was throwing for the new one. Uncle Andrew's parties were always good, but this one promised to be legendary.

"Well, enjoy yourself," she told him, looking back at the papers in front of her. "I'll be here, lining up the nails to use on this woman's coffin."

"Admirable," Hunter told her. "But the victims aren't going to be any less dead if you take a couple of days longer to track her down."

He had a point. But she felt she was on a mission. She couldn't shake the feeling that if they didn't catch this serial killer now, she might elude them forever. "They won't be," she agreed. "But maybe her next victim won't be her next victim if she gets caught," Kenzie told him.

Hunter ushered Kenzie aside, knowing she wouldn't appreciate having the others hear him lecturing her—and that was what this was going to turn out to be, he thought. A lecture.

"Using that argument," Hunter told her, "every cop on the force can never go home again because if they do, that might be the difference in capturing or not capturing a killer in the nick of time."

Kenzie raised her chin as her eyes narrowed. She was spoiling for a fight, he thought, and normally he'd just back off. But not this time.

"Why is it so important to you that I attend this thing?" Kenzie demanded, resenting that he was injecting himself into her personal life.

"It's important to me because I don't want to see you wear out. But even more important than that, I know that the chief would really like to see you there." He looked into her eyes, making his point. "This is important to *him*. This is in honor of one of his sons."

Kenzie debated just walking away, but he'd probably take that to be her running from a fight. She had never done that in her life and she didn't intend to start now. "Uncle Andrew has a great many other nieces and nephews," she pointed out. "He won't miss me. He won't even know I'm not there."

Was she kidding? He looked at her in disbelief. "Do you honestly believe that? Remember, we're talking about Andrew Cavanaugh. The man might not be chief of police any longer, but he's still aware of *everything*." His eyes continued to hold hers. "I don't think I really have to tell you that."

Kenzie struggled not to flinch. There was something about Hunter Brannigan that made her want to squirm. "No, you don't."

"Then why am I?" he asked.

He made it clear that he wasn't about to let her off the hook and that he wasn't going anywhere until she agreed to attend the chief's party. He had a personal stake in this.

Kenzie fought not to lose her temper. Sighing, she answered the question he had just thrown out. "Because you like sticking your nose where it doesn't belong," she informed him.

With that, she left the back room and went to get coffee.

She knew he was following her before she ever turned around to verify the fact.

"Speaking of sticking my nose where it doesn't belong," Hunter said, picking up the discussion when he reached the break room.

She closed her eyes, searching for strength. "Now what?"

"I talked to your brothers the other evening," he said.

Kenzie stiffened. Something inside her just *knew* what was coming even though Hunter hadn't said anything yet. Even so, she gritted her teeth and asked, "About?"

"About your engagement," he replied quietly.

Damn him. What gave him the right to go digging into her life? She turned on him, her eyes flashing.

"You're right. You stuck your nose in where it didn't belong and if you keep on talking, that pretty nose of yours is going to look like it went ten rounds with the heavyweight champion of the world."

It took effort not to laugh. He had no doubt that she knew how to deliver a punch, but by no stretch of the imagination did she come anywhere near fitting that description. So instead he continued as if she hadn't just threatened him. This was important and now that he had broached the subject, he wanted to get it all out in the open.

"Apparently, neither one of them knew what made you call off the engagement."

She could feel her temper teetering in the edge, ready to explode. "Brannigan, I am warning you—"

"They did say that they were glad that you did call it off," he told her. "Finn and Murdoch both thought that you were much too good for the guy and they were happy that you finally realized that."

She didn't want to attract any attention, but it was hard not to shout at this man. Served her right for actually thinking he might have become a decent human being.

She forced herself to dole out her words evenly. "I really don't care what they think about my engagement or the end of my engagement—and I certainly don't care what *you* think about it—or what you think about *anything*," she underscored possibly a little too forcefully because the exact opposite was true. She realized that she actually did care. Maybe even too much.

He continued talking as if she hadn't said anything. "So I did a little digging."

Kenzie stared at him in astonishment, doing her best to cover her reaction to this detective. "Didn't you hear what I just said?"

"According to your brothers, you changed after you gave old Billy the heave-ho. You became practically a workaholic. You changed departments," he reminded her. "You also started keeping people at a distance for no reason."

She didn't like his knowing so many details about her life. Denials rose to her lips, but she knew he'd just say that she was being defensive. Kenzie decided to pick her battle.

"If you're talking about yourself, Brannigan, there's a damn good reason why I'm keeping you at a distance," she assured him.

"Okay, let's talk about that," he said, following her again as she tried to walk away. "Contrary to what you might believe, I treat the women I date with the utmost respect. I don't cheat on them and I don't juggle two at a time. You can ask any of them anything you want about me. I guarantee you that they won't have anything bad to say. I never hurt any of them."

Why was he telling her all this? Not that she even believed him, she thought.

"What do you want, Brannigan?" she cried. "Applause? A good-conduct medal?"

"No, I just want you to stop looking at me as if you expect me to turn into some kind of womanizing monster," he told her. "I'm not your enemy."

Her eyes narrowed. She felt as if she was in a battle to save herself.

"You're not the answer to a prayer either, if that's what you're going for."

He surprised her by accepting her assessment. "Fair enough," he said. Hunter lowered his voice and told her, "But I can be your friend."

The last thing she wanted was this man in her life on a personal basis. Ever.

"I don't need another friend," she informed him. "I have more than enough."

"Nobody can ever have enough friends," Hunter told her.

Kenzie rolled her eyes. "Now you sound like a public service announcement."

He smiled at her. She could practically *feel* the smile curling through her system.

"Maybe I am," he told her.

"If you're through waving your gums—" she began, trying to get by him.

"Kenzie, if you don't turn up at the chief's party on Sunday," he told her seriously, "you're going to regret it."

Kenzie continued to try to tread water, but she knew that it was just a matter of time before she would be vanquished. With a very loud sigh, she blew out a breath and asked, "And why's that?"

"Because you'll be disappointing the chief," he told her, adding, "And because you really do need a little time off to be yourself again, to be you amid your family and friends."

"Friends," Kenzie repeated almost accusingly. "Meaning you?"

"The offer's still open," Hunter told her. "But to answer your question, there'll be other family friends at the gathering. You and I won't need to interact if you don't want to," he promised.

Kenzie studied him. "I have your word on that?" she asked, wondering just how far he was going to go with the charade.

"Sure. Why not?" he said with a studied carelessness she wasn't buying into. "If it means that it'll make you turn up for this celebration for the new chief of police, sure, you have my word."

Kenzie didn't believe him for a second. But he did have a point. This was important to Uncle Andrew, and the first rule instilled in all of them was that family was everything and family came first.

She just hated the fact that Brannigan was the one to remind her.

"Then I'll go," she told him.

Hunter grinned. "That's all I wanted to hear."

Chapter 16

"I thought I'd find you here."

Startled, Kenzie looked up from the report she was reading on her monitor. The last person she expected to see was walking into the squad room, heading in her direction.

Hunter.

It was Saturday and there was a skeleton crew on the floor, the way there was on every floor of the police station. Backup, if the occasion called for it, was only a phone call away. Otherwise, most of the detectives had the weekend off.

Taking his jacket off, Hunter draped it on the back of his chair and then sat down at the desk that had been temporarily assigned to him.

She didn't like the fact that for a split second, she'd experienced a glimmer of happiness shooting through her when she saw him. She wasn't supposed to react that way to him. If anything, the exact opposite should have been true.

Why wasn't it?

"What are you doing here?" she asked in a still voice. "I thought you had a hot date."

He got comfortable and turned on his computer. "I never said that," Hunter pointed out, "but now that you mention it—" his eyes washed over her "—I guess it could be described that way."

Kenzie could almost *feel* his eyes on her. She steeled herself off. "Does that line really work for you?"

"I don't know." The smile on his lips unfurled slowly, sexily. "Does it?"

She blew out an annoyed breath. She didn't have time for this. There was someone out there hacking up men and they had to put a stop to that.

"Again," she repeated, gritting her teeth as she got back to work, "what are you doing here?"

"Isn't it obvious?" he asked brightly. "I'm here to help."

She pointed out what was even more obvious. "It's Saturday."

She could have sworn his eyes were twinkling as he said, "Nothing gets by you, does it?"

She wasn't going to get anything done with him around, being Mr. Charming like this. "Go home, Brannigan."

When he didn't say anything, she glanced in his direction. There was a strange expression on his face. One she couldn't read. "You really don't make a man feel welcome," he commented.

"I wasn't trying to."

Hunter dropped his bantering tone. "Look, do you want my help or not?" he asked. "I figured you'd be here and I thought if I came in to help, you could finish up whatever you were trying to do faster. But if we're going to spend the entire time bickering back and forth, then I might as well go home," he said flatly. "The choice is yours."

This was it. This was her chance to send him on his way. And yet she heard herself doubtfully asking, "You really came to help?"

There was no sexy look, no wicked grin. There was just a simple statement. "That's what I just said."

Kenzie nodded, accepting him at his word. But even so, she still had to ask, "Why? Everyone else couldn't wait for the weekend to get here. What makes you so different?"

"That's a subject for another time." He was back in form, sporting a smile that was nothing short of incredibly sexy. "But the short version," he went on to say, "is that I'm a hell of a lot better detective than you think I am. And I don't like knowing there's someone out there hacking up his or her victims and getting away with it." Finished, he asked her, "Anything else?"

What could she say without sounding as if she was arguing with herself?

Don't nominate the man for sainthood yet, Kenzie. He might still have something up his sleeve, she silently warned.

"You can dig into that pile," Kenzie told him quietly, pointing to the stack that was on the edge of her desk.

"Okay." Leaning over his desk, Hunter reached out to grab the stack. He pulled it over closer to his desk. "I will."

To her surprise, there was a minimum of conversation. Consequently, they were able to discard a lot of the files because there were no matches to the array of torso photos the medical examiner had taken. It was progress, she told herself.

At least of a sort.

Hunter sent out for lunch for both of them despite her protests to the contrary. And, despite those same protests, she ate with gusto.

By the end of the day, having gone through a great many of the missing person files and attempting to match them to the photographs of the torsos lying in the morgue, they managed to identify another unknown torso. It turned out that Jerry Wiley had a profile on the Second Time Around website, too.

"I think that we've definitely found the black widow's hunting grounds," Kenzie said with an air of triumph.

"Just in time," Hunter commented. "It's getting late. All in all, I think this has been a really productive day." Pushing his chair back away from the desk, he stretched his legs as well as rotated his shoulders to get some blood flowing through his limbs. "What do you say we call it quits for the day?"

She looked at him, torn between wanting to say yes and telling him that she was going to stay and work a while longer.

But the truth was that she felt as if she was fading fast. Her whole body felt stiff and her eyes were really tired after reading for so long.

"Maybe you're right," she agreed reluctantly.

Hunter looked at her in surprise. "Did I just fall asleep at my desk?" he asked. "Because I could swear I was dreaming."

She was too tired to get annoyed. "I could take it back," Kenzie offered.

"No, no, don't do that," he said. Hunter switched off his computer. The light disappeared from his monitor. "Are you hungry?" he asked as he neatened up his desk just a little. "We can go grab a bite to eat," he added quickly. "I'm buying."

Kenzie began to shake her head. "That's okay," she began.

He didn't want her turning him down. They'd gotten some good work done today and his adrenaline was running high. Hunter rose from his desk and came to stand over hers.

"It can be any restaurant—your choice," he told her. "Crowded," he added for good measure, thinking that might help to seal the deal.

Kenzie rose from her seat, as well. "I think I'll just go home and turn in," she told him.

When he didn't try to talk her into changing her mind, she had to admit she was surprised. So much so that as they walked out of the squad room together, she decided—maybe recklessly so—to give him a compliment.

"Thanks for your help, Brannigan. You did good today," she added as if an afterthought.

"Okay, now I know I'm dreaming." His eyes crinkled a little as he grinned warmly in response. "But you're welcome."

Because there was no one getting on or off at this time, the elevator acted like an express, sailing directly down to the ground floor after they got on and pressed the first-floor button.

"I'll see you at the celebration tomorrow," he said, getting off behind her.

Caught up in the work today, Kenzie had almost forgotten all about her uncle's party. Surprise crossed her face as reality returned.

"Oh. Right." The words emerged in slow motion. "I'll see you tomorrow."

Hunter spared her a thoughtful look just before they parted at the parking lot, each going in the opposite direction.

"Tomorrow," he repeated.

Why did she have this uneasy feeling that she was being put on notice?

The thought haunted her all the way home and long after she had crawled into bed.

Immersed in her work from first light, Kenzie was rereading some of her notes the following morning when her apartment doorbell rang.

Suddenly alert, she looked at her watch, not seeing it at first. When the analog face came into focus, she saw that it was ten thirty.

Ten thirty on a Sunday morning.

Sunday.

"Oh damn."

The person on the other end of that doorbell had to be Brannigan, she thought, growing annoyed. She wouldn't put it past him.

Kenzie decided to ignore the doorbell and just wait him out.

"C'mon, Kenzie," a deep male voice called out to her, "we know you're in there. Open the door."

We.

Recognizing the voice, she stopped playing possum and hurried over to the door. Flipping the lock, she opened the door wide and found herself looking up at not one brother, but two.

"What are you doing here?" she asked Finn and Murdoch, both of whom towered over her.

"We're your escorts, Cinderella. Did you forget you were going to the ball, Cinderella?" Finley Cavanaugh, the taller of the two men in her doorway, asked. Not waiting for an invitation, both Finn and Murdoch made their way into her modest apartment.

"You guys have never come by to see if I was going to any of Uncle Andrew's other parties." She regarded them suspiciously. "What's up?"

"New policy," Murdoch announced. He regarded her outfit and quickly found it lacking. "Is that what you're wearing?" he asked. He and Finn exchanged looks. "You really have let yourself go, haven't you?"

"No, I haven't let myself go," she informed her brothers, annoyed. She knew there was affection behind the remark, but she wasn't in the mood to hear it. "I was just working on a case."

"Well, stop working and get yourself spruced up, Kenz," Finn told her, physically turning her toward her bedroom. "Your chariot awaits and the horses are getting restless, so get a move on."

Fisting her hands at her waist, Kenzie turned back around to scrutinize their faces. "Brannigan put you up to this, didn't he?" she asked. She half expected the detective to pop up in her doorway now as she looked around Finn's shoulder.

Finn dramatically put his hand to his chest. "Are you saying we're not capable of having independent thoughts?" he asked his younger sister.

Kenzie answered without any hesitation. "In this case, yes."

Murdoch took over. "Stop talking and get presentable," he instructed. "Uncle Andrew wouldn't care if you come wearing a shower curtain, but the rest of us would."

"Want me to help you pick out something suitable to wear?" Finn called out after her. "I'm getting pretty good at it."

Kenzie rolled her eyes. "Just stay put," she ordered. "I'll be out in a few minutes."

Finn made a show of looking at his watch. "What is that in sister language? One hour or two?" he asked.

Tempted to retort, she didn't. She knew her brother was asking that just to spur her on.

And it worked.

She hated being stereotyped. Hurrying into her bedroom, Kenzie pulled out a deep blue sleeveless dress she had bought on a whim but hadn't worn yet. After her breakup with Billy, she'd buried the dress deep in her closet. It still had the tags on it.

Pulling them off now, Kenzie slipped the dress on. It fit better than when she'd bought it, thanks to the weight that she had lost. That, too, was a result of her breakup.

She applied a smattering of makeup and quickly combed her hair. Looking herself over in her mirror, she slipped on a pair of high heels last.

Done.

Kenzie was out in ten minutes. The rather stunned look on her brothers' faces made it well worth the rush.

"Ready?" she asked innocently.

Murdoch grinned as he opened the front door for her. "You know, I forget," he told her, "you really do clean up well."

Locking her door behind her, Kenzie could only shake her head. "With a golden tongue like that," she told Murdoch, "it's a wonder you're still single."

She would have preferred taking her own car to the gathering. That way, she would have been free to leave and get back to the case whenever she felt she could slip out unobserved. Being driven to the celebration by her brothers, she knew that her fate for the next half day or so was entirely in their hands.

But, at the same time, since this promised to be one of her uncle's larger parties, finding parking within the residential neighborhood would have proved to be tricky, even if most of the residents in the development parked inside their garages.

Finding suitable parking was also one of the reasons she guessed that her brothers had hustled her so that they could arrive at the party early. While the company and the excellent food were always a huge draw, unfortunately, finding decent parking within the development was also a factor.

"I hear he's going all out," Murdoch said as they pulled up, finding a perfect spot just two blocks away. "I hear that Uncle Andrew's been getting everything prepared since yesterday."

"I think I can smell the food from here," Finn said to the others, taking in a deep breath as they got out of the car.

"You can't smell anything from here," Kenzie told him. "That's just your imagination."

Murdoch laughed. "Trust me, his imagination has no sense of smell," he said to his sister.

It wasn't unusual for them to be able to walk right into the chief's house. He left the front door unlocked specifically for that purpose whenever he held his famous gatherings.

But because this was such a special occasion, Kenzie felt that they should ring the doorbell. At the very least, that would alert the chief that more guests had arrived.

Kenzie took the initiative and rang the doorbell. The door swung open even as she was dropping her hand to her side.

It took effort for her not to allow surprise to register on her face.

Hunter was standing, bigger than life, in her uncle's doorway.

"Are you moonlighting as a doorman these days?" Finn asked his friend with a laugh.

"If you're expecting a tip, you're out of luck," Murdoch chimed in. Suddenly realizing that his sister hadn't taken a step into the house, he glanced at her and prodded, "Kenzie, get a move on. You're blocking the doorway."

"The chief asked me to open the door for him. He's got his hands full with the briskets, and Mrs. Cavanaugh's busy putting out more glasses on the side table," Hunter said, explaining why he was the one who had opened the door for them. The explanation was meant not for his friends but for Kenzie, who was looking at him with extremely accusing eyes.

"'Mrs. Cavanaugh' covers a lot of territory in this house," Finn told his friend. "I take it that you're talking about Aunt Rose."

"Right, your aunt Rose," Hunter answered like someone in a trancelike state. He hadn't been able to take his eyes off Kenzie since he'd opened the door to let them all in.

Almost reluctantly—and feeling extremely self-conscious—Kenzie walked into the house. She could feel his eyes following her every step.

"You're staring, Brannigan," she complained under her breath.

He realized that he was and cleared his throat, as if that would somehow help him clear the air, as well. Taking a breath, he told her, "You look nice in blue. The color suits you."

Kenzie made no response.

"Take the compliment and say thank you to the nice man, Kenz," Finn prompted his sister. "She's house-broken," he told his friend. "But she's still kind of skittish around strangers."

Kenzie glared at her brothers, totally ignoring Hunter as she walked past him. "I'll see you clowns later. Since I'm here, I'm going to go say hello to Uncle Andrew."

"The chief's in the kitchen," Hunter told her, falling in beside her.

Finally forced to acknowledge him, she frowned. "You don't have to guide me there. I know where the kitchen is," she informed him.

But he kept up with her. "We had a nice moment yesterday at the end of the day. Let's say, just for the sake of this occasion, we continue having that moment, okay?" Hunter suggested.

She stopped walking and swung around to look at Hunter. "I seem to recall that you said if I didn't want to see you at this party, I wouldn't."

"I can still give that a good try," he told her, "but to be honest, I forgot how crowded these parties can get." He nodded toward the kitchen, which was just a few feet away. "But let me bring you to the chief. I promised him I'd bring you to him the minute you got here."

She looked at Hunter skeptically. "The chief actually *asked* you to bring me to him the minute I got here?" She found that hard to believe.

"Would I lie?" Hunter asked her, his face looking like the very picture of innocence.

"All the time," she informed him. And then she laughed because the situation struck her as being so totally absurd. "Okay, c'mon," she told Hunter. "Let's go."

"Right this way," he said, ushering her into the kitchen.

Chapter 17

Andrew Cavanaugh was moving around his industrial-sized kitchen faster than a bead of water dropped on a sizzling-hot frying pan. Lifting lids, he was checking on the progress of the different side dishes and meals he was preparing in the various pots that were on the stove. He also looked into both of the side-by-side ovens, which were going full blast.

"It has to be hotter in here than in hell," Hunter whispered as an aside to Kenzie.

"You'd be the one to know," she responded in an equally low whisper.

Andrew, the tall, lean, muscular gray-haired man who looked more than a decade younger than his years, seemed oblivious to the heat all this cooking generated. Atypically, he was also oblivious to the fact that he wasn't alone in the kitchen.

Belatedly, Andrew saw Kenzie's reflection in one of the upper oven doors.

"Kenzie," he declared with pleasure, turning around to face her. He was all but beaming as he greeted her. "You came."

"Of course I came," she replied with a large dose of enthusiasm. "I wouldn't miss Shaw's celebration for the world."

Kenzie barely got the words out before she found herself being enfolded in a deep, heartfelt bear hug. The scent of familiar aftershave lotion seeped into her senses.

She returned the hug even as she fully expected to hear Hunter speak up behind her, saying something to the effect that she was here only because he had taken it upon himself to prod her into coming.

When he didn't, she glanced over her shoulder at Hunter, raising an eyebrow in surprise. He was looking on at the filial exchange, smiling. Kenzie couldn't help wondering what he was up to.

"You said to bring Kenzie in to see you the second she arrived," Hunter amicably told the former chief of police. "So here she is."

"Brave man," Andrew commented with a chuckle as he released his niece. "Everyone knows that Kenzie doesn't appreciate being ordered around. I'm glad you came, Kenzie," he told her warmly. Then, changing course, he told both Kenzie and Hunter, "Go, mingle, you two." He waved them off. "I've still got a lot to do before we can get dinner on the table."

"Can I help?" Kenzie asked even though she knew ahead of time what the answer would be.

"Yes," Andrew replied, then repeated more forcefully, "Go. Mingle."

Inclining her head, Kenzie turned around and retraced her steps back to the living room.

The moment she was out of earshot, she turned toward Hunter. "Why didn't you take credit for telling me to come here?" she asked.

Instead of giving her a snide answer, Hunter replied, "Because I didn't want the chief to think you had to be coerced to come here. That would ruin having you here for him. Besides," he continued in a lower voice, "I'm not nearly as shallow as you think I am," he told her.

Kenzie regarded the man beside her in silence for a moment, thinking back to several recent incidents. Maybe she *was* being too hard on him.

"I guess you're turning into a real human being after all." Then, unable to let the remark stand on its own, she added, "I didn't think you had it in you."

Hunter didn't look annoyed. Instead, he laughed under his breath and said, "Just think of me as a late bloomer," he cracked.

The remark caught her off guard and delved into her before she could stop it.

All right, back away before you say something you're going to regret, she silently ordered herself.

"I try not to think of you at all," she told him, doing her best to sound cold as she walked away.

She would have thought, Kenzie mused that afternoon, that in a place so full of people, people she knew, it would be relatively easy—emphasis on the word *relatively*—to avoid crossing paths with the one person she *didn't* want to run into.

Yet it seemed that almost every time she turned around, went anywhere, talked to anyone, there he was. Brannigan.

It didn't matter if she had made her way to the huge backyard, or the patio, to the living room, or to the recently remodeled and expanded dining room. Everywhere she went, everywhere she looked, there he was.

Or, if he wasn't, then Brannigan turned up within the next five minutes.

And the annoying thing of it was, he wasn't even looking to talk to her.

Actually, it was other members of her family whom she saw Hunter talking to.

And laughing with.

She supposed that was what got to her the most. That he was sharing moments with people she considered to be exclusively part of *her* domain, not his. This was *her* family, not his. He had no right invading it just to annoy her.

Slowly, during the course of the evening, the image she had of Hunter began to peel away. Being a reasonable person, at least in all things that *weren't* Hunter, she began to realize that he couldn't be the womanizer she'd always believed him to be, not if her aunt Rose, her aunt Lila and her aunt Maeve didn't just approve of him but really seemed to like the detective.

They, like the other women in her family, were fairly keen judges of character. Could Hunter have fooled *all* of them?

The obvious answer was no.

Still, Kenzie proceeded with caution before relenting and finally allowing herself to give him a seal of approval.

Wavering, she sought out Finn, who had always been Brannigan's biggest supporter and admirer—and as honest as the proverbial day was long.

Walking up to him next to one of the many tables laden with appetizers, side dishes and beverages, she got right to the point.

"Why isn't your pal here with his newest girl of the moment?" she asked Finn.

"Good question," Finn responded. "To be honest, I haven't seen him with anyone since he started working for the task force. Have you been keeping him chained to his desk?"

She laughed at the idea. The thought of being chained

probably appealed to some perverse side of Brannigan. "Hardly."

"Then I guess maybe he's just focused on solving the case," Finn speculated. "That cold case he had has been haunting him ever since he came into that department. Maybe he thinks he can solve it, working with you, and that's got him walking the straight and narrow. Or maybe he's just had a change of heart," Finn said. "You know, they say that all it takes to change a man is the right good woman," he told his sister. "Not me, personally," he qualified quickly, "because that's just not going to happen. But maybe it happened to Hunt." Finn looked at Kenzie for a prolonged moment.

"Wouldn't he have told you?" she asked even as she was watching Hunter talk to the chief of detectives. Whatever they were talking about, her uncle Brian certainly seemed to be amused. It was obvious that the man liked Brannigan.

She felt oddly isolated.

"Not necessarily," Finn answered.

She looked at her older brother in surprise. "I thought you guys shared everything."

"Again, not necessarily," he told her.

She sighed, frustrated. "You're of no help, you know that?"

Finn merely grinned broadly. "I do my best," he said just before he walked over to talk to the newly appointed chief of police—their cousin Shaw.

"Enjoying yourself?"

Hunter's deep voice was coming from directly behind her. The next second, he circled around to stand at her side.

"I was." Kenzie did her best to give Hunter a withering look. It fell far short of hitting its mark.

"Give it up, Kenzie. You don't dislike me nearly as much as you're trying to pretend you do," he told her. He smiled as he looked down into her eyes. "Face it. I'm getting to you."

Her eyes narrowed. Again, she couldn't quite pull it off, but she did her best to cut him off at the knees. "How do you manage to stay upright with that big ego of yours weighing you down like that?"

"I don't have a big ego," Hunter contradicted. "I just know what I'm capable of and what I'm not capable of. And you're beginning to realize that I'm more than a decent detective. Face it," he told her. "We complement each other."

She knew being nice to him was going to come back to bite her. "Look, all I said—deludedly—was that you did a good job, but if you think that—"

"I'm not talking about verbally, Kenzie," he said in a tone of voice that irrationally made her want to scream at him. "I mean in the way we work together. If you stop throwing up roadblocks at every turn, you might find out that you really do like me."

The man was an egotistical jerk, Kenzie thought angrily. "I don't—"

"As a person," he stressed, as if reading her mind. Hunter drew a little closer to her, deliberately putting a stuffed mushroom on her plate.

Kenzie drew in her breath, bracing herself. With effort, she forced herself to relax. Getting her racing pulse under control was harder.

"What are you afraid of, Kenzie? I don't bite," he told her. And then he smiled that smile that had a way of slipping in under her skin, unsettling things she could have sworn had been firmly packed away when she'd terminated her engagement. "Not unless you want me to," he said in a husky voice.

Kenzie spun on her heel, about to walk away before she wound up saying something that would give her away.

Hunter caught her arm, holding her in place. "It's a joke, Kenzie," he told her. "Relax. Look around you. This is the safest you are *ever* going to be," he stressed emphatically.

He was right. Why was she being so nervous? No matter what she thought of Brannigan, he wasn't the type to wantonly drag her behind the azalea bushes and jump her bones. She knew that if a woman said no to him, he would leave it at that.

Not that any woman would *ever* say no to him.

Except for her, she thought.

Maybe that was what intrigued him about her, she suddenly realized. She'd said no to him and he just wanted to see if he could get her to change her mind.

When hell freezes over.

She was driving herself crazy, Kenzie thought, releasing a shaky breath.

"Are you okay?" Hunter asked, peering more closely at her. "Your face just got flush."

"Just thinking about the case," she lied, waving away Hunter's concern and doing her best to throw him off the trail.

"Maybe, just for the rest of the day," he suggested, "you should forget about the case." Hunter lowered his head and whispered into her ear so that his words were for her only. "Having it consume you like this is not going to do you—or the case—any good."

She had always hated anyone telling her what to do, especially someone like Brannigan, a man she'd been at odds with for a long time. "Is that your considered professional opinion?"

"Yes. My professional opinion and my private one," Hunter added. And then he said something that really got under her skin. "You might be interested in knowing that the chief of Ds backs me up on this."

She stared at him. "You talked to the chief of Ds about the case?"

"The case, and you," Hunter added. Then, before she could ask him why he was discussing her with the chief, he said, "The chief asked how we were progressing, so I told him. The man takes an interest in all his people," he reminded her. "Remember?"

She could feel her back going up. If they weren't in such a public place, she thought she would have strangled him. A torrent of emotion flooded through her. Who the hell did he think he was?

"I don't need you to tell me about my uncle," she informed him in what sounded like, to the casual observer, an even voice. But Hunter knew better.

"I know," he said mildly. "I'm just giving you a friendly reminder, that's all. But you do need to relax, Kenzie," he told her, and she could have sworn he actually sounded sincere. "And eat," he told her. "Why don't you start with the stuffed mushrooms. I highly recommend them."

He was putting himself in charge of her, she thought. She didn't need a keeper.

"I can make my own choices, Brannigan. I don't need you—"

She didn't get to finish because he had picked up the mushroom and slipped it between her lips just as she was telling him off. Her eyes widened as both what he had just done—and the mushroom's taste—registered. In an act of self-preservation, Kenzie stopped talking and started chewing.

"This is good," she grudgingly admitted when she was finished.

Hunter beamed, pleased, although he was surprised that she'd actually admitted to him that she liked the mushroom.

"Told you. If I were you, I'd take another before they're all gone," Hunter advised. "The chief made a whole slew of them, but there's hardly anything left now. Apparently word gets around really fast. The man's culinary skills are excellent, but this time he's even outdone himself."

Well, she knew she really couldn't argue with that now.

"You're right," she said, then added, "Thank you," as he slipped the last of the stuffed mushrooms onto her plate. But just before she was about to eat the sole surviving stuffed mushroom, she looked at Hunter. "Don't you want it?"

"That's okay," he told her. "You eat it."

She was *not* going to have him give up anything on her account. He'd probably find occasion to bring up his so-called "sacrifice" over and over again and she had no intentions of suffering through that.

"We'll split it," she told him.

"Are you sure?" Hunter asked, looking from the appetizer to her face and giving Kenzie a chance to change her mind.

Why did she get the feeling that this wasn't about the stuffed mushroom and that he was asking her something else entirely? She told herself she was imagining things, told her stomach to settle down and unknot itself, but neither was listening.

"Yes," she answered, "I'm sure."

Picking up a fork, Hunter neatly cut the large-capped

stuffed mushroom into two equal halves. Then, as she watched him, all but glued in place, he picked up one of the two halves, brought it up to her lips and, for a second time, did what he had done initially.

Except this time, his eyes held hers as he fed her the appetizer.

This one tasted even better than the last one had. Better and, heaven help her, more arousing despite all of her efforts to block everything out—this included Brannigan. Or at least just focus on the way the food tasted and nothing else.

"Good?" Hunter asked, raising his eyebrow as he continued looking at her.

Her mouth went suddenly dry. She had to clear her throat before she could answer him. When she did, it felt as if her words were inexplicably sticking to the roof of her mouth. She had trouble forcing them out.

"We've already established that," Kenzie finally told him.

His eyes dipped down, indicating what was left of the stuffed mushroom. "You can have the other half, too," he told her.

"No, that's yours," she insisted. Then, seeing he was about to protest, she deliberately emphasized, "What's fair is fair, Brannigan."

"Yes, but—"

This time, she turned the tables on him and did exactly what he had initially done with the stuffed mushroom when he'd told her about it. Kenzie picked up the remaining half and, swiftly bringing it up to his lips, she fed it to him.

Kenzie wasn't prepared to have him catch her hand as she was about to drop it to her side. And she definitely wasn't prepared to feel that sharp, startling zip of electricity charging through her when he lightly kissed her fingers.

"You had some cheese on them," he explained.

There was nothing intense, nothing prolonged about what he had done, but the effect was still the same. Lethal.

So much so that even though he had quickly released her hand, her heart went into double time, mimicking the beat of a drum solo at the start of a parade.

"I'm going to have to ask the chief for the recipe for that," Kenzie heard herself saying.

It was inane, but she felt as if she *had* to say something. Otherwise, she was afraid that she was going to just give in to the incredible pull she was experiencing between them and just kiss the man she had been denouncing and derailing for the last couple of weeks.

You just couldn't actually kiss a man like that without being certifiably insane.

Could you?

Chapter 18

"May I have this dance?"

Dinner had been served and consumed as had, for the most part, the twelve-tier cake that had been whipped up expressly for this occasion.

Pleasantly full, the guests had once again broken up into smaller groups, discussing whatever interested them as law enforcement officers, parents or, for the most part, as members of a large extended and respected family of a growing community. There was music playing in the background, seamlessly accompanying the myriad mingling conversations.

Scattered about on the patio, as well as in the living room, were a few couples dancing to that music.

Apparently, Kenzie thought, turning around to face him, this was what had inspired Brannigan to sneak up on her and make the offer to drag her unwilling body around in a circle.

"No, thank you," she answered primly.

He seemed to think she was turning him down because she didn't know how to dance. The next words out of his mouth bore this out.

"It's a slow dance, Kenzie," Brannigan told her. "Anyone can do that. All you have to do is stay in one place and occasionally sway a little."

She gave him a dirty look. "Are you suggesting that I don't know how to dance?"

His smile answered her before he did. "I don't know. Do you?"

She drew her shoulders back like a cadet at attention. "Yes, I most certainly can dance."

"Oh, good," Hunter responded, lacing one hand through hers while encircling her waist with the other. He pressed her ever so slightly to him, and just like that, they were dancing. "That makes this a lot easier."

"What are you doing?" she demanded as Brannigan gently guided her around the small impromptu dance area. And then, as she realized what was happening, she protested, "I didn't say I'd dance with you."

"No, but you didn't say you wouldn't," he pointed out. The smile on his face seeped into her very soul, despite all her efforts to keep it at bay. "Go with it, Detective. It's called having fun."

She didn't want to cause a scene right here in her uncle's house, and arguing with the man seemed to be futile anyway. So, short of shooting him, she was forced to give in.

"All right, Brannigan," she said, temporarily surrendering. "It's clear you're not going to leave me alone until I agree to this, so let's do it."

His hold on her hand became a bit tighter as he whirled her around in a circle. "Why, Detective Cavanaugh, I thought I'd never hear those words from you. Be still my heart."

"Be happy you still have one," Kenzie informed him. "There are sharp objects all around and I know how to use them."

His eyes smiled at her half a beat before his lips caught up. The smile, damn him, was warm and infectious, she thought.

"Fair enough, Kenzie. Just follow my lead," he told her.

"Ha, you should be that lucky."

But, despite what she said, Kenzie continued dancing with him.

Kenzie told herself it wasn't happening, but that would be lying and she knew it. She wasn't really certain exactly when it began to take hold, but somewhere along the line during the later hours of the day, she began to understand what the mythical Brannigan charm was all about. Began not only to understand it, but to slip, at least partially, under its spell.

Not that it was anything she planned to even remotely admit to, especially not to Brannigan.

Even when he held her so close that their souls seemed to be merging and he looked into her eyes, it was a real struggle not to lose herself in him.

They danced this way for three, perhaps four numbers. And then he stopped moving. Kenzie looked at him quizzically.

"I think they stopped playing the music," he told her.

"Oh. Right," Kenzie murmured, embarrassed. "I was just lost in thought," she said belatedly.

"Yes," he told her. "Me, too." Reluctantly, he released her hand, but he continued holding her waist just a little longer as he looked around. "I think the celebration is beginning to break up," he noted.

It seemed like half the family members had already taken their leave and gone home. The rest appeared to be moving in that direction.

"Need a ride?" Hunter asked her. "I can give you a lift home."

She looked at him in surprise. "No, that's all right. I came with Finn and Murdoch."

Even as she said it, she felt a strange reluctance turning Hunter down. Maybe the wine she'd had had gone to her head. But it had been only the one glass and she had always been able to hold far more liquor than that well.

No, she decided, wine really wasn't the reason she was experiencing this feeling.

The cause was the man himself.

"So I guess that means you're going to Malone's," Brannigan said.

"Malone's?" she repeated. Kenzie looked at him, confused.

Malone's was the popular cop bar where all the local law enforcement officers went to blow off some steam after hours. Some claimed it helped to put things in the proper perspective before they went home to their families.

"No," she answered. "Why?"

"I just overheard Finn and Murdoch talking about going to Malone's with a few of the people here to cap off their evening," Hunter told her. "I take it from the look on your face you didn't know."

"No, I didn't," she replied.

"Do you *want* to go to Malone's?" Hunter asked her.

"No, I don't," she retorted succinctly as she started to head in Finn's direction.

Before she took another step, Hunter caught her arm, stopping her. "Before you go and read them the riot act, why don't I just take you home?"

He was phrasing that ambiguously and she still hadn't been completely won over. "Yours or mine?" she asked.

"Yours," he told her innocently. "Unless you'd rather that—"

"No," she said in no uncertain terms, maybe more firmly because there was a part of her that actually *wanted* to go home with him.

And doing that would only be disastrous.

"Then I'll take you to your place," Hunter told her simply. "I'll need the address."

He probably already had it, she thought. "No problem. Just let me tell my brothers," Kenzie said out loud. She watched his expression just in case this story about her brothers going to Malone's was all a ruse he'd made up.

"Sure. I can come with you—" She took a step toward him, as if to block his path. "Or not if you'd rather I just hang back."

He'd called her bluff, she thought. Even so, she still wanted to tell her brothers what she was doing.

As she began to approach Murdoch, her brother spotted her and called out, "Kenz, a bunch of us are going to Malone's. It'll only be for a couple of rounds and then I promise we'll take you home."

So Brannigan had been telling the truth, she thought. How about that. Maybe she needed to stop convicting him without the benefit of a trial.

"That's okay," she told Murdoch. "I've made other arrangements. Have fun," she said, changing direction and heading back.

"You sure?" Finn questioned.

Heaven help her, something felt as if it was suddenly falling into place inside her. For the life of her, Kenzie couldn't explain why.

She smiled broadly at her brother. "I'm sure," she answered.

She went looking for Andrew and his wife next. Locating them on the patio, she thanked them both for a wonderful time just before more of the family descended on the couple with the same intent.

Kenzie began to ease herself away. Hunter was right behind her.

"Kenzie, remember to go easy on yourself," Andrew told her just as she was about to leave.

The man still worried about each and every one of them despite having been out of law enforcement all these years. That felt comforting somehow.

"I will," she promised.

"See that she keeps her word." This time, Andrew was talking to the man behind her.

"Yes, sir," Hunter replied. "I'll certainly do my best."

Kenzie looked at Brannigan as they went out the front door. "Did you just tell my uncle that you were going to be my keeper?" she asked him.

"No," he contradicted. "What I said was that I'd do my best to see that you keep your word. The rest, as always, is up to you," he told her, then added, "But I certainly can't force you to do it."

She rolled his words over in her head. "You're pretty good at that," she said.

He wasn't sure where she was going with this. "Pretty good at what?"

"Manipulating words," she told him.

He didn't see it that way, he thought. He viewed it in another light. "It's called a survival instinct," he told her. "I learned it early on."

"How early?" Kenzie asked. She knew his reputation. But when she came right down to it, she really didn't know all that much about the actual man.

A strange smile curved his mouth. The moonlight seemed to highlight it. "Early enough to raise my father."

He didn't look it, but maybe he'd had too much to drink himself, Kenzie thought. His answer didn't make any sense.

"Come again?"

Hunter debated saying "never mind," to her. But, knowing her, she'd probably find out anyway so he decided to tell her. That way at least he'd know that she had the right story.

"My dad split for a while. My mother, never all that stable, had a meltdown right after that. She made the decision to start over—unencumbered by kids. To make that happen, she left my younger brother and me with her mother and after Grandma couldn't handle us, my dad turned up and came to the rescue, so to speak." Hunter smiled fondly. "He was a great guy, but he had a bit of a romance going with Jim Beam. So growing up, I kind of had to raise myself and my brother—and my father along the way," he added. "Does that answer your question?"

They had reached his car as he talked and were now currently on the way to her apartment, which, it turned out, wasn't that far away from the police station.

"It's a start," she told him in reference to his question.

He spared her a glance, slightly confused. "What do you mean, 'it's a start'?" Hunter asked.

"I figure we'll cover the rest of it—your background," she explained, "—while we're working together. That's what cops do, right?" she asked. "They talk to stave off the boredom."

Was she talking about the present circumstances they were dealing with? "This isn't a boring case," he pointed out. And once it was over—if they managed to solve it—he'd be going back to his division. There wouldn't be much occasion to talk then.

"No, but finding evidence is rather a slow process." This wasn't coming out right, she thought. He had a way of flustering her. She tried again. "I'm just saying that if you ever want to talk, I'll listen."

Hunter swallowed the wisecrack that rose to his lips. Whatever was happening here, he wasn't going to spoil it by being his usual self. Right now, he really didn't *want* to be his usual self if that persona was going to keep her at arm's length.

He liked talking to this new Kenzie 2.0 for however long she deigned to remain that way.

Nodding, Hunter said, "Okay. I'll keep that in mind," he told her.

Kenzie shifted in her seat. Since he had shared something personal with her, she felt almost obligated to do something in kind with him. It took her a few minutes to work up her nerve.

Just as Hunter pulled his sports car into her garden apartment complex, she slanted a look at him and told him, "You know, you were right about what you said. Earlier," she added when he made no response.

"I'm right about a lot of things," Hunter told her with a smile that for once couldn't be labeled as *cocky*. "Refresh my memory. Which 'right' are you referring to, Kenzie?"

She was about to say "never mind" but forced herself to stick it out. The man was a modern-day comic book hero without the cape. The least she could do was listen to him.

"The one where you said Billy didn't deserve me. Not to sound conceited, but he didn't. Not because of anything I did," she told him. "But because of what he did." Kenzie paused. Maybe she'd already said too much. Because Brannigan had been so open with her, she'd wanted to reciprocate. But it wasn't easy for her to open up this way.

"I'm listening," Hunter said gently when she didn't continue.

Well, she'd started this, she thought. She might as well complete it.

Kenzie took a deep breath.

"I never told any of my brothers this. I never told *anyone* this," she emphasized, then stressed, "I didn't want anyone feeling sorry for me."

Hunter nodded. “I can understand that.”

Rather than look at him, she stared straight ahead at the visitor-parking sign.

“Billy cheated on me.” Even now, the words tasted sour in her mouth. She’d actually loved Billy once, an eternity ago. “When I confronted him, he begged me to forgive him and swore he’d never do it again.”

“But he did,” Hunter guessed.

“But he did,” Kenzie echoed, still staring straight ahead. “He begged again, I forgave him again.” More the fool she, she added silently.

“They say the third time’s the deal breaker,” Hunter said.

This time she did look at him, alert. “Someone tell you this?” she asked, her guard up.

“Your face just did,” he answered.

He saw the alarm mingled with wariness wash over her features. He put his hand on her shoulder in a gesture meant only to comfort and nothing more.

“Don’t worry, I’m not going to say anything to Finn or Murdoch, or to any of the others. Because you and I both know that they would kill the SOB if they ever got their hands on him, and even though I figure the guy deserves it, they’re my friends and I don’t want to see them brought up on murder charges.

“Besides,” he added, “I figure the guy’s suffering enough for his sins.”

Her tone was still guarded. “How do you figure that?”

“Well, his stupidity cost him you, didn’t it?” Hunter said.

Kenzie looked at him. It felt as if time had suddenly stopped moving forward.

She didn’t know just what came over her. Maybe it was the late hour, or maybe she was just tired from all the long hours she had been putting in, working the case.

Or maybe because this was the first kindness in a while she'd heard directed toward her that wasn't coming from someone in the family.

Whatever the reason, she felt something, an electricity, shooting off sparks within her. And then, before she realized what she was doing, she did it. She leaned in toward Hunter and kissed him.

It was hard to say who was more stunned by that, Kenzie or Hunter. Or who was more surprised when it happened again.

She hadn't recovered her breath yet, but there she was, sealing her lips to his a second time, as if to convince herself that the first time had actually happened and that the head-spinning euphoria hadn't been something that she had imagined.

It had to be real because there it was again, taking her on another erratic-pulse journey, dilating all her blood vessels and causing her heart to pound harder than it had that time she had competed in a marathon at the police academy.

Just as she was about to draw back for a second time, she felt his hands on her face, framing it. Holding it in place as he deepened his kiss and left his mark indelibly on her.

He kissed her as if she was special.

He kissed her as if he wished she were his first.

Chapter 19

Hunter drew back.

Part of him wondered if he had suddenly been catapulted into an alternate universe. Or maybe he was asleep somewhere and this was all just part of a dream. A very soul-arousing, vivid, wonderful dream.

"Well, that was certainly a surprise," he finally said.

"For both of us," Kenzie replied, her voice only a little louder than a whisper.

She felt behind her for the door handle, as if wrapping her fingers around it gave her back an iota of control over herself and the situation.

Her legs felt shaky under her as she got out.

Get it together, Kenz, she silently ordered.

Nodding at Hunter, she told him, "Thanks for the ride."

She'd opened a door to something and he wanted it to continue. But he knew that if he made a move toward her, he'd wind up spooking her—or worse. So he remained where he was, seated behind the steering wheel.

"Don't mention it."

Kenzie turned away and began to walk toward her apartment. Three steps later, she turned around again and doubled back.

"Would you like to come in?" she asked Hunter haltingly as she leaned in toward his open window. "For coffee," she tagged on.

Hunter studied her for a long moment, doing his best to read her expression before venturing an answer. Finally, he took a chance, going with his gut.

"I'd like that."

"Then come on," she coaxed.

Hunter got out of his car and pressed the key fob in his hand. The resulting staccato sound told him his car was locked.

Kenzie led the way to her apartment. She lived on the ground floor.

"I know," she said, answering the question she anticipated him asking. "The second floor would be safer. But I didn't like the idea of lugging groceries up to the second floor." She unlocked the door to 1H. "Besides, this was only supposed to be temporary."

Crossing the threshold, she waited for him to do the same, then locked the door behind him as she flipped on the light switch.

"'Temporary' has now been a little more than three years now," she told him.

From what he could see, it looked like a nice, airy apartment. Why was it temporary? "Did you have another location in mind?" he asked her.

"Yes. A house," she answered in no uncertain terms. "When I look out my bedroom window, I like the idea of looking at a backyard, not a parking lot," she told Hunter.

Hunter nodded, as if absorbing her comment. "It'll happen," he told her confidently.

He was patronizing her, she thought. "How would you know that?" she demanded.

"Simple," he answered. Crossing to the living room section, he made himself comfortable on her oversize sofa. *Oversize, like the Cavanaugh family*, he couldn't help thinking, amused. "Because you're the type if you want something, you *make* it happen."

Opening her refrigerator, Kenzie took out the coffee tin.

"And you know this how?" she asked, popping in a filter and then measuring out both the ground coffee beans and the amount of water needed to make two cups of coffee.

He couldn't just toss words around like that without being held accountable. Even if he was trying to be comforting.

"Easy." Turning to get a better glimpse of her, he flashed Kenzie a grin. "I've made a study of all the Cavanaughs."

Kenzie frowned. She hadn't been prepared to hear him say something like that. "That sounds creepy. You realize that, right?" she said, sitting down on the other end of the sofa.

"No," Hunter contradicted, "that sounds like a man without a family who wishes he had one."

Gotcha! He wasn't keeping his stories straight, she thought triumphantly. "I thought you said you had a father and a younger brother."

He never even winced. "Emphasis on the word *had*," he told her. "My father died just before I graduated from the academy. His liver had finally had enough of his drinking and just gave out. My brother was missing for a while—and then I found out that he had died of a drug overdose six months ago." There was a rueful smile on his face although he wasn't looking at her anymore. "Your brothers are the closest thing I have to a family. And by association, that goes for the rest of the Cavanaughs, as well."

The coffee maker went through its cycle quickly, then

gave off three short beeps, indicating that it had finished brewing. Instead of saying anything, Hunter got up and crossed to the kitchen.

"Where are you going?" she asked, on her feet and following him into the kitchen.

"The coffee machine was calling," he answered.

She was at the counter, taking down two mugs. "I invited you in for coffee. You shouldn't have to pour your own."

"I don't mind. We don't need to stand on ceremony." Hunter turned to look at her. His eyes were deep, intense. "I'd say that we're way past that, wouldn't you?"

She took a breath, watching him, feeling her nerves grow increasingly more agitated. "You didn't come over for coffee," she said. It wasn't a guess.

He put the creamer down on the counter. "No, I didn't," he admitted. "But I am not about to push anything."

"So what are you doing here?" she asked, even as she felt her throat tightening farther. Her pulse was racing so hard, she was having trouble breathing.

"Following your lead," he said truthfully. "And really hoping that you *do* lead," he added.

She took a step closer to him, her heart hammering hard in her chest. Her eyes never left his face. Why did he fascinate her this way? Why, of all the men who were out there, did she have to have feelings for *this* man?

"I'm probably going to regret this," Kenzie told Hunter in a low voice as she threaded her arms around his neck.

"You don't know that," he told her, closing his arms around her waist and gently drawing her closer to him.

Yeah, I do.

Kenzie thought she said the words out loud, but maybe she didn't. Maybe she just thought them. But it was too late to find out because his lips were on hers and there were all sorts of delicious, hot explosions going on inside her at this very moment.

It was too late, much too late, for her to put on the skids and stop this.

And even if she could, Kenzie thought, she wouldn't because she didn't want to. At this particular moment in time, she needed to make love with this man, needed to feel the wild, demanding sensations that she instinctively knew he could create within her.

From the moment her lips touched his, she just *knew* that this was what she had been missing. That somewhere on some lofty plane, it was written that he could satisfy all the needs she was experiencing, all the needs that were throbbing within her.

Her fingers swiftly flew along the front of his shirt, freeing the buttons from their respective holes.

The next moment, she was tugging his sleeves off his muscular arms until he was free and unencumbered by the material.

And as she did that, she felt his hands drawing the zipper down along her back until it reached the end of its journey. Her whole body tingled as the dress she had worn to the celebration seemed to almost sigh as it floated down about her ankles.

She stepped out of the colorful blue pool her discarded dress formed, abandoning her shoes at the same time.

Her breath caught in her throat again as she tugged at the belt at his waist, uncinching it. She felt the hook at her back loosen.

Her bra slipped from her body just as his trousers did the same from his.

Kenzie could feel her skin heating as Hunter coaxed her remaining undergarment from her body. Breathing hard, she did the same with his.

And then there were no barriers, no material obstacles left to get in their way.

Nothing but naked desire to cloak them.

She fully expected him to take her right then and there. Instead, he took his time, moving slowly. Making love to her by increments.

Hunter pressed a kiss to her shoulders, her arms and the sensitive area of her throat before he moved on to other parts of her.

She struggled to do the same with him, but it was hard for her to focus when her head was spinning wildly the way it was.

He made her feel beautiful.

And cherished.

And oh so wanted.

She tried very hard not to get lost in this burning sensation licking away at her, but it wasn't easy. She was hanging on to reality just by her fingertips.

What Hunter was creating for her felt almost unreal.

This wasn't her first time.

Or her second.

But it was the first time she had *ever* felt like this.

And that was what she was going to remember, Kenzie told herself, when this was just a faded part of yesterday.

If anything either of her brothers had ever said was true, there had been an entire squadron of women moving through Hunter's life. But she was determined that he was going to remember being with her like this tonight.

She did things with him that she hadn't even contemplated doing until this very moment. For every caress he bestowed on her, she returned one in kind. For every stroke, every touch, every wild, passionate, soul-melting kiss he imprinted on her, she did the same with him, summoning just as much fire.

Or trying to.

Somewhere amid this primal exploration, she had brought him into her bedroom. Lost in each other's arms, they had almost made it to her bed. But some things couldn't be restrained.

They wound up making love with one another the first time on her floor.

After covering what felt like every pulsing, eager inch of her body with a network of hot, passionate kisses, Hunter had drawn his throbbing body along hers. Watching her intently, he entered, his hands linking hers just as their bodies formed one joined entity.

As he began to move his hips, she felt the explosion growing, getting larger and larger with each thrust. And when it came, when that final wondrous climax seized them in its grip, Kenzie wrapped her legs around his torso, holding on for dear life.

Slowly, the mushroom cloud receded, leaving her feeling as if she was glowing in the aftermath.

But that, too, faded and reality elbowed its way back in.

Kenzie lay there, breathing hard. Waiting for her pulse to level out.

She expected that now that this was over, Hunter was going to say something politely inane, then get up, get dressed and leave.

Or maybe he wasn't even going to be polite.

She braced, telling herself that she wasn't going to be disappointed. After all, she wasn't looking for a commitment, just a momentary diversion, right?

Kenzie felt Hunter stirring. It was starting. He was going to leave.

To her surprise, he moved over and continued lying next to her on the floor.

He raised himself slightly to look at her. "Are you all right?" he asked.

"Yes," she said cautiously. "Why?"

"Well, for a second at the end there, I thought you'd stopped breathing." He wasn't bragging. It was an observation. And then he actually sounded concerned as he asked, "I didn't hurt you, did I?"

This was a lot more thoughtful than she'd thought Hunter was going to be. Swallowing her surprise, she said, "I'm hardier than I look."

"Oh, there's no doubt about that," he assured her. "I just wanted to make sure that you were all right."

She realized then that Hunter had threaded his arm around her and was cradling her against him. She could feel his heart beating against her chest, and for some reason, she found that immensely comforting.

"I'm fine," she answered.

"Good," he pronounced. Hunter pressed a kiss to the top of her head.

He did it as if there was affection between them, not just torrid sex that would soon play itself out. She had no idea what to make of that. He was systematically destroying all her preconceived notions about Hunter Brannigan, lady-killer.

This was a whole different person from what she thought he was.

"So, what'll we do with the rest of our evening?" he asked her.

She had no idea why—maybe it was the way Hunter said it—but his question struck her as being funny. So much so that she started to laugh. And once she did, she couldn't stop, not until there were tears streaming down her cheeks.

"So I take it you're open to suggestions," he deadpanned once the laughter had died down.

Kenzie felt as if something almost physical reached up and squeezed her heart.

The next moment, she was swept up in her emotions and acting on them.

Turning into Hunter, she wrapped her arms around him and kissed him with every single ounce of strength she still had left in her body.

The fire that erupted between them was instantaneous, sweeping over them and taking them back to the place they had just inhabited a few minutes ago.

The lovemaking this time, if possible, was even wilder, even less restrained than it had been the first time.

They knew what was waiting for them, and they ran toward it joyfully and willingly, ready to embrace it and be part of it.

This time, they did make it up to her bed. Lost in the erotic fire they'd created, they consummated their lovemaking on a mattress. Somehow, doing it there made the act that much more official.

Hunter stayed the night and even though she was convinced she wasn't going to sleep a wink, she wound up falling asleep in his arms.

When Kenzie woke up the following morning, the spot beside her was empty.

The letdown was immediate and oppressively tremendous, almost drowning her.

Well, what did she expect? Kenzie heatedly demanded. Rose petals on her pillow? This was Hunter Brannigan, the lover of a thousand women, or so the legend went. He wasn't exactly known as Mr. Faithful.

The man wasn't about to hang around after their love-making was over. She was surprised he'd stayed as long as he had. If nothing else, he wouldn't want her getting any ideas that this was in any way a preview of some sort of domestic bliss.

He was gone the way she knew he would be.

Kenzie sat up and swung her legs off the bed. She needed to get dressed. It was Monday morning and she had a serial killer to find and catch. She couldn't do that sitting here feeling sorry for herself.

She needed to—

Kenzie stopped and sniffed the air. Was that the coffee maker?

Oh Lord, did she remember to turn it off last night? She'd gotten so caught up in what was happening, she had to have forgotten.

With visions of a fire breaking out, she ran into the kitchen, braced for anything.

Except for what she found.

Chapter 20

Kenzie's mouth fell open.

Hunter hadn't left. He was in her kitchen. She hadn't smelled the coffeepot burning. What she'd smelled was Hunter preparing breakfast.

She'd walked in on him making eggs and bacon.

He had toast in the toaster as well as a pot of coffee brewing, although at the moment, he wasn't making anything. He was staring at her.

"I take it you don't like to dress for breakfast," he observed dryly.

Suddenly realizing that she had rushed into the kitchen without putting anything on, Kenzie yelped and grabbed for something to cover herself.

But then she stopped. Covering herself after the fact was ludicrous. Hunter had already seen her naked, so there didn't seem to be much of a point for this sudden display of modesty.

Still, she moved strategically behind a chair. The high-back kitchen chair covered enough to make her feel a little more comfortable about her condition.

At least comfortable enough to explain why she had come racing in like that.

"I thought I'd left the coffee on last night," she explained. "What are you doing?"

"Making breakfast," Hunter answered cheerfully. "I thought it would be obvious." He pretended to look down at the frying pans. "Unless I'm doing it wrong."

Kenzie frowned. She hated being caught off guard like this. "Why didn't you wake me up?"

The toast popped and he began buttering the four slices. "You've been putting in all those long hours, so I thought I'd let you sleep a little longer." Hunter deposited the slices onto two separate plates. "Sorry if I crossed any lines."

Kenzie was getting to feel more and more awkward. "Um, now that I know my kitchen isn't burning down, I'm just going to go and get dressed," she told him, jerking a thumb in the general direction of her bedroom.

His mouth curved in a smile that defied being labeled. "Don't feel you have to do it on my account."

"Very funny," she muttered. The next second, she had disappeared back into her bedroom.

Embarrassed and flustered, Kenzie got dressed even faster than she usually did. She was back in the kitchen in five minutes.

Hearing her enter behind him, Hunter asked, "Change your mind about getting dressed?" Turning around in her direction, he saw that Kenzie was fully clothed. "Oh." The single word echoed with disappointment as well as surprise. "That was fast," he commented. "And just in time. Breakfast is ready," he told her, placing a dish with scrambled eggs, toast and bacon on the table. The next minute, the plate was joined by a cup of coffee. "I didn't know how much creamer you took," he explained as he sat down with his own plate and cup. "So I just put in a little."

She looked down at the lightened coffee. If this was "a little," then she was afraid to see what he considered "a lot" to be.

"Perfect." She raised her eyes to his. She couldn't resist asking, "Who *are* you and what have you done with Brannigan?"

"I told you I was a nice guy," he reminded Kenzie. "I can't help it if you didn't believe me."

She changed the subject, or at least tried to. But her mind kept being drawn back to the breakfast he'd just made for them.

"This is good," she felt obligated to say. She hadn't realized how hungry she was until just this moment. "When did you learn how to cook?"

"I told you," he said. "I raised my brother and my father. When my mother took off and my grandmother finally gave up on us, I realized that I had to learn how to cook—fast. The one time my father tried to make something, he almost blew up the kitchen. And thanks," Hunter said belatedly, thanking her for the compliment.

"I'm the one who should be thanking you." She was all but finished eating. "This is great," Kenzie told him.

"No need," Hunter began to say something, then stopped as her cell phone started ringing. He nodded at her pocket. "Sounds like duty calls," he guessed.

Just as she took out her phone and opened it, his rang.

"Cavanaugh," Kenzie responded. Turning away, Hunter answered his.

She heard Choi's voice in her ear. "Kenzie, this is Choi. A ranger picked up some really freaked-out hikers late last night."

"Okay," she said, waiting to find out why he thought this was important enough to call her.

"You're going to want to talk to them," he predicted. "Seems they went too far and got all turned around. They saw a cabin, so they decided to take shelter for the night.

They thought the cabin was abandoned. They were practically incoherent when the ranger found them."

Kenzie had a sickening feeling in the pit of her stomach. "Where are they now?" she asked.

"The ranger called the police and one of our patrol cars brought them to the station," Choi told her.

She saw Hunter looking at her quizzically. He was obviously trying to piece together her conversation. "Did you see them?" she asked Choi.

"Yeah. I got in early," Choi explained. "Those two hikers haven't stopped shaking since they were brought in."

"I'll be right there," she promised, ending the call. The second she did, Hunter filled her in on the call he'd received.

"Valdez located that tattooed victim's sister and brother-in-law. He's going to go talk to them, see if they can't shed some light on the victim and who he might have interacted with before he was killed." There was more, but he'd overheard her tone when she was on her phone. Something was definitely up. "Who called you?" he asked, nodding at the cell phone Kenzie was still holding in her hand.

"That was Choi. He called to say that some hikers had stumbled across a cabin."

Kenzie crossed over to a bookcase that was next to her flat-screen. She kept her weapon there when she came home. Securing her weapon, she turned around and noticed that Hunter had collected their dishes and stacked them in the sink.

The man just kept on racking up points, Kenzie thought.

"What did they find in the cabin?" Hunter asked as he watched her get her purse. His own weapon was already strapped in beneath his jacket. He saw Kenzie look at him quizzically. "Choi's not going to call you to report a potential tourist attraction," he pointed out.

"I'm not sure. Choi didn't go into any detail, but he said we're going to want to talk to these two people. It seems that whatever they saw, the hikers can't stop shaking. They were incoherent when the ranger picked them up."

"Well, it's for sure that it wasn't meeting Yogi Bear that spooked them," Hunter said. "What do you want to bet that our hikers came across more body parts?"

Kenzie set her mouth grimly. "No bet," she said, locking the door behind her. Desperate to lighten the mood, at least for a second, she said, "You put the dishes into the sink."

"You didn't want me to?" Hunter questioned, curious.

"No, it's just that—" Maybe she shouldn't have said anything. But since she'd started this by bringing the subject up, she knew she might as well finish. "It was just thoughtful, that's all."

His mouth curved as they walked to the parking area. "If we weren't in a hurry, I would have washed them. I learned early on that you have to take care of things as they come up or you'll wind up being overwhelmed."

In more ways than one, Kenzie caught herself thinking.

Coming up to the parking lot, she said, "I think we should go in separate cars."

Hunter nodded. "Good idea. We wouldn't want people talking."

Kenzie couldn't help glancing at him. "Someone might notice that you're wearing the same clothes you had on yesterday."

"They might notice," Hunter agreed. "But no one's going to ask anything because they know I won't say anything." He smiled at her and for a split second, it felt to her as if they were the only two people on earth. "I don't kiss and tell."

And there it was, Kenzie realized, what she was secretly worried about. That somehow, their night together would become public knowledge. "I thought you did," she confessed.

"Rumors," Hunter told her. "Rumors that are based on nothing, have no foundation and have a way of unaccountably mushrooming with a life of their own. You have nothing to worry about," he assured her. "Unless you wind up telling someone about last night, because I won't." Hunter unlocked his door and slid in behind the wheel. "I'll meet you at the precinct."

She nodded, hurrying over to her designated parking space.

Driving to the precinct a short distance away, Kenzie couldn't help thinking what a difference twenty-four hours could make.

No, she immediately upbraided herself. She wasn't going to do that. She wasn't going to let herself think about Brannigan, not in *that* way. She couldn't allow herself to be distracted. They had a killer to find.

This had been a fling, an enjoyable fling, but for all she knew, it was already over and mentally, Brannigan was already moving on.

But oh, she really hoped not.

Get a grip, Kenz. You need to be 110 percent on the job, not anywhere else.

She took in a deep breath and focused.

Parking in the rear of the precinct, as was her habit, Kenzie all but ran up the concrete steps that led to the back entrance.

Choi had really piqued her curiosity. She asked why these hikers were, as he had so eloquently put it, "freaked out."

Had they found more body parts, or was there some other reason the hikers were "freaked out"?

She walked quickly to the bank of elevators.

When she entered the squad room, she looked around but she didn't see Hunter. She hadn't seen his car either. However, there was no law that said he had to park in the back.

He was probably in the back room already, working, she guessed.

He wasn't.

They'd left at the same time, Kenzie thought. If anything, he'd left a couple of minutes earlier. Where was he?

No, she silently insisted, she wasn't going to make noises like some paranoid girlfriend. Maybe Hunter was just taking his time so it wouldn't look as if they were coming in together. She really had to learn to start giving him credit for behaving like something other than a Neanderthal.

Old habits, she told herself.

Choi was instantly on his feet when he saw her, crossing to the room's threshold.

"The hikers are in conference room one," he informed her with a note of excitement. "Wait until you hear their story."

Choi began to walk out, intending to lead the way. But he stopped when it dawned on him that Kenzie wasn't following. His brow furrowed. "Something wrong, Cavanaugh?"

"No. I just thought I'd wait for Brannigan. He is the colead on this," she pointed out. The truth of it was her competitive nature was taking a back seat at the moment.

Somehow, it didn't seem right for her to leapfrog ahead of Hunter.

"I didn't call him about this," Choi confessed. "I just called you."

"*I* called him," Kenzie lied. "As soon as I finished talking to you," she added for good measure. "He said he'd be right here just before he hung up." She shrugged. "Not everyone lives as close to the precinct as I do."

It was a lame excuse, but it was all she could think of at the moment as she tried to stall.

A feeling of relief washed over her the next moment. She saw Hunter walking into the back room. He'd changed his clothes, she realized. Even after that little speech he had given her about not needing to. He'd taken a preventive measure to forestall any questions about where he had spent the night.

Kenzie pressed her lips together to keep from smiling.

"Let's get started," Hunter said, nodding at Choi and then at Kenzie, almost like an afterthought. "Where are the hikers?"

"I put them in conference room one," Choi told the detective. O'Hara hadn't come in yet and Valdez had gone to question the tattooed victim's relatives.

"How did you find out about them?" Hunter asked as he, Kenzie and Choi made their way down the hall toward conference room one.

"Patrol called after talking to them. It seems that word has gotten around about our black widow," Choi answered.

"I suppose that's a good thing," Hunter commented, although his tone indicated that he didn't believe that in the absolute sense. It wasn't because the case was a new one. It was because this was an ongoing case that really wasn't close to being solved yet. And it was long overdue to be solved.

There was still a serial killer out there.

Choi opened the door to the pristine-looking conference room. A rather bedraggled couple was seated at the table, their body language indicating that they felt entirely on edge, as if their chairs were going to catch fire at any moment.

Bob and Cynthia Kellogg were a young—and until yesterday—robust-looking couple in their early thirties who loved spending their weekends taking in nature and hiking. They were obviously physically fit and right now just as obviously utterly shaken up by their recent experience.

Cynthia literally jumped out of her chair when she heard the door opening.

Embarrassed at her unrestrained display of terror, she flushed. But although she tried, she couldn't seem to immediately calm down.

"I'm sorry," Kenzie apologized. "I didn't mean to frighten you."

"Right now, everything frightens her," Bob said about his wife. "Not that I blame her. My own shadow makes me jump."

"What happened to you last night while you were hiking, Mr. Kellogg?" Hunter asked in a kind, even voice. "In your own words," he added. "Take your time."

"I wish there was a way to blot this out of our heads," Bob confessed. His wife gripped his hand. She seemed to be holding on for dear life. "You know, like in that movie where you stare into a flashing pen and you forget everything you've done and seen?"

Hunter looked blankly at Kenzie. She quickly picked up the thread. "I'm familiar with the movie, Mr. Kellogg," she told the man. She glanced over toward his wife, who had let go of her husband's hand and was now nervously folding and refolding hers. "I hate to make you relive something that disturbed you so much, but I need to have you walk us through it. Even the slightest detail you remember might help us save someone's life."

Kenzie leaned in, as if this was just a private conversation between two friends.

"Take a deep breath, Mr. Kellogg. Clear your mind of everything else," she told the man. "Now, if you would walk me through yesterday. You were hiking," she began, her voice trailing off as she silently coaxed Bob to start talking.

"We were hiking. I guess we hiked longer and farther than we'd planned on. When it started to rain—there was a sudden storm," he interjected.

"I know," she said, nodding. It caught the weatherman by surprise. "Go on," she urged.

"Well, I guess that we got a little off course. And really wet," he emphasized. "And suddenly this cabin seemed to materialize out of nowhere."

She could tell by the wild look that had entered Cynthia's eyes that she was letting her imagination run away with her, thinking of every horror movie she had probably ever seen. Kenzie was determined to keep this couple grounded.

"You'd never seen the cabin before?" she questioned Bob.

Bob shook his head as if trying to shed beads of water from his hair. "No."

"Could you find the cabin again?" Hunter asked.

Bob closed his eyes as if the very thought of doing that pained him. Cynthia whimpered in the background. He avoided looking at her.

"I guess I could if I had to," Bob said.

"Good. Go on," Hunter urged the man. "You found this cabin..."

"We couldn't believe how lucky we were, finding the cabin like this, because the storm started to really pick up." His mouth twisted in an ironic smile that had no humor to it. "But the second we walked in, we both knew there was something really weird about the cabin."

"Weird how?" Kenzie asked.

"There was plastic hanging all over the place. Some of it was even from the floor to the ceiling." He was breathing hard now as he spoke and his wife's whimpering had grown louder. "I swear there was blood on some of the plastic. I didn't touch it," he cried. "But we just *knew* something evil was going on in that place. And then we heard something, an unearthly screeching."

"Did you see what made the noise?" Hunter asked.

"Are you kidding?" the man asked incredulously. "Cynthia and I got the hell out of there and ran for our lives."

Kenzie exchanged looks with Hunter. Had this couple actually stumbled across where their killer hacked up his victims' bodies?

Chapter 21

Bob Kellogg really looked reluctant to act as the task force's guide back to the cabin that he and his wife had discovered. But it was Cynthia Kellogg's hysterical response to the mere suggestion that terminated the very idea. His wife absolutely refused even to entertain the thought that Bob would venture anywhere into that vicinity.

If he could remember the cabin's location. Which he told them he couldn't.

"I've got a feeling those two aren't going to be hiking anywhere anytime soon," O'Hara predicted, having returned to the conference area just in time to witness Cynthia's second and even more dramatic meltdown.

Giving the couple a moment of privacy, Kenzie, Hunter, O'Hara and Choi clustered at the other end of the conference room to talk options.

"Meanwhile, what do we do?" Kenzie asked.

Rather than bandy about possible options, Hunter turned toward Kellogg and asked, "Mr. Kellogg, do you happen to remember which direction you were going in when it began to rain?"

Holding his wife and trying to calm her down, Bob looked up.

It took a bit of doing, but the man was finally able to

give the task force a general description of the area where they were hiking.

"I left a few trail markers along the way. You know, rocks piled up on one another, in case we got lost. That was just before we saw the cabin," he remembered. "I guess I forgot about that until just now," Bob told them ruefully.

Hunter put a comforting hand on Bob's shoulder.

"'Just now' is all that counts," he told Bob.

Kenzie had a few questions of her own to ask about the cabin, but for now she thought it best not to press the couple too much. Within a few minutes, she and the others felt they had enough information to be able to find the cabin's location.

Considering that this was probably the scene of at least one if not multiple murders, she decided to request that a CSI team accompany them.

Hunter had his doubts about the wisdom of doing that. "Don't you want to make sure this isn't just two spooked hikers letting their imaginations run away with them before we get more of Aurora's finest involved?"

Ordinarily, she might agree. But her gut instincts were telling her that they just might be up against a time crunch.

"I have a feeling that if we wait, something's going to happen to that cabin. This is fire season," she reminded him. "And someone just might use that as an excuse to torch the place if they suspected it had been discovered."

She had a point, he thought. "Okay, let's go get a team together," Hunter declared.

"I just don't see what the big attraction to hiking is," Kenzie told the others less than four hours later.

She, Hunter, Choi and O'Hara, as well as the four crime scene investigators whom Sean Cavanaugh had sent with them, made their way up Big Haven Mountain, guided by the general directions that Bob Kellogg had given.

"My guess would be that's it's the view," Hunter said.

She was struggling not to slip as she was climbing, but when he extended a hand to her, she deliberately ignored it.

"I can see the same thing on the internet," she told Hunter.

"There's all this fresh air," he pointed out, undaunted.

"There're also mosquitoes," she countered.

Hunter laughed, shaking his head. "You are determined not to like this."

She realized that she was making noises like a spoiled brat, and that wasn't her intent.

"Let's just say that I like other things better." Even so, they weren't out here for pleasure. "And what I really don't like is that some psychopath sees this as their personal Shangri-la where they can wantonly do away with unsuspecting, innocent men that they lured out here."

He made her a promise. "We'll get him—or her," Hunter added, covering all bases.

Kenzie really wanted to believe him, but as she struggled onto flatter terrain, she looked at Hunter dubiously. "Are you sure about that?"

There was no hesitation in his voice or his manner. "I am."

She sighed. "I wish I was." Moving forward, she nearly slipped again. Kenzie swallowed a curse. "I also wish I was as sure-footed as a goat," she complained.

The next second, she nearly slid down the side of the mountain and might have if Hunter hadn't quickly grabbed her hand.

"Thanks," she muttered, embarrassed.

He pretended that it was nothing. "Being as sure-footed

as a goat comes with a price. You'd have to look like a goat, too, and I for one think that would be a terrible waste." Hunter had an infectious grin on his face as he said it.

"You two having fun up there?" Choi complained, bringing up the rear of their party. "You know, I wouldn't have felt slighted if you had picked Valdez to go with you instead of me."

Kenzie sympathized with her partner. "You're younger," she pointed out.

"Yeah, that means I have more to live for and I won't get to do that if I wind up falling to my death on this mountain," he grumbled.

Hunter waved at the other detective's complaint. "You're not going to fall to your death. This is hardly bigger than a hill," Hunter pointed out. "And according to the directions that Kellogg gave us," he said, looking around once again to get his bearings, "we're almost there."

"I don't see anything yet," Kenzie said, straining her eyes to take in as much of a panoramic view of the area as she could.

Hunter did the same. Ten inches taller than Kenzie, he was just able to catch a glimpse of something that might have been a cabin.

"Over there." He pointed to something on the right as he shaded his eyes for a better view. "I think that might be it."

"I sure hope so," Choi muttered. "I'm never going to complain about filing paperwork again."

"Sure you will," Kenzie told her partner. "You've got a short memory."

Choi made no response.

Going a few steps closer, Hunter was no longer wondering if he had indeed spotted the cabin that Kellogg had told them about. There it was, a sorry-looking little structure in the distance.

"This way!" he called out, raising his voice so that the others who were following them could hear.

With the end in sight, Kenzie got her second wind and practically sprinted the rest of the distance to reach the cabin.

It was a rustic-looking one-story structure, the kind people might envision when thinking of Lincoln's birthplace. Some of the wood on the sides appeared to be rotting.

Reaching the door, Kenzie wanted nothing more than to eagerly survey the cabin, but she kept herself in check long enough to pull on a pair of rubber gloves first. If she didn't miss her guess, a lot of people's fingerprints were already here. She didn't want to add to that confusion by adding her own.

When she had finished pulling on the gloves she'd brought with her just for this purpose, Hunter was standing next to her. She noticed that he already had his rubber gloves on.

"Ready?" he asked her, his hand on the doorknob.

She paused to glance over her shoulder. They had an audience of six behind them.

"So ready," she answered.

The second that Hunter opened the door, she knew that they had found the right place. She could swear that the smell of death was everywhere, even though at first glance there seemed to be no bodies visible.

At least not yet, she thought, cautiously taking a step inside.

"What do you think?" Hunter asked her after Kenzie'd had a chance to look around.

"What do I think?" she echoed. "This must be the

place," she murmured in a voice that called to mind an old cartoon.

The sound of plastic restlessly moving in the heated breeze only added to the sum total of the eerie atmosphere the scene generated. Kenzie drew closer to a length of torn plastic that was just hanging at a window.

"That's blood," she pointed out, trying not to think past that.

"There's a smattering of blood over here, too," Hunter added.

The CSI team members were already scattering throughout the cabin, photographing and documenting everything they came in contact with.

While they were doing that, Kenzie, Hunter and their two team members searched the cabin, looking for more evidence, something that was instantly definitive.

There was a main room with a sofa as well as a long table that had a couple of chairs buffering it on each side. Kenzie could almost visualize the table being covered with plastic and some other fare, rather than dinner being carved up on it.

She couldn't help herself. Kenzie shivered.

"Are you okay?" Hunter asked, seeing her shivering. "It's not cold in here," he told her.

She could almost see it, see all the death and carnage that had transpired in this cabin. Kenzie could *feel* her blood running cold.

"I disagree," she told Hunter in a whisper.

"Hey, Cavanaugh," Choi called out from the next room. "Guess what I just found."

Not another headless torso, she hoped.

She, Hunter and O'Hara all poured into the only other room in the cabin. It was the bedroom.

Choi was on the floor, on his hands and knees next

to the bed. He'd discovered something there. As they watched, they saw him pull out a hacksaw whose blade was partially broken as well as a battery-powered saw.

Getting back up, he dusted off his knees. "I think we struck gold," Choi announced.

"Or at least found another piece of the puzzle," Hunter agreed.

O'Hara had opened the only closet in the room. There was nothing in it except for wire hangers, conspicuously empty.

"Whoever used these hangers is gone now," O'Hara said.

Hunter nodded. "Luckily for the Kelloggs, otherwise we'd probably be finding their bones here today," he speculated.

But Kenzie had other thoughts. "I don't think so. They're not our killer's type. Cynthia's the wrong gender and Bob's too young. The target has always been men in their fifties."

O'Hara didn't look convinced. "Maybe under the right circumstances, the killer would have branched out," he suggested.

Lord, she hoped not, although it had been known to happen.

"Now, there's a grim thought," was all she allowed herself to say. Taking a deep breath to brace herself, she said to the others, "Let's check out the grounds while we're here."

"You never take us anyplace fun," Choi complained, mimicking a high-pitched voice of a child who was on a family vacation.

Kenzie's mouth quirked in a smile. "Next time," she promised, playing along.

There was an old outhouse located just behind the cabin.

"That has to be for show," Hunter told Kenzie. "I saw a small bathroom inside the cabin."

"Maybe the cabin came with an outhouse and when whoever bought it built the cabin up a little, they decided to leave the outhouse as a piece of history," Kenzie speculated. She cautiously drew closer to it. "I wonder if it comes with its own bats."

O'Hara laughed. "Well, there's only one way to find out."

Playing the macho male, he moved ahead of the others and dramatically pulled open the creaky wooden door. It seemed almost to moan mournfully as he opened it and looked in.

"Oh, damn."

"O'Hara, you all right?" Hunter called out, hurrying to join the man. He looked at the detective, not inside the outhouse. "You look green."

Unable to speak, O'Hara waved his hand at Hunter to step back even as he had turned away. O'Hara was able to take a couple of steps to the side before he suddenly retched and wound up purging nearly half the contents of his stomach.

Concerned about him, Kenzie came rushing over. "O'Hara, what's wrong?" she cried.

And then she saw what had caused the detective to throw up.

Kenzie sucked in air, struggling to keep the dizziness at bay.

There were body parts in the outhouse as if it was some sort of storage unit. There was an assortment of heads and severed hands. All the parts that had been missing from the torsos they had found in Aurora Park, she thought.

Hunter looked at Kenzie. Realizing that she was about

to go in, he caught her arm and forcibly turned her away from the outhouse.

"Kenzie, go get the crime scene investigators," he told her sternly, trying to break through the protective wall she had erected around herself. "Tell them to stop what they're doing and get in here."

She hardly heard him.

"This is where they were stashed," she said, her words coming out in almost slow motion, as if, if she let them out at a faster rate, her voice was going to break.

Although Hunter was trying to draw her away and he was strong, Kenzie wasn't going to let him. Struggling against the grip he had on her wrist, she kept looking into the small dark structure. Seeing the heads that couldn't look back.

"This was her trophy room," she said in a still voice. "This was where she could come in and gloat over her kills."

"You don't know that. We still don't even know if the killer's a woman. Maybe this was just a convenient place for the killer to separate the identifiable parts from the rest of the body. Pragmatic," he concluded.

"No," Kenzie insisted, shaking her head, her eyes fixed and staring into the dark interior. "That's too practical and too pragmatic. No, this was her trophy room," she insisted almost breathlessly. "I can *feel* it, Hunter. We're dealing with a monster."

"Well, you're not going to get an argument from me on that count," Hunter told her. "Anyone who can kill that many people, who could carry out what amounted to that many death sentences, can't be called anything else *except* a monster."

O'Hara had returned with the four crime scene investigators. All four—three men and a woman—had been on the job for years. Summed up, the total number of years came to a little less than twenty-nine.

But even *they* paled when confronted with carnage of this magnitude.

"Wow. This is going to take us a while," Lawrence, the senior investigator, told Hunter as he took in the number of heads and hands inside the outhouse.

"Take your time," Kenzie said, pulling herself together and doing her best not to sound as if she was sick to her stomach. "The chief will want you to be sure not to miss a thing." Turning toward Hunter, she said, "We have to find out who this cabin belongs to. It had to have been registered with the county at some point in its history. Someone's name *has* to be on the deed."

Hunter nodded. "We can start at the county registrar," he told her. "They have to have a record of ownership," he reasoned.

"That doesn't mean that the owner of the cabin is also the one who owns that head collection," Kenzie said grimly.

"Maybe not," he agreed. "But knowing who owns the cabin or who initially owned it might get us one step closer to finding out the identity of the person playing the mad butcher of Aurora." He looked down into Kenzie's eyes. "Remember, the Son of Sam got caught because of a parking ticket. We'll get this SOB," he said with confidence.

Kenzie hung on to that piece of wisdom for a long, long time.

Chapter 22

Dr. Rayburn grunted when he looked up and saw both Kenzie and Hunter walking into the morgue the following morning.

"I just want you to know that in all my years as a medical examiner, this has to be the most gruesome case I have ever had the dubious 'privilege' of working on," he told them. "Hands down," he added wryly.

In the interest of time, Kenzie, Hunter and the other two detectives with them had spent the previous day helping the CSI team collect and catalog all the evidence that had been discovered in and around that small cabin and its accompanying outhouse. In the end, twelve heads, twenty-four hands, and Kurtz's torso, were all separately bagged, labeled and brought to the morgue yesterday evening. Rayburn had left for the day before the "shipment" had arrived.

Coming into the morgue this morning and being confronted with the newest body parts had been an unpleasant discovery for him, to put it mildly.

His morning container of coffee stood cooling and untouched on his desk in the corner. He'd gotten right to work.

"Look at it this way, this makes identifying those torsos you had in the drawers a little easier," Hunter told the medical examiner.

"Theoretically," Rayburn countered. It was obvious by his expression that he had his doubts.

"What do you mean, 'theoretically'?" Kenzie asked.

"What if those heads you found belong to different torsos?" Rayburn asked. "Then what?"

It was a possibility that none of them wanted to consider.

"Then we look for those," Kenzie finally replied stoically, then added in a more hopeful note, "Until this whole thing is behind us."

Rayburn shook his head. "Your whole family is too damn optimistic for me." He paused, looking at the two detectives. He assumed they had come to see him this early for a reason. "I hesitate to ask, but do you have anything else for me?"

"Not at the moment," Hunter said. "We just wanted to make sure that all the body parts were delivered to the morgue."

"Oh, they're here all right," the medical examiner said sarcastically. "Now, if you'll leave me to do my job," he said pointedly, his eyes indicating the rear door, his meaning clear.

There really was another reason they had stopped by and it involved the folder Kenzie had with her.

She brought it up now. "We thought this might help," she told Rayburn, handing the medical examiner the folder that contained copies of the missing person files they had managed to narrow down. "We think at least *some* of those people we found are in this pile."

Rayburn sighed, eyeing the folder in his hand. He dropped it on the gurney next to the head he was busy examining. "Another haystack to go through. Thanks. Now, please leave," he requested.

Hunter and Kenzie filed out.

* * *

"I don't think he likes his job," Hunter commented once they had walked out of the morgue.

Kenzie laughed to herself. "That's probably why he has a countdown calendar on his desk. I saw it on the way in."

"Countdown calendar?" Hunter questioned. They turned the corner.

"Yes. It's a calendar that counts down how many days a person has left until retirement. From the looks of it, the doc has way too many to go," Kenzie answered.

"Too bad," Hunter commented, feeling sorry for the medical examiner. "A man shouldn't be stuck at a job he doesn't have a passion for."

"Do you have a passion for your job?" Kenzie asked out of the blue, curious.

"I wake up every morning whistling," he said without missing a beat.

The elevator arrived and they got in. She pressed for the fifth floor.

She had no idea if Hunter was being serious or sarcastic but for now, she decided not ask him any further personal questions.

Kenzie changed the subject.

"I hope that Rayburn can identify at least a few more of the victims for us," she said as they rode up to the squad room. "The more victims we know, the more information we can gather. Speaking of which, did Valdez ever get anything from the victim's brother and sister-in-law who he went to question?"

In light of the day they had had yesterday, that had completely slipped his mind.

"I haven't had a chance to talk to him yet," Hunter answered. And then he smiled at her. "As you might recall, I was kind of busy last night."

After they had finally left the cabin and made their way down the mountain again, it had been way too late to go back to the precinct. Hunter had suggested getting dinner out.

Rather than go to a restaurant, since they were both pretty tired, they had settled on takeout.

Even though they hadn't eaten all day, neither one of them was really hungry for food. Most of the takeout wound up in her refrigerator.

They were far more interested in comfort. Comfort led to other things and he stayed the night, leaving early this morning to go home and change.

She would have thought they were on the path to establishing a pattern if she didn't feel that she knew better, Kenzie mused. Hunter Brannigan was not a man to be pigeonholed and she wasn't about to make that mistake, no matter how much she wanted to believe that his behavior was changing. Changing because they had something special going on.

That happened only in movies. Grade-B romantic comedies at that. And this was life with a capital *L*.

No, she was going to just enjoy this for as long as it lasted. Kenzie absolutely refused to fall into the trap of making future plans because she knew the minute she started doing that, it would mark the beginning of the end.

"I guess we'll find out now, then," she said, referring to what Valdez had learned, as they walked into the squad room. They headed for the small room that had been allotted to them.

"I guess so," Hunter echoed with a smile that she was quickly finding had a way of just seamlessly slipping under her skin and instantly sabotaging her thinking process.

"Heard you guys had one hell of a day yesterday," Valdez said by way of a greeting. Choi was already there and had gone for coffee. O'Hara hadn't come in yet.

"I'm more interested in the day you had," Hunter told the other man. "Did you find out anything useful from the Kellys?"

Instead of answering, Valdez just grinned.

"What?" Kenzie cried. "Out with it."

"You know that grainy photo you gave me to show them?" Valdez asked Kenzie. "The one taken at the bank when Kurtz closed out his account?"

She wasn't going to get her hopes up until she heard Valdez say the actual words, Kenzie told herself. "What about it?"

"Now, Valdez," Hunter ordered when the other detective appeared to be drawing this out.

"Jenny Kelly said she thought she recognized the woman as being the same one her brother-in-law was seeing just before he disappeared a year ago," Valdez announced.

"She *met* her?" Kenzie questioned, her excitement almost palpable and getting the better of her despite her resolutions.

"Not exactly," Valdez confessed. "William Kelly was very secretive about who he was seeing, or even that he was seeing anyone," he told Hunter and Kenzie.

"So then how did she make the identification?" Hunter asked, sounding short as he questioned his partner.

"Here's the good part," Valdez said. "Seems that Jenny Kelly is the really curious type. She thought her brother-in-law was seeing someone so she decided to follow the guy. She saw him go into this woman's house, then she watched them through the window," he concluded, looking like the cat that had swallowed a canary.

"Go ahead," Hunter urged.

"Well, Jenny Kelly is pretty sure that this was the woman she saw—the woman had a different name," he added, thinking of the name the woman had used when she was with John Kurtz, "but according to Jenny, this was her."

"You said that she followed her to her house—" Kenzie said.

"That's what Jenny Kelly said," Valdez qualified.

"Did she remember the address of the house?" Kenzie asked.

"Yes—"

"Then what are we waiting for?" Kenzie cried. "Let's go talk to this woman," she urged, ready to fly out of the police station and go to the woman's house. It was too much to hope for that she was still living there, but they might find something that would help them find her.

Some of the exuberance left Valdez's voice as he told her, "Jenny Kelly and her husband already did that. They went to talk to the woman as soon as tattoo guy went missing. The woman wasn't there," he told them, disappointed. "Turns out the house had been empty for some time."

Kenzie sighed, frustrated. "Another dead end."

"Seems that way—for now," Hunter said. Undaunted, he pushed forward on another front. "Back to trying to find out who owns or originally owned that cabin with its unique outhouse collection," he told the others with a touch of sarcasm.

"You realize that depending on how far back that deed of ownership goes, finding out who actually owns that cabin may wind up being one hell of an involved treasure hunt," Kenzie pointed out.

"If this was easy," Hunter pointed out, "everyone would be a detective."

"I know, I know," she said. She shouldn't be complaining. "But there really should be a happy medium," Kenzie added.

"Who knows," Hunter speculated, "we might get lucky. Or the doc might come up with some more positive IDs for us."

She saw that accomplishment in a grimmer, more realistic light.

"That means that there'll be more people to break the news to," she told Hunter and the others. "More people to rob of any shreds of hope they might be harboring that their loved one might still be alive."

"And more opportunity to catch this cold-blooded killer, stop them from killing someone else and allowing those families to get closure," Hunter reminded her.

"Or revenge," Kenzie countered.

"Or revenge," Hunter granted. "Revenge is good, too, at least in this case," he readily agreed. He thought of the stuffy, dusty office. Not exactly a place to cheer the soul. "I can go to the county registrar's office myself," he told Kenzie.

She wasn't about to be sidelined now. She intended to see this through every step of the way.

"No, I'm coming with you," she insisted. "You might not have noticed," she told Hunter, "but I'm not any good at twiddling my thumbs, waiting around for someone else to get the results."

Right, like that could have escaped anyone's notice, he thought.

"I noticed," he laughed.

"If you're going to the county registrar's office, what do you want us to do?" Valdez asked, nodding toward Choi, who had returned with coffee, and O'Hara, who had just walked in.

Hunter had it all worked out and outlined it for the others.

"O'Hara, you go down to the crime scene lab and see if they came up with anything we can use. Choi, find out if Valri Cavanaugh has picked up on any sightings of our black widow under any of her various aliases. Valdez—" he turned to look at his partner "—I want you to go back to the Kellys'. Find out if they knew if their brother had a bank account and what bank he used. Dollars to doughnuts, it was emptied out like the others were.

"If so," he continued, "find out when this happened and the bank branch's location. Once you get that information, see if you can get a hold of any surveillance video the bank might have from that day. With any luck, our black widow stayed true to form and hovered around in the background to make sure that her mark took out every last red cent." He looked at the rest of the task force gathered around him. "If nothing else, eventually, this pattern of wholesale greed has to trip her up and lead us to her door."

"Maybe in a perfect world," Choi muttered under his breath.

Choi spoke in a low voice, but Hunter had heard him. "No," he contradicted, addressing Choi's comment. "In an *imperfect* world. People like this black widow don't exist in a perfect world," he said flatly.

They all had their assignments and went about fulfilling them.

Kenzie and Hunter drove to the county registrar's office, located some twenty-five miles away from the heart of Aurora. Hunter volunteered to drive and was surprised that she didn't offer any resistance. Instead, Kenzie readily agreed to the arrangement.

Something was up, he thought.

"You look awfully grim," Hunter noted, glancing at the expression on her face. "We might finally be closing in on some answers."

She didn't quite see it that way. Finding a name—the *right* name—and pulling it out of county records sounded just too easy. She had a feeling there was some kind of catch.

"Or those answers are just going to lead us to even more questions," Kenzie said. "Sometimes I feel just like I'm trapped in this big, recurring dream, going down a road that just leads to another road that leads to another road. And so on," she sighed, wrapping it all up in a big, unmanageable package.

"Maybe you need to take a break," Hunter suggested. "Step away and clear your head if it's getting too intense for you."

She was too dedicated to just shrug her duty off like way. "I can't step away," Kenzie insisted. He knew better than that, she thought. "I owe it to those victims to find who did this to them."

"I don't know," he said, thinking it over. "I think they'd understand," Hunter told her gently.

"Maybe," she allowed. "But I wouldn't. I *can't* slack off. I—we," she corrected herself, "have to catch this woman, this monster, before she finds someone else to hack up."

"Then focus on that," Hunter counseled. "Focus on solving the case and not any of that other peripheral stuff."

Kenzie looked at him, confused. "Peripheral stuff?" she asked.

"Yeah. The severed heads and the hands, the torsos. Get those images out of your head and just picture taking down this serial killer," Hunter told her sternly. *"Understood?"*

She laughed then. "Understood," she repeated, then said, "You know, you sound like a drill sergeant."

"Good. Because what I want is to drill that advice into your head," he told her.

He saw her mouth curve in what he affectionately regarded as her lopsided smile, although he knew better than to tell her that.

"What?" he asked.

"You've been hanging around my brothers so much, you're beginning to *sound* like a Cavanaugh," she told Hunter.

He lifted one shoulder in a casual shrug. "There are worse ways to sound," he answered with a smile.

His phone rang just then. But since he was driving, Hunter couldn't really reach for his cell phone. "Get that, will you?" he asked her.

"It's in your pocket," she said, looking at his right hip.

"So?" he asked. "What's the problem? It's not like that's unexplored territory for us, is it?" he teased Kenzie.

He'd succeeded in making her laugh. Kenzie shook her head in utter wonder. They were sharing a very intimate moment while fully clothed and seated upright in a vehicle traveling sixty-five miles an hour.

The very idea tickled her.

Chapter 23

Because the property they were looking into had initially been purchased and its deed registered sometime in the mid-1960s, the information they were trying to find was not available online. Instead, they were told by the woman in the registrar's office, the paperwork was archived in a warehouse located at another site.

They drove to the warehouse and were told that the information they were looking for was housed in a box that resided on one of the warehouse's many, many shelves, along with a ton of dust.

Arthur Calavetti, the pale, stooped-shouldered clerk who wound up guiding them through the warehouse, gestured toward what appeared to be endless rows of shelves. All the shelves were filled with myriad neatly arranged boxes.

"What you're looking for should be here," he told them.

Kenzie didn't find the term "should be" very comforting.

Hunter surveyed the area. "This place has an awful lot of boxes."

"Most of them are labeled," Arthur said. It was obvious by his expression that he was trying to be encouraging.

"Just like my tombstone will be when I die here from dust inhalation," Kenzie commented. Finding one piece of paper amid all this seemed like an unbelievably overwhelming task.

"She tends to be a little melodramatic," Hunter told the clerk.

Arthur nodded his head. "Had a sister just like that," he told Hunter. He began to shuffle toward the elevator. "If you need anything, I'll just be one flight up."

Kenzie ventured toward a row of shelves. They went from floor to ceiling. "How many people do you suppose died in here, searching for deeds they never wound up finding?"

Hunter came up behind her. "Probably not as many as you think."

"That's not exactly comforting," she told him. Turning around to face him, she asked, "How do you suggest we get started?"

"Well," Hunter said, looking at the labels on the boxes closest to him, "they seem to be arranged by years. I say let's start at the end and work our way to the beginning if we have to. You know, like a countdown."

"So basically we're setting up residence in here," Kenzie said sarcastically.

"Just for starters," he answered. "Unless you have a better idea."

"Yes," Kenzie suddenly declared as the idea occurred to her, "I have a better idea. That gremlin upstairs looks like he lives for this job."

He couldn't argue with that, Hunter thought, although he had no idea where she was going with it. "So?"

The way she saw it, Arthur was their only hope of actually finding the deed before next Christmas. "So we tell him what we're trying to find—and why. Maybe that'll spur him on to help. He *has* to be familiar with what's in some of these boxes."

"Kenzie, it's an ongoing investigation," Hunter reminded her. And the rule of thumb was that they couldn't share any information about an open case.

"An ongoing investigation that is going to go nowhere if we don't get any outside help," she insisted. "This is a clerk who probably lives and breathes these files. He's not the kind of person who would go running to some online paper to sell his story. Even if he wanted to, he probably has no idea how to go about doing that. There are still people who are technologically illiterate."

Hunter sighed, relenting. Kenzie had an offbeat point. And they did need help. "Go get the records gremlin," he told her.

She was gone before the words were out of his mouth.

When Kenzie returned ten minutes later with Arthur in tow, the clerk was completely different from the man who had left them to find their way amid the records. He looked like a livelier version of himself.

"Really?" Arthur appeared to be hanging on Kenzie's every word. "A murder?"

"Murder*s*," she corrected. "At least several."

"How many in a 'several'?" Arthur asked almost breathlessly.

"Thirteen," Hunter answered, coming up to join them. "Perhaps more."

Hunter could have sworn that the clerk appeared to be standing a little straighter now and his eyes looked as if they were going to pop out of his head.

Kenzie built on that. "You'd be doing the community a really great service, helping us catch this killer."

"What can I do?" Arthur asked excitedly.

"We need your help in locating who originally owned that cabin on the mountain and who owns it now."

Arthur scrunched up his face. Apparently this is what

he did when he was thinking. "And it's located where?" he asked.

Hunter gave Arthur the approximate latitude and longitude where they had found the cabin. Kenzie, meanwhile, had taken out her cell phone. She had pulled up a number of photographs of the cabin and the outhouse. All of them were exterior shots. She thought it prudent to spare the clerk from seeing the more gruesome photos that had been taken.

Even so, the man's hands trembled as he took the phone from her. There was no hesitation in his voice.

"I know where that is," Arthur said in a hushed whisper.

Yes!

Kenzie restrained herself from throwing her arms around his neck and hugging the man.

"We just need to know the name of the person who owns it," Hunter told the clerk. He glanced toward Kenzie. They were both banking on the fact that the information would lead, however indirectly, to the name of the killer.

Like a man on a mission, Arthur squared his shoulders and disappeared into the stacks.

Five hours later, with no small sense of relief, they finally left Arthur and the archives behind them.

Kenzie sat in the passenger seat, feeling like someone in a trance. "I can't believe we finally have a name to go on," she said, staring at the copy of the deed that the clerk had made for them.

"And it only cost us five hours and ten dollars," Hunter said with a laugh, referring to the fee they'd paid the clerk.

"Hey, rules are rules," she reminded him, using a pseudo-stern voice like an old-fashioned professor. "You have to pay a fee if you want to get a copy of the deed," she said. "If you ask me, that's a small price to pay if it winds up getting us some answers. Or *the* answer."

"Well, I wouldn't be sending up fireworks just yet if I were you," Hunter cautioned. "We need to verify just where this Cameron Bishop presently is and what he's been doing all this time. I can't believe that he's been the sole owner all this time," he marveled.

Kenzie slanted a look at him. "I guess the killer's a guy after all."

"Don't get ahead of yourself," Hunter cautioned again. "I didn't say that either. Maybe *Mrs.* Cameron Bishop is the guilty party. Or it could be that one of their offspring is responsible for the carnage. We don't know anything for sure yet."

Kenzie suppressed a sigh. "I get it. We need the full details," she replied, too excited to take offense. Any other time, she might have felt that he was lecturing her. "It's just that, you know when you're running a marathon and you think you see the finish line, you suddenly just want to pour it on and sprint, to get that feel of the tape against your chest before someone else does."

"Well, just hold yourself in check, Desiree Linden," Hunter told her. "You'll get to cross that finish line soon enough."

She stared at him in confusion. "Who?"

"Desiree Linden," Hunter repeated. "She's the woman who won the 2018 Boston Marathon."

Despite her excitement that they had actually located the deed, she stared at him, astonished. "Your head is just this big jumble of information, isn't it?" Kenzie asked in amazement.

Hunter flashed her a grin. "I do try my best," he said.

Kenzie wanted to tell him that he didn't have to try. That his "best" was already more than good enough for her. But she didn't want to say anything that would wind up scaring Hunter off. There was a reason why all the women whom he'd been with had never managed to land him. He wasn't the type to allow himself to be cornered. So she did what she usually did—she went back to talking about work.

Kenzie leaned forward and pulled her phone out of her pocket. Holding it in her hand, she said, "I'm going to call Valri and ask her to find everything she possibly can about this Cameron Bishop."

Hunter glanced at the clock on the dashboard. "Isn't it a little late to be calling Valri at this hour? She might have already gone home."

"The computer tech department never really goes home," Kenzie quipped. "They just reset."

He laughed. "Cute." He thought back to the last time they had brought Valri a request. "But I don't think that Valri will find that very amusing."

"Let me worry about my cousin," Kenzie told him, then added very seriously, "This is why we're in this game—to get the bad guys off the street and behind bars before they hurt anyone else."

"Simplistic," Hunter commented. "But accurate."

Kenzie placed her call. She was just beginning to think that Hunter was right and her cousin had gone home when Valri answered on the fourth ring. Kenzie instantly brightened. "Valri, it's Kenzie."

"Talk fast, Kenzie, I'm on my way out. I've been as tense as an ice pick all week and Alex promised me a massage when I got home," Valri said, talking about her husband.

Kenzie struggled to speak coherently. "I think we've found a person of interest in those murders, Val. Or at least the family of a person of interest," she qualified for

Hunter's benefit. After all, the players hadn't been properly identified and labeled yet.

"Bring it to me tomorrow, Kenz. I'll get to it as soon as I can."

She was disappointed that Valri wasn't as excited as she was. "No, *now*. Valri, this is really important," she stressed. "This killer carves her victims up and she won't stop until we can get her and haul her away," Kenzie insisted.

"Her," Valri repeated. "Then you're sure it's a woman?"

Kenzie could tell by the lack of background noise over the phone that Valri had stopped moving. She finally had her cousin's attention.

"Yes. We found the cabin where the victims were killed and we have the name of the person who bought the cabin. Now we need your help in tracking that person down." Kenzie was almost pleading now.

She heard Valri sigh. Her cousin was surrendering! "Give me the name. I'll see what I can do. Just don't expect miracles."

Kenzie could feel herself grinning like the proverbial Cheshire cat. "I always expect miracles from you, Valri. Just see what you can find out," she requested eagerly, then gave Valri the name that was on the cabin's deed.

"Okay, got it. I'll give you a call when I have something," Valri told her. "Just so you understand, this might take some time. Don't sit waiting by the phone tonight," she warned.

Kenzie laughed. "You know I will. Thanks, Val. You're one in a million," she told her cousin, then ended the call.

Curious, Hunter asked her, "You will what?" as she put her phone away.

"Wait by the phone. Valri told me not to, but..." Kenzie's voice trailed off as she shrugged her shoulders. "Kind of hard not to, given the circumstances."

She expected Hunter to tell her to listen to her cousin.

Waiting for a call that most likely wouldn't come for at least a day was counterproductive and they didn't have that sort of time to waste. There were details to see to and look into.

She didn't expect Hunter to say, "I've got an idea how to make the time go by." And she certainly didn't expect him to look so damn sexy as he said it or for her heart to practically jump up into her throat, beating like a drum solo.

"Oh? How?"

"How do you think?" he asked with a wicked grin.

She heard herself saying, "I have some thoughts on the matter."

"So do I."

Hunter's laugh seemed to curl all around her, embracing Kenzie.

Valri called her in the squad room a little after ten the next morning. Kenzie and Hunter lost no time in getting down to the computer lab.

"You look as exhausted as I feel," Valri commented when Kenzie walked in with Hunter behind her. "Didn't you get any sleep last night?"

"I was working on the case, trying to put the pieces together," Kenzie told her cousin.

It was a lie, really. But she couldn't very well come out and say that she'd spent the night making love with Hunter. That lovemaking was his way of trying to get her mind off the case for a while. The moment she even hinted at anything like that, she knew it would be over. Admitting that they had spent the night together was tantamount to giving away Superman's secret identity. Once it was out there, his crime-fighting days, as he knew them, would be over.

It was official, Kenzie thought the next moment. She was losing her mind.

"So what do you have for us?" Hunter was saying. "Do you know where we can find Cameron Bishop?" Hunter asked Valri.

"Haven't a clue," Valri admitted.

There was no way to describe how incredibly let down Kenzie felt.

However, Hunter was scrutinizing the computer tech's face. "But you do know something, don't you, Valri?"

"I know that this guy disappeared off the face of the earth," she told them, then added, "And if he hadn't, you wouldn't want to find him. I get the feeling that he was a really terrible person."

"Define 'terrible,'" Hunter urged, interested.

"I managed to put together his background. Cameron Bishop never married. For the most part, he lived in the shadow of his brother, Steve, a self-made millionaire. And then his brother and sister-in-law died under what I can only call suspicious circumstances. When they did, 'Uncle' Cameron jumped into action. He took in his niece as well as the trust fund money Steve had left for her care."

"I have a feeling we're not going to hear that they lived happily ever after," Kenzie said.

"Well, over the years, child services was called in a number of times, but apparently none of the allegations that were made by the neighbors ever stuck."

"So his niece wasn't taken away?" Hunter questioned.

"No, each time Cameron managed to charm his way out of the charges. He had child services believing that his niece, Camille, would fall apart if she was removed from his house—actually her parents' house because Cameron had moved in there to take care of Camille. He had them convinced that Camille needed the stability that he could provide for her. Meanwhile, it seems that he was slowly siphoning away Camille's trust fund."

"Why was child services involved in the first place?" Kenzie asked.

"There were rumors of child abuse," Valri told her. She paused for a moment, as if she was steeling herself before saying, "*Sexual* child abuse."

"So what happened?" Hunter asked, although in his mind he was already filling in the blanks. "Did Camille eventually run away?"

"Not exactly. She didn't run away. But for all intents and purposes, Cameron did. He disappeared. He supposedly left her the one thing he owned outright—the cabin—to remember him by.

"It took some doing," Valri continued, "but I found a picture of Camille Bishop taken by child services from the last time that they had been called in." She pulled out a rather blurry photograph from the file she'd put together and placed it in front of her cousin and Hunter. She watched their reaction as they looked at the photograph. "Look familiar?"

Chapter 24

Kenzie's eyes widened as she stared at the photograph that Valri had pulled from the file and printed for their benefit.

"Oh my Lord, she could be the little sister of the woman who stole Kurtz's money," Kenzie cried.

"Or, given when this photo was taken, it could be that same woman as a teenager," Hunter speculated.

Kenzie could feel her brain going a mile a minute as the scenario surrounding the serial kills began to fall into place.

"And you said there were rumors of sexual abuse?" she asked Valri.

Valri nodded. "According to the records, nothing was ever really substantiated, but yes, there were rumors."

"Is this guy's DNA on file anywhere?" Kenzie suddenly asked. "Like because he had any surgeries, or ever gave blood for any reason. Maybe there are some lab tests on file somewhere."

Kenzie realized that she was just shooting in the dark but maybe, just maybe, she could hit something that would yield answers.

Hunter turned to look at Kenzie. "What are you getting at?"

She took a breath, trying to sound coherent and doing

her best not to get ahead of herself. She had a tendency to do that and she knew she had to be clear.

"Those severed heads we found in the outhouse," Kenzie began. "This woman's 'uncle Cameron' might have been her first victim. Maybe he takes her up to the cabin, their 'special place,' and this time his niece fights back. She snaps and in her rage doesn't just kill him, she carves him up." She could see that she had both their attentions. "What do you want to bet that his head is in that collection? If we have his DNA on file, that'll give the ME something to use as a comparison when he runs his tests."

Hunter slowly nodded. "It's a long shot," he warned her.

Kenzie didn't think so. "You were the one who brought up Son of Sam and the parking tickets, remember?"

Valri looked from one detective to the other, lost. "Say what now?"

"Long story," Kenzie said, putting her cousin off for now. "I'll tell you when we have more time. Meanwhile, Brannigan and I need to talk to Doc Rayburn about running those DNA tests, then see if we can track down Camille Bishop."

"Or Sheila Gibson, Dorothy Wilson, Penelope James, Colleen Alexander, Sally Marco, Miriam Howe and Rebecca Robertson," Valri said, reading the woman's other aliases from the list she'd made for them. She raised her eyes to meet Kenzie's. "Those were just the current aliases I could come up with."

"She might be using a new one by now," Hunter pointed out to Kenzie.

"Just a little ray of sunshine, aren't you?" Kenzie quipped. "No matter what she calls herself, she's still that damaged little girl, Camille Bishop, underneath it all." She headed toward the doorway, then glanced back at Hunter. "Let's go talk to Rayburn."

* * *

"Don't ask for much, do you?" Rayburn grumbled after he had heard Kenzie and Hunter out.

"Then you can't run the tests?" Kenzie asked in surprise. "I thought I heard you say that you prided yourself on specializing in doing the impossible."

"I didn't say that," Rayburn denied. "The difficult I can do. The 'impossible' takes a little longer—as long as you can get me that sample of Cameron Bishop's DNA."

"Working on it even as we speak," Hunter told the medical examiner.

Before coming here, he'd given the assignment to Valdez, who was currently in the process of digging up any and all medical records pertaining to Cameron Bishop.

"Okay," Rayburn announced. "Get out of my morgue. I've got work to do."

The two detectives left the room and went down the hallway to the elevator bank.

"Okay," Kenzie said as she pressed the elevator button to get them aboveground again, "now all we need is a way to track down our black widow. Any suggestions?" she asked Hunter.

He thought for a moment. "What is the one thing she keeps doing?"

"Hacking up the men she lures into her cabin," Kenzie answered dryly.

"Besides that," Hunter said, waving away her response. As they rode up to their floor, he leaned in to her, creating an incredibly intimate space that contained just the two of them. "C'mon, Kenzie. You know the answer to this."

Irritation flared in her eyes. She didn't have time to play any guessing games—and then it dawned on her. "The black widow is bringing her victims back to the cabin. Her uncle's cabin. I think she's killing her uncle all over again. What do you think?"

"Looks like it," Hunter agreed. "All her victims are older men."

"And to top it off," she cried, feeling as if she was on a roll, "before she even kills them, she steals their money."

"Just like her uncle stole hers," Hunter declared.

Now that they had laid it out, it all seemed so obvious. He couldn't help wondering how they could have missed it.

Kenzie realized what Hunter was thinking. "You want to stake out the cabin," she guessed.

"She's bound to come back there," he told her. "It's the one pattern she keeps repeating. Killing those men at the cabin completes her need for revenge." He looked at her to see if she agreed with his take. "Like you said, her uncle probably brought her there, promising her an outing, and instead he took her innocence from her. She needs to bring her victims to the cabin to satisfy her desire for payback."

They got out of the elevator. Kenzie shivered at Hunter's interpretation.

"She had other recourses," she insisted. "She could have called the police, told child services the truth when they came, anything but stayed where she was, enduring his repeated abuse."

"It was complicated, Kenzie," Hunter countered. "Cameron was her only family after her parents died. She found herself in an ongoing love/hate kind of relationship that she couldn't extricate herself out of."

"Maybe," Kenzie allowed. "But she still didn't have to kill those other men," she maintained.

"No, you're right, she didn't," Hunter agreed. "But by

then she was pretty damaged. Who knows what was going on in her head.

"Okay," he said, clapping his hands together. They'd come a long way and he felt as if they were about to start on the homestretch. "Why don't we tell the chief of Ds what we've found out so far and get him to approve this stakeout. We're going to need at least two teams, maybe three, of two people each to watch that cabin those two hikers stumbled across until our black widow brings her latest victim there."

Hunter had a point, she thought.

"I know this sounds terrible, but I hope it's soon. And I hope that we're the ones who are there to bring her down." She saw Hunter looking at her in silence. He probably thought she was a little crazy, Kenzie guessed. "There's nothing I want more than to stop that woman cold," she told him. And then she searched his face for some sort of a sign that he understood. "Does that sound bloodthirsty?"

Her heart practically leaped up when she saw a quiet smile curve his lips. "No," he told her. "That sounds like me."

That gave them something in common, Kenzie thought. She found that infinitely comforting.

Brian Cavanaugh was quick to approve the stakeout and the request for extra teams to relieve the ones on watch duty.

"Great work so far, you two. Keep it up," he told Kenzie and Hunter as he sent them out of his office. "I had a feeling putting you two together would help solve this thing."

With Valdez tracking down Cameron Bishop's available medical records, that left Choi and O'Hara to form the other stakeout team. Initially, there were to be two twelve-hour shifts. If it took the black widow longer than a week to find and bring back her new victim, more teams would be tapped to join stakeout duty.

"Camping out is seriously having less and less of an appeal for me," Kenzie told Hunter as they sat in his car, watching the cabin from high ground. From this vantage point, they were able to see anyone approaching the cabin from either direction.

Sucking in air, she slapped the side of her neck, killing another insect. "I don't know which is worse, the bugs or the heat."

"And here I thought my company would get you to forget about all that," Hunter said.

"You forget, I can't exactly 'do' anything right now with your 'company,'" she reminded Hunter. "We're on a stakeout, not at a lovefest."

"Well, if we remain alert, we could probably do both," he told her with a laugh.

Kenzie had no idea if he was kidding, or actually serious. All she knew was that when she was in his arms, nothing else in the world existed for her.

Which was why she couldn't risk making love with him while they were on stakeout. Never mind that doing it out in the open in the forest had myriad minuses to it.

She could feel herself growing progressively more restless. "We've been on stakeout watching her damn cabin for almost a week now. I'm beginning to think our timetable is off. Maybe the black widow's decided to change things up a little. Or maybe she's decided that twelve victims are enough."

"Thirteen," Hunter reminded her. "You're forgetting about John Kurtz," Hunter pointed out. "We found his head away from the collection."

"I'm forgetting *nothing* about this case, especially not how itchy it's making me," she said, trying to reach the far side of her left shoulder blade. She shifted in her seat, leaning forward.

And then she stopped.

"Hunter, look down there," she told him excitedly, pointing to the far side of the cabin. "Someone just pulled up in a Jeep." Her eyes widened as she stared at the figure emerging from the driver's side of the vehicle. "It's her." The words came out in almost a hushed gasp. Kenzie's eyes widened. "And she's got another one with her."

Hunter had already zeroed in on the two people. "Well, he's still walking on his own power, so that's a good sign."

"If she's running true to form," Kenzie said, "he won't be for long."

They watched as the woman whom they were still referring to as their suspect linked her arm through the arm of the unsuspecting man who had accompanied her to the cabin.

If they didn't know what they did about Camille Bishop, the two people they were watching looked like a typical couple, Kenzie couldn't help thinking.

Camille whispered something in her intended victim's ear and he seemed to pick up his pace. They walked into the cabin together.

"Now!" Kenzie whispered into Hunter's ear.

He didn't have a chance to respond. Kenzie was already heading down the incline, all but sliding straight down. He hurried so that he could catch up to her. Hunter had a feeling Kenzie was going to go in like gangbusters if he didn't stop her.

Though it almost seemed ludicrous to think in these terms—and he knew she'd resent it—he wanted to protect Kenzie. The woman he had come to know so well in the last few weeks was far from helpless, but for all they knew the black widow could have a gun with her. There was no question in his mind that a gun, pulled out and discharged at the right moment, could render anyone helpless in an instant, no matter how damn clever and able they were.

He reached the bottom at the same time that Kenzie did and together they sprinted toward the cabin.

With Kenzie taking the front entrance and Hunter taking the rear, each of them took a door and on the count of "Three!" they entered at the same time, kicking the doors in.

The doors gave easily. Their hinges were completely rusted.

They immediately realized that they had made their entrance at just the right moment. If they'd waited for even a couple of minutes longer, the knife that Camille had in her hand would have severed her latest victim's throat.

"Put it down, Camille," Kenzie ordered. "That's not your uncle. You killed him a long time ago."

Stunned beyond words and looking incredibly frightened, Camille's latest victim seemed to suddenly realize just how close he had come to death. With a horrified cry, the man stumbled away from Camille and practically dived behind the muscular shelter that Hunter's body provided.

An anguished, enraged guttural shriek escaped Camille's lips. Frustrated because she was robbed of her latest kill, Camille looked wildly around at the two intruders with eyes that were filled with hatred and didn't quite appear to be human.

Kenzie thought she had managed to disarm the woman by wrenching away the knife from her. She didn't see the hidden gun tucked into the back of her waistband until it wasn't hidden anymore.

Cursing loudly, Camille pulled out the weapon and aimed it at Kenzie. Seeing the gun, Hunter lunged for Camille, putting his body between the other woman and Kenzie. The gun discharged while he was grappling with the black widow.

The gun discharged twice. The second bullet narrowly missed Kenzie and she could only assume that it whizzed by her body. Still grappling with Camille, Hunter grabbed her arms and pinned them behind her.

"Cuff her, Kenzie," he ordered in a voice that sounded oddly hollow and strained.

Kenzie happily did as he ordered, cuffing their serial killer—she couldn't bring herself to refer to Camille as a suspect any longer—then pulled out her cell to call command for backup.

"It's over," she announced to the chief the second he came on the line. "We got her. Send in the B team," she said with a laugh, as she turned to look at Hunter. As she did, she saw Hunter sinking down to his knees. The next second, he keeled over. "Hunter!" she cried out, suddenly more terrified than she had ever been in her life.

Her terror instantly escalated when she saw the blood that was soaking into his shirt.

"Omigod!"

"Kenzie, what is it? What's going on?" Brian's deep voice rumbled against her ear. "Talk to me," he ordered sternly.

"Send an ambulance," she heard herself saying. "Hunter's been shot. That bitch shot him!" she accused, turning to look at the woman who was lying facedown on the ground, her arms cuffed behind her. "Forget the ambulance," she amended. "Send in a medevac," she said, referring to the helicopter transport service they used. "I don't think Hunter can wait for an ambulance. And, Uncle Brian," she said in a voice grew stone-cold, "if the B team isn't here before the helicopter arrives, I just want you to know I'm not leaving that woman alone here to wait for them. I'm shooting her."

"Kenzie, don't do anything you're going to regret," Brian told her.

"Don't worry, I won't. I'm not going to regret shooting her at all," she told her uncle. Her hands were shaking as she terminated the call.

"Kenzie, you can't," Hunter said weakly. He'd managed to overhear her call to the chief and struggled to rally, to try to talk some sense into Kenzie's head.

"Yeah, I can. She shot you, I shoot her. I'll say it was self-defense."

"You can't say that. She's handcuffed," he pointed out in between sucking in air.

"I'll take the cuffs off." She fought to keep from crying, terrified that Hunter was going to wind up being the black widow's collateral damage. "And you, don't make things any worse by talking. Save your strength. Although your brain is gone, you know. That was a stupid stunt to pull, getting in between her gun and me." Her throat felt as if it was closing up. "That bullet was meant for me, not you."

"I know."

"You're an idiot, getting shot like this. You know that, don't you?" she cried, losing the battle she was fighting to keep from crying.

Hunter was having a great deal of trouble sucking in air now. "A simple…thank-you…would be…nice."

Kenzie's tears were falling freely as she sat there, cradling him in her arms. "I'm not going to thank you for getting shot on my account. And the second that you're better, I'm going to beat you senseless for being so dumb, you hear me?"

The last thing Hunter managed to say to her, albeit in a hushed voice, before passing out was, "I…look…forward…to…it."

"Idiot," she retorted before breaking down in gut-wrenching sobs.

Chapter 25

Kenzie felt as if time was moving by on the back of a tortoise, and she was terrified that Hunter was going to die in her arms.

The medevac finally touched down ten minutes after she had called the chief of Ds. It was a frantic ten minutes that she'd spent begging Hunter to open his eyes and stay with her.

By the time she heard the helicopter landing outside the cabin, Kenzie was convinced that she had lost Hunter.

And then she thought she felt a movement. Hunter's fingers weakly brushed against her wrist. Joy mingled with paralyzing fear. Kenzie could hardly breathe.

"Hunter, don't give up, you hear me? They're here. The medevac is here! You can't give up now," she ordered the unconscious detective.

She tried to move him, but there was no way that she could get him out to the helicopter. The medical attendants were going to have to come into the cabin to carry him out.

"We're in here!" Kenzie yelled at the top of her lungs, trying to be heard above the noise and the whirling helicopter blades.

"I'll go get them," Donavan Reese, Camille's almost-victim quickly volunteered.

Caught up in trying to keep Hunter alive, Kenzie had almost forgotten all about the other man, the one who had almost been slain.

"Hurry," she cried, nodding.

Within less than a minute, Reese was back. With him were two medical attendants and Murdoch.

Her brother was at her side immediately. "What happened?" he asked, looking at Hunter's pale face.

"The big dumb jerk got in the way of a bullet saving me," she told Murdoch. She was crying again and she didn't even bother wiping the tears away.

"He's going to be all right, Kenz." Wrapping his arms around her, he eased his sister out of the way so that the medical attendants could do their job. "He's too ornery to die, you know that," Murdoch told her.

Kenzie blinked, trying hard to stay focused and not give in to the hysteria growing in her chest. "He better not, if he knows what's good for him." Her words came out in a shaky whisper.

"We're ready to go, Detective," Edwards, the taller of the two medical attendants, told Murdoch.

Kenzie snapped to attention, shrugging out of her brother's hold. "I'm coming with him," she declared. Her tone left no room for argument.

The attendant looked over her head at Murdoch, who nodded his assent.

"I'll stay here with the prisoner. Backup should be here soon," he told Kenzie. Belatedly, he glanced at Reese, the man who had brought them into the cabin. "Who's this?"

"The man who was about to become victim number fourteen," Kenzie said as she hurried out of the cabin behind the two attendants carrying Hunter out on a gurney.

In the background, she heard Camille laugh. "Number fourteen? There are more than just thirteen dead men buried on this mountain." Her statement was followed by more hysterical laughter.

The attendants were loading Hunter's gurney into the helicopter. If they hadn't been, Kenzie would have rushed back into the cabin and grabbed Camille by the throat, squeezing it until the black widow told her where all the dismembered bodies were buried.

She left that job up to Murdoch.

Nothing else mattered except for saving Hunter.

"I want him taken to Aurora Memorial," Kenzie told the attendant closest to her, raising her voice again to be heard above the roar of the helicopter blades.

"The chief already called ahead and made those arrangements," Edwards assured her. "They're waiting for us."

"Hear that?" Kenzie asked, bending over Hunter's gurney and talking into his ear. "You've got people waiting for you to arrive. They're going to fix you up. Even better than new."

Less than ten minutes later, the medevac landed on the helicopter pad that had been recently added to Aurora Memorial Hospital's tower building.

Kenzie felt the wind whipping right through her as she got out of the helicopter. She ran alongside the gurney as the waiting hospital staff took over, taking its precious cargo directly to the elevator.

"Looks like we just can't get away from riding elevators together, Brannigan," she told him with a pained smile.

She was holding on to his hand so tightly, she couldn't feel her own fingers anymore. Except to get on and then off the helicopter, she hadn't let go of Hunter's hand during that whole time. She couldn't shake the feeling that if she broke their connection, Hunter would slip away from her.

In some way she couldn't begin to explain, she knew that she was anchoring him to life.

Aurora Memorial's operating rooms were all located on the first floor. It was there, just in front of OR 3's double doors, where she finally had to let go of Hunter's hand. But it wasn't for lack of trying to hold on.

"You can't come in here, Detective. We need to operate on Detective Brannigan," Dr. Rogers, a surgeon she vaguely recognized from another lifetime, was telling her. "We'll take good care of him, Detective," the doctor added kindly.

She had no choice. Although everything within her screamed "No!" Kenzie finally had to release Hunter's hand.

"I'll be right out here, Brannigan. Waiting," she called after Hunter as the orderlies whisked his gurney into the OR. "Don't you dare stand me up, you hear me?"

Her voice broke as she uttered the last words.

"He's going to be fine, Kenzie. This is one of the best hospitals in the country."

She realized that she was hearing Brian's calm voice. He was standing right behind her. Wiping the back of her hand across her eyes, she turned around to face him.

"They've treated half the police department here at one time or another," her uncle told her.

Brian hadn't come alone. He'd brought his older brother, Andrew, and his nephew Shaw with him, as well as her aunt Maeve and several of the younger Cavanaughs.

Glancing toward them now, their faces all blurred and ran together for Kenzie.

"He shouldn't be the one being operated on," she told her uncles. "That woman was trying to kill me, not him."

Her voice rose a little as her anxiety heightened. "Hunter took the bullet that was meant for me."

"There's no point in going over what happened, Kenzie. Just focus on Hunter getting better, understand?" Maeve instructed.

Unable to speak, Kenzie could only nod. When her aunt took her into her arms, Kenzie just melted into the warmth and support she felt there.

By the time Hunter's surgery was over, some two and a half hours later, the floor was jammed with police officers, detectives and, in some cases, their spouses.

Eve Cooper, the head nurse on the floor, surveyed all the bodies that seemed to be jammed into a relatively limited space. She appeared far from pleased.

"Oh Lord, Regina Henderson warned me about this when she retired," Eve told the young assistant standing next to her. "At the time I thought she was exaggerating. Turns out that she didn't begin to do justice to this chaos." Eve pressed her lips together. "She said to just go with the flow, but I can't let these people act like they're human roadblocks. People," she cried, raising her voice.

When she failed to get their attention, Eve tried again, louder this time.

"People!" The noise stopped and heads turned in her direction. "That's better," she said with a sigh. "You've got to go into the waiting area. You can't just stand around like this. Better yet, pick a person or two to act as your liaison and convey the patient's condition when updates are available. *The rest of you go home*," she ordered.

Andrew saw the look that came over Kenzie's face when the head nurse told them to go home. He knew trouble when he saw it and immediately stepped in to avert any problems in the making.

"Nurse Cooper," he said, reading her name tag. "I understand that you have a hospital to run, but these men and women are concerned about one of their own who was shot earlier today while apprehending an extremely dangerous serial killer. They just want to make sure he's going to make it. You know how nerve-racking it can be, waiting for that phone call to come, the one that lets you find out what's happening," he told the head nurse, speaking to her as if they were both on the same side rather than opponents. "I promise you, once Detective Hunter Brannigan is out of surgery and in his room, you won't see most of us here any longer. We'll clear out," he told her.

The head nurse looked at the former police chief. The frown on her lips receded. "I guess I can't singlehandedly carry you all out of here."

"No, ma'am, I'm afraid you can't," Andrew said, agreeing with her.

Cooper, more than a foot shorter, looked up at him. "And I have your word you'll clear out once he's out of surgery?"

"And back in his room," Andrew added. "Yes, ma'am, you have my word."

"All right," the head nurse sighed. "But at least try to cluster together in groups, not just all over the first floor. Could you try to do that, Chief?"

"Yes, ma'am," Andrew told her. "We can try to do that."

"Looks like you still have that charm going for you, big brother," Brian said with a warm laugh, coming over to join Andrew once the head nurse had disappeared from the general area.

"She's just doing her job as head nurse and I'm just doing mine as head of this family," Andrew said good-naturedly.

"Head of this family, eh?" Brian echoed. "Don't let Dad hear you say that," he warned with a chuckle.

"Don't worry. I don't have a death wish," Andrew told his younger brother.

Over in the corner, Kenzie was standing to one side just next to the operating room doors. For the most part, she hardly heard what anyone had said or was saying. Her brothers and sister had come by, offering their support and encouraging words. She nodded and smiled, but she really hardly heard them either. She hadn't taken her eyes off the door that had closed, separating her from Hunter an eternity ago.

While having what amounted to her entire extended family here helped her cope, it didn't, ultimately, erase the icy fear that resided in the pit of her stomach. Only being told that the surgery had been a total success and that Hunter was going to make a complete recovery would return the color to her face.

When the surgeon finally did come out to give them an update, Dr. Rogers was cautiously optimistic.

"We got the bullet out." He told them the part that Kenzie had somehow known in her heart to be true. "There was a lot of internal bleeding going on, but we managed to stop that, too. I don't mind telling you that if Detective Brannigan wasn't in such excellent physical condition, it would've been a completely different story.

"As it is," the surgeon continued, "the next forty-eight hours or so are going to be crucial. But I see no reason why, barring unforeseen complications, that your detective won't make a full recovery."

"Thank you, Doctor," Shaw told the man, speaking for the officers and detectives as a group. He shook the surgeon's hand. "That's really encouraging news."

"He'll be in Recovery another hour, then they'll take

him up to his room," Rogers concluded. He looked toward Kenzie, whom he recognized as the bloodied detective who'd wanted to come into the OR. He smiled at her encouragingly. He'd learned a long time ago that family and friends played a large part in his patients' recovery. "You can go see him then," he told her.

"Thank you, Doctor," Kenzie whispered, unable to say anything more in a louder voice.

"Why don't I drive you home so you can change out of those dirty clothes, honey," Maeve suggested once the surgeon had left.

"No," Kenzie answered, her voice still hoarse. "I'm not leaving here until Hunter opens his eyes. But thank you for the offer," she added with a weak smile.

"Oh, honey," Maeve said, putting her arm around her niece. "You don't need to thank me. We're family." The older woman looked into Kenzie's face. "And so is he," she added in a quiet, firm voice that did more to comfort Kenzie than anything else had.

Although she knew that she looked like someone who had been involved in a heated, bloody battle, Kenzie was as good as her word. She refused to go home until Hunter regained consciousness.

She stubbornly sat in his room and spent endless hours talking to him. When she ran out of things to say, she read to him. And on those few occasions when her energy completely petered out, she fell asleep in the chair she had pulled up next to Hunter's bed.

But she didn't sleep long. It was as if she was subconsciously afraid that he would open his eyes and she would miss it.

Her sister went to her house and brought her a change

of clothing on the second day she spent keeping vigil next to Hunter's bed.

"You don't want to scare anyone in the hospital with that bloodied shirt of yours, Kenz," she told Kenzie when she brought her the clean apparel.

Nodding, Kenzie took the clothes and went into Hunter's private bathroom to change. When she came out again, she was carrying the bloodied clothes bunched up in her hands.

"I don't know if I can get those things clean," Skylar commented, frowning as she looked over her sister's clothes.

"Don't bother trying," Kenzie told her. "Just throw them away. Seeing them will just remind me how close Hunter came to dying," she told Skylar grimly.

Her sister nodded. She shoved the bloodied clothing into the shopping bag she'd brought.

"Well, I've got to get back. Everyone at the precinct sends their love," she added as she began to take her leave. Stopping in the doorway, she looked at her sister. She was aware how worried Kenzie was because Hunter hadn't regained consciousness yet. "He's going to be okay, Kenz. You've got to believe that."

"Yeah," Kenzie answered a bit too quickly. "I know." She glanced down at her new clothes. "Thanks for bringing these."

"Anytime I can make you look less scary, just let me know," Skylar said with a grin.

And then she left.

Kenzie moved her chair in closer to Hunter's bed and she looked at his face. His expression hadn't changed from the time they had brought him in here. Despite the optimistic words that everyone who came into the room offered, Kenzie couldn't tamp down the fear that was growing in her chest.

That he wasn't going to wake up.

"Okay," she said in a small voice, looking up toward the ceiling, "I was hoping he was going to come around by now, but every day that goes by, he just stays the same. I know I should be more patient, but I'm not. You know that. You made me this way.

"You know that I don't usually ask for anything. I can't even remember the last time I did. But I'm asking now. I'm asking you to wake him up for me. I'll do whatever you want me to." She tried to think of what people who prayed for miracles offered in exchange. "I'll make charitable donations. I'll volunteer at a shelter. I'll become a nun if that's what you want, but please, please, *please* bring him back to me.

"I can't live in a world without him in it. Please," Kenzie whispered, her voice breaking. "Please."

Closing her eyes, she prayed in earnest. Prayed the way she hadn't prayed since she had been a little girl.

Prayed harder than she had ever prayed before.

Tears seeped through her lashes, sliding down her cheeks.

She prayed until she lost track of time.

"Kenzie? What are you doing?"

Certain she was imagining things, her eyes flew open anyway.

Hunter's green eyes were open, as well, and he was looking right at her.

Epilogue

Once he regained consciousness, Hunter's recovery went amazingly fast. So fast that even his surgeon felt he needed to comment on it.

"Never has anyone come around so fast once they opened their eyes after being in a coma for two days," Dr. Rogers said, making a final notation on Hunter's chart before having it input on the computer. "You are really amazing."

Hunter slanted a glance toward Kenzie, who had arrived a little while ago to take him home. "I get that a lot," he told the doctor.

"Looks like he's getting delirious again, Doctor," Kenzie said to the surgeon. "Maybe you should keep him here for another few days for further observation."

"No, he's ready to go home. I've already signed all the necessary paperwork," the doctor told her. "Take care of yourself, Detective," he said, shaking Hunter's hand. "And stay away from bullets."

"I'll do my best," Hunter promised. And then he grinned at Kenzie as Dr. Rogers left his room. "Looks like I'm going home."

"Looks like," she agreed as she pulled out a small traveling case she had brought to the hospital yesterday. It contained a change of clothes for Hunter, including underwear and shoes. The clothes he'd worn when they'd flown him here in the medevac had been cut away in the name of efficiency. There was no saving them and they had been thrown away. "Get dressed, Brannigan. I'm going to be driving you back home."

As Kenzie went to get his few personal possessions in order to pack them up, Hunter caught her by the hand. She looked at him quizzically.

"Look, while we're still alone, I need to ask you something," Hunter said, feeling oddly tongue-tied. This was a completely new feeling for him. Insecurity had never been part of his makeup before.

Kenzie smiled brightly at him. "Yes, I'll drive your car while you're recovering."

"That wasn't what I was going to ask," he told her, "but good to know."

He looked serious, she thought. Uneasiness slipped in. She had no idea what to expect. "Then what were you going to ask?"

"Well," Hunter began slowly, measuring each word, "I figure since you've seen me at my worst and didn't go running off, screaming, I thought…I thought maybe we could make it official." He realized that he was holding his breath as he waited for her reaction.

"Make what official?" she asked.

"Damn it, Kenzie, I'm trying to ask you to marry me before you find someone else a little less damaged to partner up with," he said, irritated, as he unconsciously glanced down in the general area where he'd gotten shot.

Kenzie pressed her lips together. When she finally answered, she said, "I can't marry you."

That stunned Hunter. But then he rallied. "Can you give me a good reason why not? Because I need a good reason. Otherwise, I'm not going to back off or stop asking you until you say yes."

Kenzie sighed, and then with a straight face, she told him, "I can't marry you because I made a deal with a higher power. I told him that if he let you live, I'd become a nun."

Hunter stared at her, not knowing if she was actually being serious or putting him on. She looked so incredibly serious, for a split second he thought she really meant it.

"You'd make a lousy nun," he finally told Kenzie, hoping against hope that she was pulling his leg.

And then her serious expression gave way to a grin. "Funny, that was what he said when I made the offer. I guess he brought you back as a consolation prize for turning me down."

"You're an insane person, MacKenzie Cavanaugh," he told her, relieved.

She considered his remark. "I guess, then, we're a good match because no sane man would ever throw himself in front of a bullet like that."

A ray of hope flashed in his eyes. "Then it's yes, you'll marry me?" Hunter asked her.

"No," she answered. And then she laughed. "It's *hell yes*, I'll marry you."

"That's all I wanted to know."

The next moment, still seated, Hunter pulled her into his arms and kissed her. Hard. He had two days to make up for and he fully intended to start now.

* * * * *

Don't forget previous titles in the Cavanaugh Justice series:

Cavanaugh Cowboy
Cavanaugh's Secret Delivery
Cavanaugh Vanguard
Cavanaugh Encounter

Available now from Harlequin Romantic Suspense!

SPECIAL EXCERPT FROM

HARLEQUIN®

ROMANTIC suspense

After fleeing her abusive father, pediatric PA Miranda Blake never dates in order to keep her real identity a secret. But as she works closely with Tad Newbury to save a young boy, will she finally be able to let someone in? Or will Tad's secrets endanger her once again?

Read on for a sneak preview of USA TODAY *bestselling author Tara Taylor Quinn's next book in the Where Secrets are Safe miniseries,* Her Detective's Secret Intent.

"You're scaring me."

"I'm sorry. I don't mean to. I just have something to tell you that I think you'd want to know."

"Are you leaving Santa Raquel?"

"Make the call, Miranda. Please?"

Less than a minute later, she had him back on the phone. "All set. You want to go to my place?"

"No. And not mine, either. You know that car dealership out by the freeway?" He named a cash-for-your-car type of lot. One that didn't ask many questions if you had enough money, which made her even more uneasy.

"Yeah."

What was he doing? What could he possibly have to say?

Unless he'd found out who was watching her…

HRSEXP0819

"Head over there," he told her. "I'll be right behind you."

"You're sure I'm safe?"

"Yes."

"You're really scaring me now, Tad."

"Call Chantel," he said. "She'll assure you that my request is valid."

"You've talked to her today?"

"I had to tell her I wouldn't be at the High Risk meeting."

Oh. So he was leaving. Which didn't explain why she was on her way to a car lot.

And suddenly she didn't want to know. Life without Tad was inevitable. But did it have to happen right now? When the rest of her world could be caving in?

HRSEXP0819